The
IRISH ADOPTION HOUSE

BOOKS BY MICHELLE VERNAL

BRIDES OF BOLD STREET SERIES
The Dressmaker's Secret
The Dressmaker's Past
The Dressmaker's War
The Dressmaker's Chance

THE LITTLE IRISH VILLAGE SERIES
Christmas in the Little Irish Village
New Beginnings in the Little Irish Village
A Christmas Miracle in the Little Irish Village
Secrets in the Little Irish Village
Saving Christmas in the Little Irish Village

The Little Irish Farm

LOVE ON THE ISLE OF WIGHT SERIES
The Promise
The Letter

THE IRISH GUESTHOUSE ON THE GREEN SERIES
O'Mara's
Moira-Lisa Smile
What Goes on Tour
Rosi's Regrets
Christmas at O'Mara's

A Wedding at O'Mara's
Maureen's Song
The O'Maras in LaLa Land
Due in March
A Baby at O'Mara's
The Housewarming
Rainbows over O'Mara's
O'Mara's Reunion
The O'Maras Go Greek
Mat Magic at O'Mara's
Matchmaking at O'Mara's
Cruising with the O'Mara's

When We Say Goodbye
Staying at Eleni's
The Traveller's Daughter
Sweet Home Summer
The Cooking School on the Bay

The
IRISH ADOPTION HOUSE

MICHELLE VERNAL

bookouture

Published by Bookouture in 2025

An imprint of Storyfire Ltd.
Carmelite House
50 Victoria Embankment
London EC4Y 0DZ

www.bookouture.com

The authorised representative in the EEA is Hachette Ireland
8 Castlecourt Centre
Dublin 15 D15 XTP3
Ireland
(email: info@hbgi.ie)

Copyright © Michelle Vernal, 2025

Michelle Vernal has asserted her right to be identified as the author of this work.

All rights reserved. No part of this publication may be reproduced, stored in any retrieval system, or transmitted, in any form or by any means, electronic, mechanical, photocopying, recording or otherwise, without the prior written permission of the publishers.

ISBN: 978-1-83618-997-8
eBook ISBN: 978-1-83618-998-5

This book is a work of fiction. Names, characters, businesses, organizations, places and events other than those clearly in the public domain, are either the product of the author's imagination or are used fictitiously. Any resemblance to actual persons, living or dead, events or locales is entirely coincidental.

PROLOGUE

The pony and trap bounced along the rutted roads under cover of darkness, bar the waning moonlight. Father Doyle grasped the reins firmly, flicking them toward Dublin, and Maudie huddled down inside her coat next to him, willing herself not to look back. A flash illuminated the sky, and she'd barely registered the distant explosion when cracks like thunder made her jump and clutch the seat. Gunfire, or something bigger? She didn't know, but she was terrified and, despite Father Doyle's proximity, had never felt more alone in her life.

Only you're not alone, Maudie O'Connor, she reminded herself, wrapping her arms around her belly and silently vowing to protect her unborn babe.

They rattled on, ignoring the distant fighting, Father Doyle – his jaw set in grim determination – steering them ever further from the only home Maudie had ever known. Would she ever see her sister or Ronan again?

She realised the trap was slowing, and as the priest allowed the pony a few minutes' rest, his sanctimonious voice began to intone a prayer for her repentance and forgiveness.

Maudie defied him by keeping her head held high and thinking not of sin but of her beloved Ronan. She remembered secret caresses and lovingly whispered words. No amount of praying by pious Father Doyle could wash her memories away. She stared out into the night, knowing Ronan was out there somewhere, waiting for her and their child.

'I suggest you spend the next leg of our journey thinking on the sinful deed that's brought you to this, Maude,' Father Doyle finished, picking up the reins once more.

She'd do no such thing! She'd think of the home she'd create with her family of three, but the cottage – with its smell of peat and soda bread, echoing with a happy baby's gurgle – faded as the country road eventually merged into cobbled city streets. Maudie needed to focus on the route they were taking, to commit it to memory so she'd be able to find her way back. Ronan would get word to her sister as to where he was, and she'd go to him with their newborn son or daughter.

Maudie's heart felt like it was being crushed in a vice as, having wound their way past unfamiliar streets filled with strange sights and sounds, they clip-clopped alongside a high wall. Father Doyle pulled at the reins, and, with no warning, the pony and trap disappeared inside those walls via iron gates, left open presumably in anticipation of their arrival. The blood began to thunder in her ears as the wheels crunched over loose gravel toward the gloomy outcrop of buildings illuminated by the moon. This was to be her prison, and she knew the vista would be equally bleak come morning.

'Whoa.' Father Doyle slowed the pony, and they juddered to a stop outside the entrance of a building where a light glowed through the ground-floor window of St Patrick's Mother and Baby Home.

Maudie clambered down from the trap, staring fearfully up at the institution she'd been brought to, and placed a protective hand on her belly. She didn't belong here – though she knew her ma and da would say she was exactly where she belonged.

At a home for fallen women.

PART ONE

IRELAND

1

IRELAND, 1985

Maudie O'Connor hadn't thought she'd ever step foot on Irish soil again. She'd left the Emerald Isle decades ago, vowing never to look back and to leave the story of what had happened there behind her. There was nothing left for her in Ireland anymore – or so she'd thought. The ghosts were still here, though, and it was time to lay them to rest. Besides, if she'd learned anything in her eighty-three years on the planet, it was that you never knew what was waiting around the corner. And look, here she was in Dublin's fair city in her golden years, with her feet planted firmly in the foyer of the Shelbourne Hotel no less.

It had been important to Maudie that they stay here at the city's iconic hotel, with its courteous doormen and concierge – somewhere she could never have imagined setting foot in her youth. The woman travelling with her, whom she knew better than she knew herself, hadn't argued – only nodded her agreement, as she had from the moment Maudie first mentioned her need to return to Ireland.

They'd arrived at the hotel late yesterday afternoon, the journey from Savannah, Georgia, very different to the ship passage she'd embarked on to America as a naive, frightened but determined girl all those years ago. Despite the passage of time and the advent of air travel, it seemed to Maudie that modern travel was more arduous. By the same token, it was miraculous that two days ago they'd been in the southern United States, and now here they were in Ireland! Their trip had entailed a domestic flight to Atlanta, where they'd overnighted in a hotel, then a transatlantic flight to London. It had all been very quick and tiring, but a good night's sleep between crisp sheets had remedied that.

When they'd first sat down with their travel agent, Bonnie, Maudie's travelling companion had suggested spending a few days in London to see the sights. But in the end, Maudie – who had the final say – had vetoed the idea. She didn't want to dilly-dally and be distracted with things like Tower Bridge or Buckingham Palace. Dilly-dallying was not a luxury she could afford at her time of life. Besides, this trip wasn't a holiday; it was a pilgrimage.

So instead of unwinding in England's capital city, they'd no sooner disembarked at Heathrow than she'd been deposited into a wheelchair and whizzed across to the gate where their flight to Dublin was due to leave any minute. It had been touch and go as to whether they'd make it, and the murmurings of having words with Bonnie about the ridiculously tight turnaround had only been silenced by their first glimpse of an eiderdown of misty green below. For her part, Maudie's throat had tightened with emotion upon seeing the Emerald Isle stretched out beneath her, a land she'd never thought to see again, and she was grateful for the warm hand encasing hers.

Today was the day Maudie would confront her past, speak her truth and finally close the door on a painful history she'd tried so hard to put right. The enormity of what lay ahead swelled up, causing her to hesitate in the hotel's entrance and feign great interest in the watery blue sky outside. She needed a moment to compose herself and focused on the scudding clouds while the doorman, holding the door, waited patiently for her to exit.

Ireland – you're back in Ireland, Maudie affirmed silently, as trepidation and nostalgia swirled inside her. A lifetime might have passed between what had made her leave her country's shores and this day, but still it felt like yesterday, like she was still the same determined young woman inside, even if her body disputed it.

'Have you got your wrap, and did you put your umbrella in your bag like I told you to? Tara on the front desk was saying it might get chillier after lunch and we're in for a shower or two.'

'Stop fussing,' Maudie grumbled in response. That was another thing about getting old. You were treated like a child. She didn't mind though, not really.

'There's the car.'

The hire car was brought round to the grand entrance by a valet, and Maudie allowed herself to be led outside, but then she froze under the red awning and inhaled deeply. Sixty-four years ago, an aroma of horse dung undercut with the sweetness of hay, tobacco smoke and hot bread had filled the air. Back then, the streets had smelled both feral but hopeful too. Today, she could smell diesel, cigarette smoke and, yes, there it was, the whiff of hot bread. It dawned on her as she allowed the gentle tug on her arm to lead her to the car that it was the scent of hope.

'They make the seats so low,' Maudie grumbled as her travelling companion helped her into the passenger seat, feeling a wistfulness for the pony and traps of her youth. Still, she knew full well she'd need a forklift to get up into one of those these days! Her seat belt was clicked into place, and a few seconds later her fingers were gripping the seat for dear life as the car lurched forward and shot out into the traffic.

'Heavens to Betsy!' she chided, the Southern phrase she'd heard so many times over the years tripping off her tongue with ease, her Irish soul causing her to add, 'Janey Mack! You're not in America now. Irish roads are different – do you hear me? They're narrower for one. So slow down.'

'I'm not used to sitting on the right-hand side – or driving on it.'

What that had to do with pressing the accelerator like a speed demon was beyond Maudie, but nevertheless her order was met. She was a good girl, Maudie thought. She was still clutching the seat though, needing something solid to hold on to. Today was going to be a day of happy, sad, frightening and painful memories, she thought, bracing herself as she stared out the windscreen. Only, instead of seeing the car farting black exhaust fumes in front of them, she saw a young girl with fiery red hair and emerald-green eyes who was full of passion for the freedom of her country and love for her man. A girl who had no idea what her country would rob her of.

2

RUSH, COUNTY DUBLIN, 1920

The door to the shop jingled open, bringing a whisper of salty air inside. It was carried on the April breeze from the coast of Rush, County Dublin's North Beach. In the doorway, Maudie saw the outline of Ronan Quinn's rangy frame blocking the sunlight, and his signature scent of warm soil, sun-dried hay and the muskiness of physical labour teased her senses.

The effect Ronan's presence had on Maudie was immediate, and she reacted like a deer freezing at the sight of a hunter. Her hands clenched so hard her nails dug grooves into her palms, and the ground beneath her feet no longer felt solid. She wanted to throw herself at him, yearning to stretch up on her tippy-toes and kiss those shapely lips of his.

Of course, she didn't dare show her 'base' instincts and dug her nails in even harder. Her boss, Mrs Hughes, couldn't be trusted. Maudie was certain her employer, in her dual role as postmistress, on occasion steamed open letters she thought might hold some juicy piece of news. If the ferret-like woman were to get an inkling that her young shop girl was smitten with Ronan Quinn, she'd gleefully drop it into conversation the next time she saw her mam.

Maudie's mam and da had expressly forbidden her to have anything to do with Ronan, a known member of the IRA.

When it came to the lad she loved, her mam was fond of saying, 'He's a dose of the divil in him. Sure, all the Quinn lads do now their poor departed mammy, good woman that she was, is no longer here to rein them in. And then there's the poor mister bedridden with the consumption.'

As for her da, well... The last time her younger sister had mentioned having seen Maudie talking with Ronan Quinn, he'd glowered across the table and said that the O'Connors might come from a long line of smugglers, but these days they kept their noses clean, and their stance on the war was neutral. Maudie would do well to remember that.

Meanwhile, Mam, dishing up stew, had made it clear she didn't want the likes of that Quinn lad sniffing after Maudie and firing her brothers up with all his fierce talk of independence for Ireland and putting their family at risk. She'd heard rumours he was hiding weapons on the family farm.

What Mam and Da didn't understand was that love, true love, didn't give you choices. She didn't have any choice where Ronan was concerned because she loved him with everything she had. And at least Ronan and his brothers were doing something. They were putting their words into actions.

Paudie and Jocelyn O'Connor's neutral stance was born of fear of reprisals. The Black and Tans sent over to assist the Royal Irish Constabulary wouldn't just deal with the Quinn men should suspicion of involvement with the IRA's Fingal Brigade fall on them – anyone known to associate with them would also be punished.

The violence had stepped up of late with more targeted attacks on the RIC in and out of nearby towns, and with each passing day, the threat of discovery for those involved or who sympathised became more likely. Nobody could be trusted.

Especially not Mrs Hughes, Maudie thought, hearing her

tsking and tutting over a salacious titbit of tattle with Mrs Nolan, the indiscreet cook at nearby Foxbourne House. It was no doubt over Miss Cecelia, the wild eldest daughter of the aristocratic Altringham family, who gave the cook plenty of gossipy fodder.

She allowed herself to meet Ronan's gaze, hooded beneath coal-black brows. His blue eyes were luminous against his fair skin, making her think of the sky washed clean from the rain, and as he stepped inside the shop, letting the door close behind him, he pulled a silly face at Mrs Hughes then winked at Maudie.

Maudie bit her bottom lip as her fears for him were swept away and, stifling a giggle, fixed her eyes firmly on the woodworm swirls on the boards she was standing on.

Maudie kept her voice neutral as she dropped her dusting rag and stepped behind the counter. 'Good afternoon, Mr Quinn.'

Ronan doffed his cap at her, an unmissable glint of mischief in his eyes. 'I've come to settle the account, Miss O'Connor, and I'll be needing a bag of bran while I'm at it.'

'Certainly, Mr Quinn.' Maudie was giddy, like she was play-acting for her audience of two. The nuns who'd taught at St Catherine's, the school she'd attended until she was fourteen, had always said she'd a quick brain, and it served her well at times like this. Though nervous giggles threatened, she opened the accounts book and did the maths in no time. 'That'll be nine and six you'll be owing us with the bran included, thank you.'

Ronan fished around in his pocket and counted out the coins before pressing them into Maudie's outstretched palm. Only that wasn't all he passed her.

Excitement surged as her fingers closed around the note. Heart racing even faster, she checked Mrs Hughes's back was turned and slipped the note into her apron pocket before opening the register to fetch his few pence change. 'There you go, Mr Quinn.'

'Thanks, Miss O'Connor.'

Maudie wondered if her eyes held that same cheeky twinkle as Ronan's as he hefted the sack of bran onto his shoulder.

He nodded at Maudie and the two other women. 'Have a fine day now, ladies.' Then he was gone.

Mrs Hughes and Mrs Nolan ignored him, although as Maudie returned to her dusting, she did catch the words 'Quinns' and 'trouble' in the same sentence. Normally that would bother her. But not right now.

Ronan's note was burning a hole in her pocket. She was desperate to read it but didn't dare risk doing so in the shop, not when a customer – or worse, a Tan – could barrel in at any second.

She couldn't wait though. There was nothing for it. She'd have to make an excuse.

'Pardon me, Mrs Hughes, but I've a call of nature in need of answering.'

The woman's mouth puckered as she grudgingly flapped her hand toward the back of the shop, muttering, 'Be quick about it.'

Maudie didn't mess about, hurrying through the cluttered rear of the shop, out the back door and down the path to the wooden outhouse. Only when the door was closed and the bolt slid into place did she retrieve the paper. She held the note up to the chink of light sneaking in through the gap at the top of the door.

Meet me at our place on your way home and make sure you're not seen.

Maudie pressed the note to her lips. She had known Ronan

for as long as she could remember, falling in love with him the moment he'd defended her.

As they'd flooded out St Catherine's gates one afternoon, John-Paul Hennessy, the local doctor's son, had loitered, waiting for her in the lane to taunt her about being a witch, with her red hair and freckles. She was no pushover and she'd have defended herself, even if he was twice her size, only Ronan had beat her to it and shoved him over. John-Paul, or JP as they called him, had landed on his arse in a puddle, and everybody had laughed. Except, of course, for him. He'd looked murderous.

Even now, all these years later, he held on to that grudge, scowling at Ronan on his visits home from Trinity, where he was following in his father's footsteps and training in medicine. He no longer called her a witch but had a sneering, superior manner on the mercifully few occasions he came in the shop.

His mother's ill health had brought him home from university in recent times. The word was Mrs Hennessy, a sparrow-like woman always trying to please her husband and only child, wasn't long for this world. If he'd been a different kind of man, she'd have felt sympathy for him, but the only empathy she could rustle up was for his long-suffering mother.

These days, she wasn't intimidated by him and saw him for what he was: an unpleasant, pompous man with a boulder of discontent at the expectation he'd take over his father's practice resting on his shoulders.

It had taken Ronan a little longer to reciprocate the feelings this incident had sparked in Maudie. He'd stopped seeing her as the annoying little girl who'd follow him about with the devotion of a puppy shortly after her eighteenth birthday. One afternoon, he'd sauntered into the shop and everything had changed. He couldn't explain it, he told her later, other than he felt like he'd been struck by lightning, looking into her green eyes and suddenly seeing the beautiful young woman she'd blossomed into. The banter they'd exchanged as his need for tobacco, tins of beans and wedges of cheese increased overnight had soon blossomed into courtship. Until her mam and da had both put their foot down.

Then the furtive note-passing in the shop had begun, along with the clandestine meetings. Maudie would never give Ronan up. He understood her in a way no one else did, recognising the fire in her that refused to be satisfied with the status quo. Like her, he wanted to see and experience more than their tiny eastern pocket overlooking the Irish sea.

They'd lain in the sand dunes, hidden in their secret place, her hand in his, watching clouds scudding overhead, momentarily forgetting about the fight for freedom as they dreamed of marrying then travelling to America.

Maudie longed to stare up at the Statue of Liberty, while Ronan daydreamed of wandering amongst the skyscrapers he'd heard were being built in New York. They both knew Ireland's misty shores would bring them home, and then, as the eldest son, he'd take over the running of Quinn Farm, which would pass to him when the tuberculosis claimed his daddy.

First and foremost, though, Maudie understood Ronan's need to be part of changing things. He wanted freedom for Ireland, true freedom, as did she with every ounce of her being, and they'd made a pact, linking their little fingers and sealing it with a kiss, not to marry until this was achieved.

What would it be like to be his wife? She sounded the name out in her head. *Maudie Quinn.*

A smile played at the corners of her mouth, the note still held to her lips as she imagined a time when those kisses of Ronan's that left her full of want and need didn't have to end.

There was no more time for daydreaming, however – not if she didn't want Mrs Hughes hammering on the door. So Maudie tore the note into tiny shreds and let them float down into the dank depths of the privy. Then she unlocked the door, stepped outside and gulped the fresh air, aware the hours between now and when she could at last turn the sign in the window to *closed* would crawl by slower than Father Doyle's droning of the Eucharist Prayer.

Surely her parents couldn't object to them being together when Ireland was at peace as an independent nation? And, if they did, she knew she'd marry him anyway.

3

Maudie was wrapping sausages in greaseproof paper and counting down the minutes until she could turn the sign in the shop window to *closed* and shout out goodnight to Mrs Hughes. She desperately wanted to hurry away to meet Ronan.

As she placed the sausage package in the wooden crate along with the other items on the list young Liam Lynch had presented her with, her eyes swivelled across the shop floor to where Mrs Hughes was engaged with a salesman. He was scribbling down her order, and Maudie bit her bottom lip, hesitating. Was it safe? It was now or never, she decided.

Her cheerful demeanour belied her anxiety as she began tallying up Mrs Lynch's shopping list in her neat handwriting. She halved the weight of the flour and potatoes, added a turnip and bag of carrots, omitted the sausages altogether and slipped in two cans of salted fish and another of peas to the order. Maudie had a system whereby she'd place the extra items onto the accounts of those customers in town who could well afford them, and so far no one had picked up on the discrepancies and quibbled over their account. Ronan had told her she was a modern-day, female Robin Hood, robbing the rich to give to the poor. Robbing was a strong word, Maudie had thought, not seeing herself as a thief but rather as doing her bit for the cause.

She closed the small accounting book with a snap. 'Here we go, Liam.'

The lad was barely twelve years old, with tufts of gingery hair protruding from his cap. As the oldest Lynch child, he'd been sent to collect the staple supplies by his poor work-worn mammy, who'd too many mouths to feed and no husband to help. Liam's smile of thanks dimpled his cheeks, but it didn't light his eyes. The lad was grieving, having lost his da and his childhood simultaneously by having to step into shoes he should never have had to fill. Eamon Lynch had been shot dead for his part in the RIC patrol ambush on the road into Skerries earlier in the year. He might be a hero to those who wanted freedom for Ireland, but he'd been a husband and father too.

Liam's nose was runny, and he looked pale as his grubby hands reached for the crate, his gaze flitting past her to linger longingly on the colourful jars of sweets on the shelf behind her. The urge to grab the sherbet lemons and add one for him and each of his siblings to the family's groceries made her ache, but the odds of getting caught were too high. Mrs Hughes's sharp-eyed gaze wouldn't miss her fetching the jar down, and her end-of-day inventory would pick up on the sweets not having been added to the Lynches' on-tick tally. Maudie couldn't afford to get caught. The little extra she managed to send home to those in need was too important to risk for the sake of sherbet lemons. So, in an attempt to drag the young boy's attention away from temptation, she said, 'Be sure to remember me to your mammy now, Liam, won't you?'

Liam blinked, coming out of his sherbet-induced trance. 'I will, Miss O'Connor.'

'And, Liam?'

'Yes, Miss?'

She dropped her voice to a whisper. 'There's an extra carrot in there for Pip.'

His face lit up upon hearing this, and Maudie's heart lifted a little. At least his pony was in for a treat. Then he dragged the crate from the countertop and gave a soft 'oof', staggering beneath its weight. All that was visible of him now were spindly legs protruding from his patched short trousers as he took a few stumbling steps backward before steadying himself and turning toward the door.

'Liam Lynch, tell your mam there'll be no more on tick if she's late paying her account again this month! I'm not a bank giving out free money,' Mrs Hughes called after him.

'Don't mind her, Liam,' Maudie whispered, holding the door for the young lad and glimpsing his waiting pony and trap. 'Take care now.'

She'd no sooner picked up a dusting rag, intending to wipe the tins of fruit, when the door burst open. Three Black and Tans – so named for their mismatched uniforms of dark green jackets, which appeared to be black, and tan military trousers – barged in reeking of ale, their gazes sweeping over the shelves to see what they could help themselves to. Maudie shivered, feeling as though the temperature in the shop had plummeted.

The salesman, who seconds earlier had been full of blarney, seemed to shrink, while Mrs Hughes uncharacteristically ignored the muddy prints the Black and Tans' boots were leaving on her floor. Nor did she greet the young men.

'Afternoon, all,' the taller of the trio said in an accent that leaned toward cockney as he rubbed his hands together like he was warming them by a fire. His gaze alighted on Mrs Hughes, whose lips tightened, while the salesman attempted to blend in with the dry goods. The British recruit skipped over him, pinning Maudie with his pale-lashed stare. She shivered, despite her determination not to be cowed, as his eyes raked over her body far too slowly for her liking before returning to her face with a smirk.

He abruptly turned back to Mrs Hughes. 'Now then, Missus, you Irish are known for your hospitality, so do you have anything stronger than tea to warm myself and the lads up with? It might be spring but we're not used to the wind off the Irish sea.'

'What you see here on the shelves is all I stock.' Mrs Hughes's tone was clipped.

'Have you forgotten something, Missus?' His tone was playful, but there was no mistaking the steel that lay beneath the words.

For a moment, bewilderment flickered over Mrs Hughes's face, and then she realised what the bully was angling at.

Maudie willed her not to bow and scrape. *Don't say it!* she shouted silently.

'Sir.' Mrs Hughes spat the word.

'That's more like it. Did you hear that, lads?' He turned with a swagger to his associates, who were hanging back uncertainly, clearly taking their lead from him.

The shorter of the two nodded. 'We did, Art.'

'These Paddies need to learn who's in charge and show us some respect.'

'They're too busy trying to blow us all up for that,' the other lad muttered.

Maudie burned with indignation, and her toes were curling inside her boots to the point of cramping. These men were common thugs and did not deserve their respect. Still, she wasn't stupid enough to speak up, and there was nothing she could do other than watch as they helped themselves to tobacco, ale and other supplies.

Occurrences like this were nothing new since the Tans, as they called them, had begun arriving in force last year, but she'd not seen the ringleader of this particular trio of brutes about town. There was cruelty in those pale-lashed eyes of his, and his stare had made icy fingers creep up her spine and her scalp prickle. It was predatory, and she sensed she would have to watch her back from here on in.

4

Maudie's heart was thumping, still jittery from her encounter with the Tans, as she hurried along North Beach's deserted shoreline. She couldn't stop glancing back over her shoulder, her eyes watchful as her boots sank into the dry sand. Her path would have been easier if she could have moved down the beach to where it was damp and packed, closer to the sea's edge, but she couldn't risk being spotted.

On her left, the low-lying dunes separated the beach from the cluster of limewashed fishermen's cottages near Rush Harbour, one of which was her home, partially hiding her. At this time of day, the harbour and shoreline were deserted, with the menfolk either home tucking into dinner or at the pub. The pub, with any luck, was where the Tans were now too.

To her right, the faint shushing of seawater being sucked out with the tide was almost drowned out by the stiff breeze settling in for the evening, and the sky was shot through with gold as the sun sank low. Seagulls circled lazily overhead as Maudie abruptly veered left into the dunes. The salt wind was stinging her eyes, making her feel alive. She could almost believe she was wild and free as she pretended to be Emer, wife of Cú Chulainn, the warrior of legends. This land was hers and the Irish people's, she thought, picking her way through the sand hills, and Ronan a warrior to be feared.

There was no marker, but she knew these dunes intimately, where she'd played since she was a dot, and the way to her and Ronan's secret place – a hollowed dip in the undulating shoreline where they could be together. There were no prying eyes to see them there, shielded by mounds of sand and waving grasses.

He wasn't there, and hoping he wouldn't be long because the sun wasn't far off setting, she unknotted her scarf, flapping it out before laying it down to sit on. The sand beneath it and the stiff cotton of her dress was still warm as she pulled her knees to her chin and wrapped her arms around her stockinged legs. Here, she was sheltered from the breeze, and cocooned in the hollow, the jittery feeling abated. She began softly singing 'The Foggy Dew', and the protest song swept away the lingering fear the pale-lashed Tan's gaze had left her with.

'Maudie!' Ronan sank down next to her a minute or two later, and she started, not having heard him approaching.

'What if I'd been one of the Tans?'

Fear made his voice sharp, and Maudie grabbed his hand. 'But you weren't.'

Ronan pulled free from her grasp, shaking his head. 'Don't make light of it. They're everywhere. You've to keep your wits about you. Do you hear me?'

'What have you heard? What's going on?'

He set the satchel he carried everywhere aside and took his cap off, holding it loosely between his legs, which were bent like hers. She reached over to ruffle his thick, black hair – kept short because otherwise it hung straight in his eyes.

This time, he caught hold of her hand and held it tight. 'You're to take extra care, Maudie. That's all you need to know.'

Maudie huffed, deciding she wouldn't tell him about the Tans' visit to the shop this afternoon and the uneasiness it had unlocked. It would only worry him further, and he already had so much on his plate, looking after his da on top of everything else. She knew it was worry behind Ronan's steadfast refusal to bring her in on his clandestine activities with the Fingal Brigade. He was adamant the less she knew, the better, but it was a bone of contention between them. He argued that it was too dangerous and he wasn't prepared to risk her safety; Maudie fired back that it was a risk she had to live with every day where he was concerned.

'Is it not equally dangerous for you?' Maudie said now, raising the tired argument. She was unable to keep the irritation out of her voice but mindful of not raising it.

'Don't worry about me. I can look after myself.'

Maudie dug the toes of her boots into the sand. 'Oh, and I can't – is that it? Sure, you know yourself young Liam's da, Eamon Lynch, said the same thing, and he's dead and buried.' She folded her arms defiantly. 'And don't speak to me like I'm a delicate waif, Ronan Quinn.'

'Maudie—'

'No. It's a wasted opportunity and you know it.'

There was no need to explain what she meant. Maudie had said it until she was hoarse. Her job at the shop meant she was in an ideal position for passing information. She was wasting her breath once more, though, because Ronan's jaw was set in that infuriatingly stubborn manner. His stubbornness frustrated her as much as hers did him. They were kindred spirits in that department. This time, however, Maudie wasn't backing down, having had all afternoon to formulate her argument.

'What about Countess Markievicz and all she's done along with all the other women working behind the scenes? Is it not dangerous for them?'

Ronan opened his mouth, but Maudie didn't let him reply. 'Women are acting as couriers and intelligence gatherers, Ronan. They're out there fundraising, nursing, even taking part in direct combat. And what am I doing to help? Nothing. That's what.' She folded her arms across her chest.

'Are you finished?'

She was a long way from done, but she'd momentarily run out of steam.

'Those women are brave – I'm not disputing that or that you are too. It's your fearlessness that frightens me. But those women, Maudie, they aren't you.'

Maudie prided herself on not being wishy-washy and weak, but when it came to Ronan, she turned to jelly. She recognised the softening of his face as he leaned in toward her, tracing a finger gently down her cheek.

'I don't want to fight with you.'

His voice was husky and his breath warm on her face. Maudie's lips parted in anticipation, but frustration overrode desire. Enough was enough. This time he wouldn't bring her round with his sweet kisses. She was sick of feeling useless, and she needed to make a point.

Maudie clambered to her feet, scooping up her scarf and shaking the sand off it. Was it frustration or anger choking her? Either way, she was determined to make Ronan see sense and let her get involved, and if the only way to do that was to leave him here stewing, so be it.

She was yanked roughly to the ground once more, and her lips peeled back in protest, but before she could make a sound, his hand clamped firmly over her mouth. The urgency in his eyes conveyed the need for silence.

They weren't alone.

5

Maudie read the urgency in Ronan's eyes. His pupils had dilated, and his eyes appeared more black than blue as he raised his index finger to his lips. She nodded in understanding, and he took his hand off her mouth before angling his head toward the wall of sand. Following his lead, she crawled over to it, and they crouched with their backs against it. If whoever was out there was to stumble across their hollow, the best they could hope for would be that they didn't see them until it was too late and fell in. Then there was a chance of escape. Maudie squared her shoulders, knowing she had to be ready for whatever came next.

It was a blessing that the much-cursed easterly blowing off the Irish sea would have carried their earlier whispers downwind from their uninvited guest and in turn had served to give them forewarning of the person's approach. Out the corner of her eye, Maudie saw Ronan's hand snaking toward his satchel. The pistol he retrieved made her hands clammy and her stomach bilious. She hadn't known he carried a weapon, and from his confidence handling it, she could tell he knew how to fire it, should he have to. Had he killed with it? Would he kill now if he had to? She eyed his tensed muscles, realising with a jolt that there were sides to him she hadn't seen before. Ronan was her heart, but he was also a soldier.

The air around them tasted thick, and if fear had a smell, then this was it. Maudie was certain her heart, which was beating louder than a bodhrán, would give them away.

The crashing about and muttered curses didn't belong to any Irishman, and as they grew nearer, she held her breath, biting the inside of her lips so hard salty blood trickled forth. It had to be a Tan. Her chest grew tight with desperation, and light-headedness threatened. She was only moments away from gasping loudly for air, the instinct for survival primed to take over, when whoever was out there began to move away.

Maudie inhaled in a hot, desperate rush as the sounds grew fainter, until Ronan, pistol still at the ready, risked raising his head above the hollow to look.

It took a moment for the circulation to return to Maudie's frozen limbs, and when it did, she shuffled over to Ronan, leaning against him to peer over his shoulder. Through the wavering grasses on the shoreline sloping away from their hiding place, a lone figure weaved his way down the beach toward town. Her body stiffened – she knew who it was. Maudie was certain the man on the beach was the Tan called Art – presumably short for Arthur. She could only see his retreating back in the fading light, but she recognised his ramrod gait, and if he were to turn around, she knew he'd have pale-lashed eyes.

'He was looking for someone.' Ronan didn't take his eyes off him.

Maudie backed away to the far side of the hollow, eager to distance herself from the man on the beach. Ronan was right. Was it her? Had he followed her from town? The thought filled her with a sick dread, but she could think of no other reason for him to have been here given his drunken state. At the memory of how his eyes had grazed over her in the shop, she shivered.

'He won't be back. Not tonight at any rate.' Ronan slid back down on his haunches, the pistol by his side. 'You're shaking, Maudie.'

'It was a close call is all. I'm all right.'

'No you're not. What is it?'

Sometimes Maudie thought he knew her better than she knew herself. 'Nothing.'

He reached out for her, cupping her chin gently with his hand and tilting her head so she'd no choice but to look at him. 'Tell me.'

She couldn't lie, not to Ronan, and swallowing against the dryness of her throat, she relayed her fears. 'I recognise him. He and two other Tans came in the shop shortly before closing this evening and helped themselves. His name's Arthur. I think he followed me, but I was so careful, Ronan. I always am.' Her eyes held his, beseeching. 'I checked and there was no one about.'

Ronan's Adam's apple bobbed as he studied her. 'What else?'

'That's it. I've told you everything.'

'Maudie, c'mon. This is me.'

Her eyes slipped away as she hesitated, but knowing Ronan wouldn't let it go, she resigned herself with a sigh. 'There was something about the way he looked at me. It frightened me.'

Only then did he release her chin. 'You're right to be frightened. What if I'd been held up or couldn't make it and you'd been here on your own?'

He sounded angry, and he didn't need to say anything more. He was only voicing the dark thoughts she couldn't stop pinging through her mind, and she rubbed the goosebumps on her arms when she noticed he was still holding the gun.

'Put that thing away.' She pointed at the weapon, not liking what it had opened her eyes to – the reality of what Ronan was prepared to do and that because of it his life was in danger. She lowered her gaze, worried he'd be able to pick up on her suspicions that the Tan had been trying to find her and that things could have turned out differently if he'd found not just her but Ronan too.

'Not before you learn how to use it.'

Maudie's gaze shot up, and she watched him unload the magazine and check the chamber before holding the pistol out to her.

'C'mere.' He patted the ground in front of him, and she didn't hesitate in reaching forward to take the handgun, her fingers curling around the grip before she moved to sit between his legs, her back resting against his chest. His arms reached around hers as he showed her how to use her left hand for support before unlocking the trigger guard.

'Breathe in, steady yourself and aim straight ahead.'

She did so, locking on to an imaginary target.

'Now, slowly does it. Ease the trigger back with an even pressure.'

There was resistance, but she kept her pressure on it steady, and then the trigger gave way. It was followed by a sharp click.

'Good girl, yourself, and I hope you never have to fire it again.'

Ronan took the pistol from her, and Maudie twisted round to face him as he slipped the handgun back in his satchel. 'We've been fools taking risks like this thinking we could get away with it.'

'Don't say it.'

'I have to. You know I do. We mustn't meet again. Not until the Tans are beaten back. It's too risky.'

'No, Ronan, I couldn't bear it.' Maudie's voice tangled in a sob. The shock of their near miss and the thought of not seeing Ronan other than fleetingly in the shop was suddenly too much.

'And I couldn't bear it if something happened to you. Listen to me.' He pushed the curls that had worked their way free of her bun gently back from her eyes, his hands coming to rest either side of her face, thumbs caressing the line of her jaw. His eyes never left hers. 'I love you, Maudie Jean O'Connor, and one day soon you'll be my wife. Then nobody will be able to keep us apart.'

Maudie felt as if she was falling into twin pools, and as the earnestness in his eyes gave way to a deeper longing, her breath quickened, her lips parting in readiness as he pulled her toward him. Anxiety mingled with need, her eyes fluttered shut and the lapping of the sea at the shore faded until the only sound she was aware of was their breathing. The muskiness of his skin was intoxicating, and Maudie pressed her body against his, wanting more. This evening would be the last time they'd be together for who knew how long. Anything could happen. These were fraught times.

She broke free from his embrace and began to unbutton her dress.

Ronan was mesmerised by her hands, and she could see the effort it took for him to look up and whisper, 'Are you sure?'

'I'm sure.' And Maudie slipped her shoulders free from her dress.

6

This was happiness. This was what it meant to love, Maudie thought, trying to memorise the tickling of Ronan's sleepy breath on her hair and the strength of his arms, honed from hauling hay onto the horse and cart along with the hours of manual labour working on his da's farm. She wanted to be able to pull this here and now out again and again because it was all she was going to have until independence was won. Just for a little while, they'd shut the world out tonight, but as the three-quarter moon emerged from behind the clouds, it crept back in. Maudie knew her mam would be going spare, wondering where she was and what might have happened, and her eyes flickered open. If she didn't arrive home soon, Da would head out looking for her, thinking the worst.

'Ronan.' She rolled onto her side, and her fingers began tracing an outline around his birthmark: three ruby-red, petal-like dots clustered together on the side of his neck she'd once told him reminded her of a shamrock. She hoped it was a lucky sign for him, for them both and their future together.

'Mm.' His voice was heavy with drowsiness.

'We've got to go.' She couldn't believe she was saying it when all she wanted to do was stay there with him forever.

He pulled her closer for a moment, kissing the top of her head before letting her go, and as they hurried to dress he asked, 'What will you tell your mam and da?'

'I don't know. I'll think of something.' She laced her boots before holding her hand out to him to help her up.

'I've been putting a little aside whenever I can, Maudie. An emergency fund, like.'

'For America?'

He nodded. 'There might come a time I'll need to run.'

'Not without me you won't. I love you, Ronan Quinn, and I'll follow you to the ends of the earth if I have to.' She stood on tiptoes and kissed him softly, but this time her lips didn't linger. They needed to go.

The easterly was once more on their side, sending clouds scudding across the misshapen pearl hanging in the sky so they were blanketed by darkness, and Ronan held her hand tightly as he led her to the coastal path. He set a brisk pace, which she would have struggled to match if not for his pulling her along, until they reached the top of the lane lined by the row of fishermen's cottages. Ducking behind a thicket of thorny blackthorn, they could see it was empty, save for the stone door stoop where Tommy O'Rourke was hunched over snoring. This wasn't an uncommon sight and one that suggested Tommy had whiled away the day in the pub instead of fishing, and his wife had locked him out. Maudie would have been amused if she wasn't frantically trying to conjure an excuse for her lateness.

All worries about the dressing-down she was in for the moment she stepped over her cottage's threshold vanished as Ronan hugged her to him fiercely.

'Promise me you'll stay safe, Ronan,' Maudie whispered into the dip at the base of his neck, her hands pressed to his chest, knowing as the words left her mouth that they were unfair.

'Only if you promise me the same.'

'I do. I promise.'

'Me too.'

They both knew the words were hollow as his lips sought hers one last time.

'Go.' Ronan's voice was hoarse as he broke away and stepped back, and Maudie knew she'd no choice but to face the music.

As she picked her way down the lane, she could picture the scene inside her family's cottage. Her father and eldest brothers, twins Jimmy and Shane, followed by Fionn along with her younger siblings, Joe and Caitie would be seated around the table, waiting for dinner. The evening meal wouldn't have been delayed on her account, and she'd tell Mam she'd been sent on deliveries by Mrs Hughes. Maudie knew she'd never be suspected of being bold enough to lie. Still, if she was out too long after dark, Mam would eat the face off her. She'd be having words with Mrs Hughes too – because these days, nothing good happened after dark.

Lying to her mam and da didn't come easy to Maudie, and she longed for the day she could be transparent about her relationship with Ronan. Thankfully, she'd found a confidante in her older sister, Nora, who'd married a local farmer, Martin Gallagher, and was now expecting her third child. Her sister seemed to have been permanently pregnant these last few years, and they lived a simple but happy life nearby on their smallholding. If it weren't for Nora, sometimes she thought she'd go mad with having to keep all the things she felt for Ronan locked up inside.

Hopefully, the need for secrecy would end soon. The Tans were growing more brutal by the day, and Ronan said that was proof they were running scared. The Irish were winning. That may be so, but she lived in daily terror of him becoming the target of their brutality.

As she reached her cottage, a tingling at the base of her neck alerted her to a presence, and she swung round half expecting to see Tommy O'Rourke on his feet and staggering about, but he was still slumped in his doorway. Someone was there though – she was sure of it, so she lifted the latch on the door and hurried inside.

Maudie's eyes refused to close as she lay in her bed later that night, her younger sister Caitlin fidgeting in her sleep above her. A curtain screened her off from the bed Jimmy and Shane shared with Fionn. The two older boys had staggered in from the pub then crashed about getting ready for bed but had fallen asleep as soon as their heads hit the pillow. As for Fionn, the middle brother, he'd sleep through anything. Joe, the youngest O'Connor lad was in Mam and Da's room next door, and tonight her da's low, rumbling snores, usually a source of rhythmic comfort on those nights when sleep wouldn't come, were setting her teeth on edge.

It wasn't her heathen brothers or da keeping her awake though; nor was it the wind rattling at the window like it wished to come in. Fear was the culprit because each time she closed her eyes, wanting to relive the tender look on Ronan's face, all she could see was the Tan's, insipid eyes, and that feeling she'd had earlier of being watched returned. Maudie wasn't a seer, but she'd a sense something bad was coming.

The windows rattled once more, louder this time, and she whimpered as the wind carried an eerie keening.

The banshee was calling.

7

For three nights in a row, Maudie's slumber had been broken by the banshee's cry. The sound was like fingernails down a blackboard and a forewarning something bad was coming. There'd been no sign of the tall Tan searching the dunes for something or someone the other night, but still she had this pervading sense of doom and wished for the opportunity to steal away to Quinn Farm to be with Ronan. As she'd helped clear the breakfast things that morning, she'd been unable to keep her agitation to herself, convincing herself her mam would tell her the banshee, female spirit, omen of death malarkey was superstitious nonsense and that her imagination was running away on her.

But Jocelyn O'Connor had said no such thing. Instead, her face had gone as white as the limewash of their cottage, and the bowl she'd been carrying to the basin had fallen from her hands as she'd crossed herself. Maudie had bent to pick up the enamel dish rolling about on the flagstones, regretting having spoken up. 'Mam, sure, you know what I'm like. It's probably just the wind's whistle I'm after hearing.'

Neither woman had been convinced, and now the yawn

Maudie attempted and failed to stifle felt like it came all the way from her boots. She was tidying the shop's shelves, bringing old stock to the fore. Her head ached, and she was bone-tired; nor had she managed much in the way of breakfast. Awareness of Mrs Hughes's eyes boring like bullet holes into her back saw her all fingers and thumbs as she fumbled the tin of beans she was holding.

'Keeping yer awake, am I?' Mrs Hughes huffed from behind the post-office counter, where she was sorting the mail.

Maudie wasn't in her good books. The shopkeeper had given her a talking-to yesterday about her head being in the clouds when she'd short-changed Mrs Sheedy, who'd been quick to point out the oversight – loudly – in front of the waiting customers.

'I'm sorry, Mrs Hughes. I've not been sleeping well.' Maudie placed the beans on the shelf. She was only now beginning to dry out after getting soaked on her way to work. She reached for a tin of fruit, knowing her employer wasn't interested in excuses.

'Do you think you can manage to stay awake long enough to keep an eye out while I drop this in to Mrs Moore?' Sarcasm laced the older woman's voice as she flapped an envelope at her. 'It's from her daughter in America. She'll be eager to receive it, and that rain's finally gone off.'

In other words, Mrs Hughes wished to hand deliver the letter to the woman who lived a stone's throw from the main street so she could hear the latest instalment of Niamh's new life in New York first-hand.

'Yes of course.' Maudie nodded meekly, all the while silently calling her a ferret-faced auld busybody.

Mrs Hughes pulled her apron over her head as she made her way out the back of the shop, returning a moment later wearing her coat, scarf in hand to guard against today's cold snap.

'I expect that delivery unpacked by the time I get back.' She indicated the crate by the flour sack. Then she glanced out the window as she slipped Mrs Moore's letter into her pocket before carefully folding her scarf into a triangle. 'That north-easterly's blowing in straight from the Arctic today, so it is.' She draped the plain scarf over her scraped-back hair, which was the colour of wood ashes, and was tying it into place when a blast of frigid air and the aroma of damp wool blew into the shop.

Maudie twisted her neck toward the entrance. Her face fell when she saw it wasn't Ronan standing in the doorway but rather an ill wind that had blown in.

'Well, if it isn't young John-Paul Hennessy himself,' Mrs Hughes simpered. As the doctor's son, he was greeted as though Jesus himself had called in with his glass bottle to be filled with milk from the churn. She laid her hand on his forearm, all tea and sympathy. 'How's your poor mammy? She's been in my prayers, so she has, and you be sure to tell her I'll be saying a Hail Mary for her.'

Indecision played out on Mrs Hughes's face, and Maudie knew she was torn as to whether she should stay and see to JP so as not to miss the latest updates from a dying woman's bed or deliver the letter personally to Mrs Moore and be the first to hear the news from New York. In the end, the decision was made for her.

'Thank you, Mrs Hughes. There's comfort in knowing Mother's in your prayers. Now, please, don't let me keep you.' JP, who seemed to have developed a plum in his mouth since leaving Rush for the hallowed halls of Trinity, held the door open to sweep her past.

'You be sure to look after John-Paul here – and give him a quarter of those Bullseyes while you're at it,' Mrs Hughes flung back at Maudie then, directing her attention to JP once more, she said, 'I remember how fond you were of the sweets as a little lad.'

'I still am,' JP replied, his eyes twinkling, 'and that's very kind of you, Mrs Hughes.'

'Not at all.'

Mrs Hughes reluctantly stepped outside, and he shut the door behind her.

Maudie had already abandoned her tins and was waiting to serve him, eager to see him on his way. 'I'm sorry about your mammy, JP.' She took the bottle he'd set down in front of her, noting the twinkle in his eyes had disappeared. 'I'll have this filled for you in just a tick.'

'It's John-Paul. Nobody calls me JP these days.'

A leopard didn't change its spots, Maudie thought, the words bouncing off her back as she strode toward the dark, cool corner in the back room where the churns were kept. They were full and therefore heavy, but she managed to fill the bottle without spilling a drop. A blessing because she didn't want to give Mrs Hughes further cause for complaint.

True to her word, she presented the bottle filled with fresh, creamy milk in next to no time before fetching the sweets. 'That will be four pence, please, *John-Paul.*'

JP's lips gave a sardonic twitch at the emphasis Maudie placed on his name as he fetched the correct amount from his trouser pocket.

'Thank you.' She rang the princely sum up on the register, dropped the coins in and closed the drawer, fully expecting him to turn and leave. Instead, JP thrust his hand back in his trouser pocket and began jangling the remaining loose change all the while whistling softly.

Maudie's back stiffened. 'Was there something else you were after?'

'I saw Ronan, quite by chance, in Dublin a few weeks back.'

Ronan having been in Dublin was news to Maudie, but she kept her expression neutral. 'So?'

'So, what would a farmer's boy be doing in the city? I wondered. Especially in these turbulent times.' He placed his hand on the counter and drummed neatly trimmed fingernails on it, faux concern creasing his brow. 'I followed him to see for myself. All the way to Church Street, to St Michan's to be exact. What business could he have there? I wondered, watching him disappear inside the auld church.'

'Perhaps he'd gone to light a candle.' Her eyes pretended innocence because two could play this game, but her insides had turned to ice.

'Hmm. Odd though that he should have a bag he wasn't carrying before with him when he left the church less than five minutes later. 'Tis a mystery as to what was in it.'

His tone said it was anything but, and Maudie braced herself for what he would say next.

'I've been thinking maybe I should drop by the barracks and see if a local farmer lad visiting a church in Dublin empty-handed and leaving with a large bag might be of interest to them.'

Then he sauntered from the shop, leaving Maudie alone, his veiled threat lingering in the air.

8

'Urgh.' Maudie wiped her mouth and straightened, having just emptied the remains of last night's dinner along with the mug of tea she'd supped at breakfast into the bucket she'd dived for as her stomach heaved. She'd worked herself up into a state of anxiety, unable to think coherently for panic during the hour that had passed since JP had left the shop and Mrs Hughes had sailed back in.

All the while, Mrs Hughes watched on with her hand covering her mouth and her back pressed against the counter, trying to put distance between herself and Maudie. She eyed the bucket with distaste.

'I'm sorry, Mrs Hughes.' Maudie blinked to clear her vision, her eyes burning. 'I'll go and wash this out.' She dragged herself upright and picked the bucket up, desperate to clean up her mess and use having been sick to her advantage. It would be the excuse she needed to get away and warn Ronan.

'What on earth brought that on? There was nothing wrong with you earlier,' echoed after her, but Maudie didn't reply.

The nausea had passed, but she was freezing in that way no amount of blankets would fix, and her head still thumped as she made her way back into the shop, having splashed her face with cold water, in time to see Mrs Hughes wielding a broom. The cold water had done nothing to alleviate her panic over JP's visit, but the sight of her employer jabbing Francis McMahon with the handle end of the broom brought her up short. The rank smell of a man needing a good wash along with his favoured tipple, poitín, as he staggered backward made Maudie gag once more.

The drunk eejit tripped over his own feet as he was nudged out of the shop, landing on his arse in the muddy, rutted gravel of the road. This should have made her giggle behind her hand, but it didn't because although her head felt foggy, she knew she had to act. Maudie had to warn Ronan about JP's suspicions over what was hidden on Quinn Farm. They both knew he couldn't be trusted – he'd had it in for Ronan for years. He could be whispering in the ear of a Tan now while she dithered, and the need to reach the farm and warn Ronan saw raw energy course through her veins, fighting off whatever she was sickening with.

'And don't you be coming back into my shop when you've been on the batter and stinking like a pig again, Francis McMahon,' Mrs Hughes shouted, flapping the door back and forth so the air blew the fumes from the shop.

Maudie moaned, staggering and grasping the counter to steady herself. 'Oh, I feel terrible, so I do, Mrs Hughes.'

Alarm registered on her employer's face. 'You do look peaky. I hope you're not contagious. What did you have for your dinner last night?'

'Fish.'

'Could it have been off?'

Maudie shrugged, willing the older woman to say she should go home so she could head up to Quinn's Farm. She had to find Ronan.

Mrs Hughes crossed herself frantically. 'What an afternoon.

Francis McMahon carrying on about wanting tobacco on tick and you grovelling about on your hands and knees being sick.' She gave a firm shake of her head as though trying to make sense of it all. 'G'won with you, Maudie O'Connor. Get yourself off home, and don't come back until you're able for work.'

Maudie croaked, 'Yes, Mrs Hughes. I'm sorry – I don't know what brought this on.'

For someone supposedly poorly, she moved with lightning speed to fetch her coat, pulling her hat on as she hurried out the door.

'And I'll be docking your pay!'

Outside, Maudie was grateful for the spectacle Francis McMahon was creating as he got to his feet and began hurling profanities at the crowd of bystanders, who, in turn, were lapping up the drama and egging him on. She kept her head low, adrenaline having pushed aside her earlier fatigue as she resisted the urge to take the faster route and run straight up the main street. It would only draw attention to herself. As it was, her shoulders were knotted with the expectation of a meaty paw clamping down on one of them at any second – someone demanding answers as to what the rush was as she splashed through fresh puddles, only breathing easier once she'd erred left.

The narrow alley tucked between buildings was a reprieve from the cold wind, but it was full of shadows, and she stifled a cry as a mangy cat on the prowl emerged with an annoyed mewl. Her feet barely touched the ground until she surfaced on the lane at the bottom that would lead her away from town and closer to Ronan.

It wasn't long before the humdrum noises of life in the town of Rush faded, replaced by the lonely bleat of sheep behind low-lying stone walls and whistling wind rushing across the countryside – other than that, the only sound was Maudie's heavy breathing. She was slipping and sliding her way up the *bóthar* leading to Quinn Farm, knowing better than to take the risk of being seen on the lane leading to the farm. She was trying to avoid the brambles that were determined to snare her clothes, not stopping even upon hearing the material of her skirt tear.

At last, she caught sight of the ramshackle buildings thirsty for rethatching and could see the farmhouse in the background. She stumbled out onto the sweeping lane of stony gravel the Quinns used to transport goods to town. On either side of her were empty fields. The drying turf and mingling manure tickled the back of her throat as she scanned the vista for signs of life. But there was nothing other than two pigs rolling in the mud, and she hared toward the house, shouting Ronan's name though she knew her voice would be lost on the wind.

Daniel, the youngest of the brothers, heard her, however, appearing outside the barn with tufts of hay clinging to him, which suggested he'd been taking a sneaky nap, as Ronan had confided he was apt to do. He was rubbing his eyes and stared at her like he might be dreaming. 'Maudie?'

'Where's Ronan?' There was no time for pleasantries, and when he scratched his head and yawned, she wanted to shake him hard. 'Where is he, Danny?'

The panic in her voice infiltrated his dozy demeanour. 'He's probably in the house seeing to me da because my stomach's after telling me it's lunchtime. What's brought you here in such a flap?'

Maudie didn't know if Daniel, the baby of the family, had any part in the business of Ronan and his other two brothers, Malachy and Colm. She didn't want to unload her fears on to him if he was unaware of their involvement with the Fingal Brigade, so she was already picking up her skirts.

'Maudie?' Daniel was wide awake now.

She didn't look back as she ran toward the house, bypassing the mooching hens and the donkey waiting to be put to work.

There was no time to knock, so she pushed the door open and called out.

The deserted kitchen she ran into first was in a sorry state. Mairead Quinn would be turning in her grave. But there was no sign of Ronan.

Hearing movement upstairs, Maudie retraced her steps, her legs sagging as she saw Ronan at the top of the stairs, his hand resting on the bannister.

'Thank God!'

'What are you doing here, Maudie?'

Ronan's expression was unreadable as she cried, 'It's JP. He knows about what you and the lads have been doing.'

Before she could say any more, a rasping voice drifted from the open door on the landing.

'What's happening, son? Who's there?'

'Nothing to worry about, Dada. Go back to your soup.'

Maudie understood Ronan didn't want to frighten his da in his poorly state, so she called up the stairs with a joviality she didn't feel, ''Tis only me, Mr Quinn, Maudie O'Connor. Mammy sent me up with a jar of her jam. Sure, we've damsons coming out our ears and enough jam to keep us going all winter. She thought you might enjoy a dollop on a slice of bread.'

'She'd be right – I would. You be sure to tell your mam I said she's a good woman.' His voice quavered into a coughing fit, and Ronan, his foot already on the top tread, hesitated.

Maudie was about to tell him to go to him when the barking eased and Ronan descended the rest of the stairs two at a time, taking hold of Maudie's elbow when he reached the bottom. He steered her outside to where a veil of misting rain had set in.

'What does JP think he knows?' Ronan rallied on her.

The door, catching on a squall, banged shut behind them.

'He came in the shop while Mrs Hughes was out earlier and took great pleasure in telling me he saw you in Dublin. He followed you to St Michan's Church and waited until you came out again.'

The colour draining from Ronan's face confirmed the conclusion JP had jumped to about what Ronan had been carrying when he'd left the church and the rumours Maudie had heard whispered about weapons being stored here at the farm.

'Do you think he's said anything?'

Maudie shook her head. 'I don't know, but he was enjoying himself, like a cat playing with a mouse.'

'He could have already told the Tans.'

Ronan was thinking out loud, Maudie realised, voicing the fears that had brought her scurrying to the farm.

Ronan took stock of her muddy feet and torn skirt. 'You took the *bóthar*?'

She nodded. 'I couldn't risk being seen.'

He grasped hold of her upper arms, his fingers pressing hard. 'Listen to me now, Maudie. Put JP and what he said out of your head. You're to go home and carry on as usual. Do you understand?'

'But where will you move the guns? You have to move them, Ronan. The Tans could be on their way now. You said yourself JP's a liar.'

Hysteria was rising, and Ronan shook her as she'd wanted to shake Danny minutes earlier.

'Maudie, stop it!'

There was a whimpering sound, and it took a moment for Maudie to register it had come from her.

Ronan's voice softened. 'It's safer if you don't know anything. You're not to worry – do you hear me?'

'How?' She choked back a sob.

Ronan, the dampness curling the ends of his dark hair, kissed her then, and she clung to him. They held each other tightly, and she could feel his heart beating through his shirt, but all too soon, he plucked her hands from him.

'You have to go.' He spun her round in the direction she'd come and pushed her gently, and the urgency lacing his words propelled her feet toward the *bóthar*. He was right – she needed to leave him to deal with things here, and as she formed excuses to tell her mam about the state of her appearance, she saw Malachy and Colm, with Daniel bringing up the rear, striding across the field toward the farmhouse.

As she disappeared back down the bramble-strewn path, she knew all that was left for her to do now was pray Ronan and his brothers would stay safe.

9

The rain was lashing now and driving toward Maudie, making progress hard and blurring her vision. She couldn't see further than the length of her arm. The Tan called Arthur. She sensed he was coming for Ronan and his brothers. Her skirt and blouse clung to her; her coat was sodden, and her boots squelched with each step, her body leaden. That was when she heard her, the sound all around her. She cast about wildly, even though she knew she wouldn't see anything, but the thin keening, a lament full of sorrow, rang inside her head.

Was it her the banshee was calling for? Or had she been too late to save Ronan and his brothers? Were the Tans' heavy boots marching toward the farmhouse this minute? You couldn't outrun the banshee, but fear made her try, spurring her on despite the mud and thorny brambles doing their best to stop her, tracking the ground so as not to lose her footing.

Maudie was breathing heavily, her heart banging and her teeth clenched so tightly they hurt. She risked raising her gaze momentarily, but all she could make out was the curving of the path ahead, further blinding her as to what lay around the corner. The wailing made her feel like she was losing her mind, and she covered her ears with her hands as she smacked headlong into a presence too solid to be otherworldly.

The wind was sucked from her lungs like the bellows of a Uillean pipe being squeezed hard, and she stumbled backward, barely managing to stay upright. It took a moment for Maudie to comprehend the warning behind the banshee's cry because it was no apparition blocking her way but *him*.

Those pale-lashed eyes mocked her beneath his peaked cap, beads of water rolling off it, and her stomach clenched tighter than a fist ready to punch. JP must have gone straight to the barracks after he left the shop. It was the only explanation for a Tan to be using the *bóthar* rather than the lane in this downpour. He wanted to approach the farmhouse by stealth. Others were no doubt on their way too.

Suddenly, a calm inner voice penetrated the maelstrom inside her head. *You mustn't let him sense you're afraid of him, Maudie. Animals can always sense weakness.*

'You startled me.' *Show no fear, Maudie.* She recovered her breath and raised her chin, but not before she saw the pistol tucked into the waistband of his trousers through his open coat. Any decent man would have asked if she was all right, but this was a man without a shred of it. Somehow she found the courage to look him in the eye, revulsion coursing through her.

'What's your hurry?' His lip curled.

There was a canine quality in the flash of teeth, putting Maudie in mind of a wolf as she stood her ground. She pushed this thought aside, knowing for Ronan and his brothers' sake she needed to stall him because she'd begged to help, and this, now, was her chance. 'It's Arthur, isn't it? I saw you in the shop I work in the other day.'

There wasn't so much as a flicker at the use of his name.

The words babbled forth. 'I was sick earlier, so I was. Into a bucket no less. I think it was on account of the salt fish I had for me dinner last night, although I'll not be upsetting my mam by telling her that.' She deliberately rambled on like a thick eejit, hoping Ronan was using the precious seconds she was gleaning him wisely. 'Mrs Hughes told me to go home, so you know I must have been poorly. But it was the funniest thing, once I got there, I felt better, and my mam sent me up to the Quinns' farm with a jar of jam for the mister.' Her words ran into one another as she played the part of simple village girl to the hilt. 'He's fond of her damson jam, so he is. And the poor man's terrible sick with the consumption. I don't think he's long for this—'

'You Bog Irish are all liars.' The Tan cut her off and took a step closer, a malevolent presence blocking her path.

Maudie instinctively stepped back. Her hands were clenched by her sides and her body coiled tight ready to run if she needed to.

'You think I don't know who lives at the farm you left town in such a hurry to visit? Rebel scum. We've been watching them.' Spittle foamed at his mouth.

'You followed me?' It slipped out. In trying to warn him, she'd put Ronan in danger.

His eyes narrowed. 'I've seen you sneaking about. I saw you in the dunes and today ducking down that alley, checking behind you to make sure you weren't noticed. You're not so clever, are you?'

Maudie stayed silent.

'When I'm done with you, I'll go back to the barracks and tell them what I think that Paddy of yours has stashed up at that farm.'

Awareness of being all alone here on the *bóthar* with the enemy prickled. It dawned on Maudie that he'd said 'when he was done'. It wasn't Ronan and his brothers he'd come for. It was her. He'd followed her to the farm then lain in wait, knowing she'd come back the same way. Every nerve ending in her body screamed at her to run. Now!

She made to sidestep him, but his boots were planted firmly.

There was nowhere to go except back where she'd come, and he'd be on her before she could turn heel. The only hope she had was to talk her way out of this, and so she steeled herself, continuing to play her role.

''Tis a small kindness my mam had me doing is all, sir. She'll be worried about me now the weather's turned and will have my brothers out looking. I'd thank you to let me pass so I can be on me way.'

The slap rang out like a pistol retort and saw Maudie reel backward, her boots grappling with the sodden earth as her hand flew to her face. Something warm oozed from the corner of her mouth, and she stared at the Tan, wide-eyed, before railing on him. 'Bastard!' White-hot hatred for this man and what he symbolised swept her terror aside. 'Only a blackguard would hit a woman like so.'

A pulse throbbed at his temple, and his nostrils flared as his lips curled into a parody of a smile. Maudie knew then she was staring evil in the face, and as she made a desperate attempt to duck past him, her feet left the ground before her back slammed down onto the path, winding her a second time. There was no time to react before he was on her, and even as her brain reconnected with her body and she began to flail at him with her fists, he was grabbing her arms, pinning them over her head with one hand. His leg rammed between her thighs as she thrashed beneath the suffocating stench of wet wool, tobacco and ale. It wasn't the banshee whose scream ripped through the air but hers.

Maudie knew what would happen next as he tore her underwear, the rough skin of his roaming hand scraping her skin. His pupils had dilated, filling his eyes with blackness as he panted overtop of her, and when he rammed his way inside her, filling her body with pain, she left her mind, not wanting to come back.

Her instinct for survival was stronger, however, and as he

rolled off her with a grunt, she knew this was her one chance. Maudie reared up, intending to run for her life but registered his handgun, discarded while he did his worst. They dove for it at the same time, but Maudie was quicker, and though she fumbled it momentarily given its slickness from the rain, she didn't hesitate. Her finger found the trigger and squeezed it.

The Tan's mouth widened in disbelief as his hands clutched his stomach, those pale-lashed eyes never leaving hers. Maudie fired again, this time keeping her eyes open and her hand steady, before scrambling away as he fell forward into the mud. Somewhere, someone was sobbing, and she was oblivious to the gun still in her hand, lying limp in her lap.

'Maudie!' Ronan swooped down on her, kneeling in the mud and prising her fingers from the gun. He set it aside.

'I had no choice.' Maudie realised it was her she could hear sobbing as she collapsed against his chest. 'I had no choice. He – he—'

'Shush.' He rocked her gently in his arms. 'You did what you had to do.'

She had no idea how long they stayed there, but her sobs eventually eased into shuddering breaths, and Ronan let her go then rose to his feet. He nudged the immobile body with the toe of his boot before crouching down and putting two fingers to the Tan's neck. 'He's dead. I would have killed him myself if he hadn't been.' It was then he looked back at Maudie and saw the blood on her face where her lip had split. He fetched his hanky and wiped it away gently.

'I killed him.' Maudie felt as if she were in a trance as drops of rain mingled with the tears staining her cheeks. The world felt disjointed and dreamlike as Ronan thrust out his hand and helped her to stand. Her legs buckled, and once he'd steadied her, he placed his hand on her forehead, his brows knitting.

'Jaysus but you're burning up. That's more than shock. You're sick, Maudie.'

She tried to focus, but it was hard as her vision swam. She had to tell him what she knew. 'He followed me to the farm then waited for me here, and once he'd – once he'd—' She couldn't bring herself to say the words out loud.

'Shush now. I know. Was he alone?'

She nodded. 'When he'd finished with me, he planned to go back to the barracks and tell the others about you and your brothers.' Her eyes wavered to the lifeless form, and panic bubbled in her throat. 'What will we do?'

'I want you to put this out of your head. It never happened. Get home to your bed now. Go.'

For the second time that day, he gave her a gentle push, and Maudie staggered down the path. She fell twice before somehow picking herself back up and, with her wits about her enough not to want to draw attention to where she'd come from, crossed the fields instead of the road, taking the back way to the cottage.

The fever that had been building all afternoon was a raging inferno by the time she fell in the door, collapsing in a heap on the cottage floor and lying so still at her mother's feet she could have been dead.

10

Maudie's eyes fluttered open. Disorientated, it took her a moment to work out where she was.

A ray of sunlight filtering through the window of the room she shared with her brothers and sister was the first thing she registered. She watched the twirling dust motes trapped in it as things started to fall into place. She was in bed at home in the cottage where she'd always lived, and for reasons she was too exhausted to work out, this filled her with relief.

How had she got here?

It hurt to think and so she didn't, croaking her mam's name instead then letting her head fall back against the pillow. Attempting to swallow, she winced. Her throat was drier than a bone, and a slow beat drummed inside her head. She was cold too and, lifting her head slightly, saw the quilt bunched around her feet. The simple cotton nightdress Mam had made her felt damp and clung to her skin.

Jocelyn O'Connor must have sensed she was awake as she swished into the room not a minute later. The random thought that the last time she'd been outside it had been pelting down popped into Maudie's head as her mam's cool hand rested against her cheek briefly. She wanted to grab hold of it and keep it pressed there because it made her feel safe.

'Thanks be to God, your fever's broken. The blessed Mother must've been watching over you, Maudie O'Connor.'

Maudie looked at her mam's gently lined face and saw it was creased with concern. And something else. There was something in her eyes she didn't recognise. But her mind was addled, she decided, as a hazy memory of being sent home from the shop by a disgruntled Mrs Hughes floated forth.

She'd been sick – she remembered that much at least. There'd be time to mull over the rest of how she'd come to be here later, but right now she needed a drink because it hurt to talk too. 'Could I have a cup of water, please?'

'Of course.'

Jocelyn returned with a tin cup and bossy orders, more like her usual self. 'Now don't sit up too quickly and only take a small sip to start with, or you'll bring it back up. You've been supping a little these last three days but not nearly enough. This will do you good.'

Maudie registered her mam's words, but the desperation for water saw her leave that alone for the time being to ease herself up on her elbows. The cup was held to her mouth and her lips, cracked and sore as they settled over the rim, but the cool liquid was bliss, and it was hard not to gulp at it.

'There we go. That will do you for now.' Jocelyn took the cup away and set it down on the stool beside the bed. 'I'll leave it there for you.'

Only now she'd drank her fill did her mother's words sink in. Three days! She'd been sleeping for three whole days.

'I've been sick then, Mam?'

'It's the flu you're after having, Maudie. We had to send for Doctor Hennessy, and the aspirin he prescribed broke your fever.' She was clasping her hands tightly and speaking quickly.

'I've a cough syrup too for when you need it, and he says a poultice to the chest will help draw out any congestion.'

'I don't remember much, only leaving the shop.'

'That's a blessing in itself.'

'Why?'

Jocelyn didn't answer, tugging the quilt up and over her. 'You've been a divil for kicking it off, and it's important you keep warm.' She clucked about, tucking it in around her daughter. 'You're to keep your fluids up and take plenty of bed rest too. Doctor's orders.'

Her mother's voice as she rattled off her instructions made Maudie's head threaten to explode, and exhaustion swamped her. She tried to fight against it, wanting to swim to the surface and grasp hold of her thoughts because hearing Doctor Hennessy's name had triggered another memory and not a good one. It was something to do with his good-for-nothing son, JP, she thought as fatigue won the battle and her eyes closed once more.

The light had shifted the next time Maudie awoke, and seeing Caitlin sitting on the stool, holding the seat with her hands and kicking her legs out as she stared at her, made her jolt back to consciousness unpleasantly.

'Jaysus, Caitie, you frightened me!'

'You're awake.' The younger girl was unrepentant. 'And you sound like a man, croaking away like so.'

'Make yourself useful and pass me the water Mam left, would you?' Maudie suspected Caitie wasn't supposed to be in their bedroom.

Caitlyn scooted off the stool and picked the cup up from where she'd set it on the ground. Maudie tentatively hoisted herself upright and was relieved to find she felt much improved from the last time she'd opened her eyes. The headache had eased, and her chest no longer had a tight band wrapped around it. She drank the remains of the water greedily then handed the empty cup back to her sister, who hesitated, eyeing it with disdain.

'I suppose you'll expect to be waited on hand and foot this next while, and Mam will have me skivvying doing your chores as well as my own.'

Maudie would have been amused by her sister's hard-done-by act under other circumstances, but she'd no energy for her carry-on in her current state. She shook the cup at her. 'Just take it, would you? What are you doing in here anyway? I could be contagious.' Each word was an effort.

Caitlin did so, huffing a sigh. 'I've the constitution of an ox. Everybody says so. And it's you giving people terrible frights. Poor Mammy didn't know what to think when you arrived home in such a state.' Her eyes were owlish with the drama of it all. 'The Lynches are all sick with the flu. Mrs Hughes says Liam was in the shop the other day and that's how you came to catch it too. She says it's a miracle she didn't catch it and all.'

Maudie frowned, trying to keep up. 'You were here when I came home?' Her last clear recollection was leaving the shop early with a flea in her ear from Mrs Hughes about docking her pay.

Caitlin, seeing her sister struggling to piece together what had happened, jumped in, curls bobbing gleefully. 'No, but I heard Mammy telling Dada you were covered in mud and soaked to the bone. She couldn't get a word of sense out of you. Me, Fionn, Jimmy and Shane were sent to stay with Nora. You've the whole room to yourself. I wouldn't like that at all. I'd not be able to sleep with only my own breathing to listen to.'

The thud of her sister's boots against the stool legs was beginning to set the pounding in her head off again.

'She says that after Mrs Hughes sent you home, you must

have wandered off through the fields and fallen – that's how come you're all bruised and battered.'

Was she? Maudie's fingers moved to her face, gently exploring the tenderness on the left side as she became aware of a soreness in her private parts.

'Mammy said 'tis a miracle you got home at all.' Caitlin swelled with importance as she divulged more. 'You were crying out some awfully strange things in your sleep, Maudie, so you were. I wasn't supposed to peek in here, but I did. Awfully strange things.' She tapped the side of her head, implying her big sister was touched, cocky because Maudie was too weak to clip her.

'Like what?' Unease permeated through the fog.

'It was like you were tussling with someone, crying out "no" like a madwoman, you were. That's not all you were crying out either.'

Thud, thud, thud went her feet, and she twirled a lock of hair around her finger, waiting for Maudie to ask what it was she'd been shouting.

'Tell me, Caitie,' Maudie rasped, no choice but to oblige her annoying little sister.

'Only if you give me tuppence.'

'I'll give you five pence if you stop kicking that stool.'

Caitlin grinned, slid off the stool and fetched the money from the jar Maudie kept her meagre savings in, which sat on their chest of drawers. Her sister might look like a wee cherub, but she'd a touch of the divil in her, all right, Maudie thought, watching her slip the pennies into her pocket. This time, she perched on the edge of the stool.

''Twas Ronan Quinn's name you were crying, and you sounded ever so frightened.' Caitlin adopted a pious look, hard to carry off at twelve years of age. 'Sure, you know yourself, Maudie, if you've been carrying on with him behind Mammy and Dada's back after they told you not to, there'll be murder.'

'Well, I'm not.'

'If you say so.' A sly look flitted across her face. 'I've more news – if you want to hear it, that is?'

Caitlin's voice had an annoying sing-song quality.

'Tell me.'

'A Tan's missing.' She gave a short, dramatic pause. 'There's a curfew, and there's been raids.'

Maudie was suddenly desperate for her tittle-tattling sister to disappear and let her be. She needed to assemble the fragments floating about inside her head. 'Caitie, I'm not able for this. I've to rest. The doctor said so.'

Caitlin didn't budge from her perch – she was having too much fun. But as if by magic, their mam appeared, hands flying to her hips when she spotted her youngest daughter.

'What are you doing in here?' Jocelyn demanded shrilly. 'Do you want the flu and all? I swear your ears are painted on, Caitlin O'Connor. There's you staying with your sister and her expecting.' She shook her head. 'You're a thoughtless child, so you are. Now get in that kitchen and make yourself useful. There's potatoes need peeling.'

Caitlin scuttled from the room before the stinging smack to the back of her legs came.

'Are you feeling a little better now?' Jocelyn asked, clearly exasperated as she fetched a fresh set of underwear from the drawer once Caitlin had gone.

Maudie was wracked by a round of chesty coughing before she could reply, which saw Jocelyn set the undergarments down and sort her with a spoonful of sickly-sweet honey-and-lemon syrup. It soothed her ravaged throat, and once the coughing had subsided, Jocelyn helped her from the bed.

'Lift your arms up, Maudie. That's a good girl.'

Maudie did as she was told, grateful to be rid of the damp nightdress but shivering in her nakedness. The underwear her mam helped her into was crisp and smelled like fresh air. She fancied the simple comfort of fresh undergarments had more healing properties than anything Doctor Hennessy could prescribe.

'Maudie?'

The hesitancy in her mam's voice saw her raise her head.

Jocelyn reached out and touched the tender side of Maudie's face. 'Do you remember how you came to be in such a way?'

Maudie closed her eyes, swaying as she was hit by a kaleidoscope of images. JP, Quinn Farm, Ronan, the Tan, a gun. Something bad had happened, something terrible, but she couldn't put her finger on what. 'No. I think I must have fallen over.'

'Yes. I think you must have.' Jocelyn was nodding firmly as though confirming this to herself.

'Where are my things, Mammy?' Maudie wanted the clothes she'd been wearing. Holding them might help her remember.

'They're gone. I burned them.'

Maudie's mouth fell open. 'Why would you do that?' They could ill afford that.

'Because your skirt and underwear don't get torn in a fall.'

Horror settled over Maudie as she recalled being slapped and thrown to the ground. He'd hurt her. She shut her eyes, allowing the image of what had happened in. *Dear God!* It hit her then. She'd shot him. The Tan was dead.

Maudie's legs buckled as the events of three days earlier crystallised in her mind, and she crumpled to the ground.

11

A pair of capable arms helped Maudie to her feet. She was woozy, and the floor seemed to tilt, but as she swayed like a young sapling on a blustery day, Jocelyn kept a firm hold of her, her fingers digging into the flesh of Maudie's upper arms.

'There, you're all right. I've got you.'

'I don't know what happened, Mam.' Oh, but she did. She remembered it all now.

'It was too soon to get you up and about. That's what happened. You've not eaten in days, so you're bound to be wobbly on your feet.' Jocelyn skipped over the words lightly.

A wave of panic cleared her fuddled head. She'd been in bed for days – anything could have happened in that time. This time, her cry for Ronan was silent.

'I'll warm you a nice bowl of stew and we'll see if you can manage to eat a little of that. It will set you on the road to recovery. In the meantime, my girl, it's back to bed with you.'

No! Maudie had to find out if Ronan and his brothers were safe. What had he done with the dead Tan's body? He'd have moved him surely, but he'd still be missed, and there'd be repercussions. All hell would be let loose, and no mercy would be shown to those suspected of having had any involvement in Arthur's disappearance. Had he told anyone he'd been following her? Had JP informed on Ronan? On her? Her thoughts ran into one another. 'Help me dress, Mam. I have to go!' If anything had happened to Ronan, she'd not be able to live with herself.

Jocelyn was having none of it. 'I see. You know better than Doctor Hennessy, do you? Bed rest he said. Sure, you're in no fit state for anything else.'

Maudie tried to protest, but her mam was stronger, and she was hustled back under the quilt, aware that even if she managed to get dressed, she wouldn't make it further than the end of the lane. If she was to be of any use, she needed to be strong.

Jocelyn tucked the quilt tightly around her daughter. Then, glancing behind her to make sure little ears weren't flapping, she kept her voice low and brusque. 'These are terrible times we're living through, Maudie, and 'tis a terrible thing that's happened to you, but there's nothing to be gained by speaking up. Nothing at all.'

Maudie stared at her mam through hollow eyes, hearing the warning that laced her words. A tear leaked out the corner of her eye as it dawned on her what she'd seen reflected in her eyes earlier. Shame. To Jocelyn O'Connor – indeed, to most of those who occupied their small island – as an unmarried young woman, it wouldn't matter whether she had been brutalised by a Tan or given herself willingly to the man she loved – she was no longer pure. Maudie was spoiled goods.

'None of that now. It won't help.' Jocelyn's tone was sharp.

In that instant, Maudie saw not her mam standing over her but a stranger with hard lines tugging her mouth down. Her heart ached with something she didn't understand, but all sense flew from her head as her mam's fingers dug into her shoulders before shaking her hard.

'Do you hear me, Maude Jean? Not a word. I'll not have you bringing shame down on the O'Connors' good name.'

It took a moment for Maudie's teeth to stop rattling so she could gasp, 'Yes, Mam.'

Jocelyn let her go but still hovered over her like some sort of avenging angel. There wasn't an ounce of warmth coming from this woman who'd brought her into the world. 'If word of this gets out, no decent man will have you. Put it from your mind.'

Maudie reeled as if she'd been slapped a second time, only this time the wound wasn't superficial. This wound wouldn't heal. Jocelyn O'Connor, the woman here before her now, was a stranger. In these last few seconds, she'd lost her mam. She couldn't lose Ronan too.

'Right so. I'll go and see about that stew.' Jocelyn swept from the room, leaving Maudie feeling more alone than she'd ever felt in her life.

The door creaked open. 'Maudie?' a tentative voice called softly into the gloom.

'I'm awake, Nora.'

'Your voice is rougher than bark, so it is.' Her sister's ample frame waddled in. She pushed the door to behind her and set down the bowl she was carrying to pull the curtain and fling open the window, letting a burst of crisp spring air in. 'That's better.'

It looked to be a clear day outside, and now Nora had let the light in, Maudie could see her properly. She was a sight for sore eyes with her rosy cheeks and enormous belly. Her hair, the same shade of fiery red as Maudie's, was thick and lustrous, whereas Maudie's hung limply about her face. Nora was blooming, while Maudie felt like she was wasting away.

'Mam's worried about you. She says you're to eat if you're to get well. I've some porridge. Will you have a little? For me, Maudie. I've been so worried.'

Maudie was suddenly ravenous, and she nodded, watching as Nora picked up the bowl and settled herself on the stool – no easy task given her girth.

She sighed. 'I feel like a great big cow.'

'Moo.'

Her feeble joke made Nora smile.

'That's more like it. I've been desperate to see you.' She spooned a little of the oats up and slipped them into Maudie's mouth, not giving her a chance to say how pleased she was to see her too.

To both their surprise, she made short work of the porridge, and once Nora had scraped the bowl clean and Maudie had licked the remnants from the spoon, Nora spoke up. 'Mam says you took sick at work and were sent home, and Caitie told me you'd fallen taking a shortcut home through the fields.' Her green-eyed gaze, so like Maudie's own, was shrewd as she studied her sister. 'But there's more to it. Isn't there?'

'Sometimes I think you know me better than I know myself.' Maudie plucked at the quilt. She was torn between desperately needing to unburden herself and not wanting to burden her sister given her present condition.

Nora set the bowl aside and took hold of her sister's hand. 'I've broad shoulders. You can tell me anything. It won't leave this room.'

Maudie swallowed and started at the beginning with JP's cloaked threat when she'd been alone with him in the shop. She stuttered her way through everything that had unfolded, trying not to wince as Nora squeezed her hand so hard it hurt when she relayed how the Tan had followed her and lain in wait – only in this story she was telling, he never got the chance to do what he did to her. Nora gave a tiny gasp when Maudie told her how, seeing her chance, she'd picked up his pistol and squeezed the trigger.

'God between us and all harm,' Nora said softly.

'And then Ronan was there, Nora. He must have sensed something wasn't right and come after me, only he was too late – the Tan was already dead.'

'He got his comeuppance – nothing more, nothing less. When I think of what he might have done to you...' Nora crossed herself.

Maudie resolved to never think of what he'd done to her ever again because if she clung to the version she'd told Nora, perhaps she'd come to believe it herself. 'That he deserved it won't matter to the RIC. Caitie told me there's a curfew and there's already been raids.'

Nora nodded. 'They think the IRA are behind his disappearance – they've been ransacking homes looking for evidence.'

Maudie threw her hands up. 'Nora, what have I done?' She couldn't live with herself if others were to suffer because of her actions. 'I must confess. Perhaps they'll let things be when they hear why I did it.'

'Pull yourself together, Maudie O'Connor.' Nora was sharp. 'Those blackguards haven't an ounce of mercy running through them, as you well know. They'll shoot you on the spot, and don't believe for a minute there wouldn't be reprisals for us, your family – or anyone who knew or associated with you. So you'll do no such thing.'

Nora was right, and the futility of her situation saw her pummel the bedclothes. When her energy was spent, the tears flowed.

'I'm going to tell you something now.' Nora had fetched a hanky from her pocket and was wiping her sister's face. 'Mam's right. The best thing you can do is put all of this out of your head. It never happened because whatever the RIC do next is out of your hands.'

Maudie's heart broke a little more that her sister, the stalwart she'd always been able to count on, should side with her mam.

'You need to forget Ronan Quinn too.'

The words sliced through her heart. It was too much. 'I can't do that,' Maudie cried. 'I can never do that.'

Caitlin burst through the door, causing both women to startle, her cheeks high with colour. 'It's the missing Tan, Maudie! An RIC officer patrolling the beach found him an hour ago. Dead as a doornail, washed up on the shore. Now the Quinns' farmhouse is on fire. The Tans lit it with the mister still in his bed, so they did, and they're searching for Ronan and his brothers. They raided the property and found weapons.'

The sickening realisation settled over her that JP had indeed done his worst and reported what he'd seen in the city. If Ronan and his brothers were found, they'd be shot or hanged for trying to cover up what she'd done, and she could do nothing to stop it. All she could do was pray they got away.

12

The smoke from the smouldering ashes of the Quinns' farmhouse had spiralled into the sky for days afterward. It had served as a funeral pyre for poor Mr Quinn, who'd perished in his bed. And a sobering warning.

Three weeks later, the town was still under strict curfew, and they had been the longest weeks of Maudie's life. She went about her days in a trance, following a simple pattern of chores. While she was physically present behind the grocery-shop counter, her mind was occupied with thoughts of Ronan and his brothers – spirited away, she hoped, to an IRA safe house.

Nora had told her routines were the only thing that kept people sane in times like these, and Maudie had felt profoundly sad her sister's new baby was going to be born into them. She'd heard the phrase *sick with worry*, and that was what she was. There were some mornings the smell of eggs or porridge turned her stomach, and of an evening, she couldn't keep her dinner down. And she was tired. So very tired.

With no word from Ronan, everything around her was bleak as she made her way along the street, now beginning to wake up for the new day. The image of his face was so sharp it was an almost biblical vision. But when she blinked, it was gone and she was standing outside the back door of the shop.

That happened a lot lately – chunks of time lost thanks to the turmoil inside her.

Maudie let herself into the shop, glad of the half hour to herself each morning as she readied the shop for business while Mrs Hughes had a slow breakfast. By the time Mrs Hughes appeared with a curt, 'Good morning, Maudie,' she'd swept and mopped the shop floor.

Maudie waited for the go-ahead then swung the sign around.

The door seemed to open instantaneously, and it didn't stop opening and closing until midday, when they hit a quiet spell. Mrs Hughes disappeared upstairs to check on the dinner, leaving Maudie with the salubrious task of picking mouse droppings out of the flour sack. Mrs Hughes wasn't worried, given hers was the only grocery shop in town. Still, she'd not risk word spreading that she ran a dirty establishment.

The tell-tale jingle sounded then, and Maudie was glad to pause her picking. But, looking up, she froze.

It was JP Hennessy.

Maudie hadn't seen him since the day he'd told her about having followed Ronan in Dublin. To her surprise, he'd lost his cock o' the walk self-assuredness and was rattling the loose pennies in his pockets, his stance awkward. He was just standing in the entrance like he didn't know where to put himself. She'd heard Mrs Hughes lamenting his mother's passing a week or so back, but her own emotions had still been too dulled by recent events to really react. And his part in her own grief of not knowing where Ronan was and when she'd see him again prevented her feeling too sorry for JP directly – though his mother was blameless in that of course.

Now she straightened and appraised the man she held responsible for all the horror that had unfolded since he'd last stood in the shop. He seemed diminished, and the burning hatred she'd expected to consume her didn't come.

'What is it you're after, John Paul?' Her voice was weary. She didn't know how she'd get through the afternoon.

There was a tremor in the muscles beside his mouth as he continued to tinkle the pennies. 'I, ah, I came to tell you it wasn't me. I didn't report Ronan.'

His speech was wobbly, off-kilter and, to Maudie's surprise, genuine. She met his gaze unblinkingly.

'I'm not a traitor,' he carried on. 'I wanted to rattle you is all, and I'm sorry for all that's happened.'

What was she expected to say? It didn't matter now, and auld Mr Quinn had paid with his life for the ball JP had set rolling. She searched inside herself, but the only words she could dredge up were, 'I'm sorry for the loss of your mam.'

JP stared at her a moment longer then murmured his thanks and left.

The door hadn't closed behind him when Maudie nearly toppled the flour sack in fright as Mrs Hughes's voice sounded behind her.

'Maudie, did you give poor John-Paul a quarter of the Bullseyes like I told you to?'

'I'm sorry, Mrs Hughes. I forgot.'

Mrs Hughes swept out of the shop, calling after John-Paul and muttering about Maudie being useless.

Maudie went back to her mouse droppings. It didn't matter whether JP was a traitor or not. What had happened had happened, and she'd still had no word from Ronan.

13

'Maudie's getting fat like Mrs O'Rourke's pig,' Caitlin pronounced, wriggling out from under her mam as she tried to tame her unruly mop for Mass. Maudie was filled with a childish urge to prod her, purely to annoy her little sister as much as she was annoying her.

Still, Caitie was only speaking the truth, she thought, tugging at her dress before slipping her coat on overtop. The sickness that had plagued her in those first months after she'd heard the banshee's call had passed. She'd never have thought it possible, but five months after she'd staggered through the door of the cottage half dead, though nausea had plagued her for another couple of months, her appetite had returned with a vengeance.

They followed the troop of other townsfolk to St Maur's. Maudie felt a little lighter of spirit today. Not because of the interminable service looming inside the chilly church's stone walls, but because afterward she would go home with Nora and her growing family. The little ones helped take her mind off Ronan.

They told Mam it was so Maudie could help out for a few

hours, what with the new babby, bonnie Noelle. The truth of it was the sisters would enjoy catching up on their week over a cup of tea while Noelle, an easy baby who hadn't even cried during her baptism, slept.

Martin, kind man that he was, would take her niece and nephew out to the fields with him after they'd eaten, leaving the sisters to chat in peace. Nora had made a good match, Maudie often thought. She deserved her happiness. Unlike Maudie. Murdering the Tan would plague her as long as she lived. She was sure God was punishing her for it by keeping Ronan away.

This morning, Father Doyle'd had plenty to say, and by the time they exited St Maur's, Maudie's knees were sore from all the kneeling. Poor Joe had got a clip from Mam for fidgeting and had scampered off to play with his pals. Nora was talking with Deirdre, a dear friend, whose small tribe were all tugging at her skirts, complaining they were hungry. It might have been icy, but they spent a good half hour sending plumes of white breath into the air outside the church while they milled about in conversation. Maudie lost count of how many matronly types poked their noses inside Noelle's tightly wrapped swaddling to give Nora advice. Given her sister had already weaned two other robust tots, she took it with more grace than Maudie would've. At last, however, as the children's protests about being hungry grew, people broke away to make their way home.

The eldest O'Connor girls, with their green eyes and red hair, made a fine-looking pair, and as Nora's little ones ran ahead, making sure to splash through every puddle under their da's watchful eye, Maudie linked arms with her older sister. They never saw Mrs Finney clipping her husband around the ear as he stared moony-eyed after the pair, but both turned upon hearing running steps behind them.

'Can I come with youse?' Caitlin, cheeks pinkened from her efforts, panted. Her new friend Mary-Kate, who'd come to live on her aunt and uncle's farm after being orphaned, hung shyly behind her.

Maudie, who wanted a few hours' reprieve from her little sister's bothersome company, shooed her and Mary-Kate away. Then Nora and Maudie carried on their way, neither noticing Caitlin's clenched hands or the flare of anger in her eyes as she watched her big sisters walk away from her.

'You've a sparkle back in your eye and colour in your cheeks, Maudie. It's good to see.'

Nora and Maudie were tidying the dinner things away, and Martin had wrapped the children up once more and swept them outside.

'And you're eating well.' Nora poured the tea.

'Don't you start.'

Maudie's retort saw her sister glance up, eyebrow arched, pot in hand.

'Caitie only announced I was getting fat like Mrs O'Rourke's pig this morning. I'll swing for her one of these days, so I will.' Maudie's eyes narrowed when she noticed her sister's mouth twitching. 'And it's not funny, Nora.' Bantering with her sister felt good. She'd done her best to cast the spectre of those pale-lashed eyes from her mind, though they still came for her in her dreams.

'Sorry. She's incorrigible, that one.'

'Don't I know it.' Mollified, Maudie accepted the tea Nora slid toward her. 'It's true though. I am.'

'I hadn't noticed.' There was a chinking as Nora stirred her tea.

Maudie sighed, dropping her gaze to her stomach. 'My dress is getting awfully tight.'

'Finish your brew and I'll take a look. See if I can't let it out a little for you.'

That cheered Maudie – her elder sister was a handy seamstress.

The sisters drained their cups, and then Maudie, not wanting the conversation to fall into dangerous territory, asked, 'Will you look at my dress now?'

Nora nodded. 'Stand up and move into the light over there where I can see better.'

Maudie did so.

'Now hold your arms out to the side and turn around slowly for me, so I can see how it hangs on you.'

'I'm like a scarecrow.' Maudie laughed, the tinkling sound foreign to her ears. 'All I need is an old cap on my head.'

As she turned to face the door, she heard Nora's sharp intake of breath. She spun back to face her. 'What is it?'

Her sister's hand was pressed to her mouth, her eyes wide.

'Nora, you're frightening me.'

At last, Nora dropped her hand and asked quietly, 'When did you last have the curse?'

Maudie's stare was blank, but her mind was churning. She tried to recall when she'd last been plagued by women's troubles. The cramps could be crippling at times. It truly was a curse. But the realisation she'd not had them in some time saw her shake her head. *I can't be.* The ground shifted beneath her feet.

'Sit down, Maudie. You've gone chalk white.' Nora shook off her shock and took charge, steering her sister to the nearest chair. Then she clattered about at the table before returning to Maudie's side with a cup of sweetened tea. 'Drink this.'

But Maudie's hand was shaking too much so Nora held the cup steady and helped her sip it. After a minute or two, as the sweetness hit her veins, she found her voice. 'It's been months – before Ronan disappeared.' She thought of how they'd come together in the dunes. She wouldn't regret that. Not ever, and he'd come back for her when it was safe to do so. But then she thought of *him*, the other, with those pale-lashed eyes... no! She wouldn't even consider it.

Nora nodded, her tone gentle. 'You're with child, Maudie.'

'But I can't be.' A note of hysteria rang out, and her head began playing games, telling her it was the shock of what she'd done and how it had led to Ronan vanishing that had stopped her curse. She lived with the constant fear of him being caught. He'd be shot if he was, and it would all be her fault. 'It was only the once, Nora.' Maudie had almost convinced herself this was true, but at night the nightmares would come, reminding her what had happened on the *bóthar*. Surely, though, an act filled with hatred couldn't be counted?

'You'll not be the first girl to have said that. Sometimes that's all it takes.'

Her screams over being powerless to make the Tan stop echoed in her ears, and her throat grew tight. That stoat had taken her choices away. *And you took his life for it*, a voice whispered in her head. She could choose to believe this baby was Ronan's though. All the while, the implications of what having a baby would mean began filtering through her racing thoughts.

She wasn't married, no matter that she felt married in her heart.

Ronan was in hiding, along with his brothers, and she'd no way of getting word to him to tell him he was to be a father.

If he knew, he'd marry her right then and there. But that couldn't happen until Ireland was free. If Ronan was to take her as his wife, she'd be a widow no sooner than she'd said, 'I do.' The Crown was baying for blood and would see to that.

Nora was rubbing her hands between her own, trying to offer comfort, but she wrenched them free and placed them on her belly.

'You must be around five months along.'

This baby had to be Ronan's. She wouldn't let it be any other way. Her child would be born of love, not violence.

There was a part of Ronan growing inside her. Maudie allowed a sense of wonder to replace her initial shock and fear as she tenderly rubbed her tummy.

Nora watched her sister's face. 'Oh, Maudie, don't. It's impossible. You won't be able to keep the babe.'

'But I can't lose this little one. He or she's part of Ronan!' She prayed silently this was true, full of fear as to how she would feel about the child if she was wrong.

Nora looked as stricken as Maudie. She tried to reach for her hands again, but Maudie wouldn't have it. Hot, heavy tears filled her eyes, and she cried into her hands, her brain scrabbling for solutions.

She grabbed Nora's hands as an idea struck her. A vain hope. 'I could go away and have the baby. You could pretend to be carrying again and take my baby on as yours and Martin's.' Being an aunt would be better than being nothing, no one.

She was oblivious to hurting Nora, so tightly was she squeezing her hands, her eyes pleading with her sister to go along with her mad plan.

Nora was crying now too. 'I can't.'

'Yes, yes you can. We'll talk to Martin when he comes in.'

But Nora was shaking her head.

'Don't do this to me, Nora. Please.'

'Maudie be fair. I wish more than anything I could help you. But you know yourself Martin would never go along with such a deceit.'

She couldn't find it in her to be fair though, not right then. Life was far from fair.

Ronan should be here.

But she'd nobody to blame but herself for him not being by her side now.

She was the one who'd committed murder.

14

'You're going to have to tell Mam, Maudie.'

'No!' Panic and fear saw Maudie press her eyes so hard they bulged in their sockets, and when she opened them, she could see nothing but stars. Her sudden outcry made placid little Noelle begin fretting, and Nora shushed her.

It wasn't just her mam she was frightened of. She was terrified she might have to pay for her sins in taking a life, even that of a monster, for the rest of hers by carrying his child. *No!* Her internal voice cried. This was Ronan's baby – it had to be.

'I'll come with you. You've no choice but to tell her.'

'But she'll send me away.' Her sister was coming back into focus, and she could see Noelle's little hand curled around her mother's. 'Ronan won't know where to find me – us – when he comes back.' She was scrabbling to stay what felt like her execution.

'Oh, Maudie.' Sympathy flashed across Nora's features. 'You won't be gone forever, and one day, God willing, Ronan will come back and you can start afresh together.'

'You don't know that. Sure, what about poor Sheelagh McDonagh and the lies everyone was told about how she was staying with her aunt and uncle in Dublin, helping them in their shop? She was in the family way, even if we all pretended otherwise, and no one's seen her since. Her mam and dad could have knocked her off for all we know.' Maudie knew she was being ridiculous, but she couldn't stop herself. 'You know yourself when anybody asks Mrs McDonagh how Sheelagh's getting on in the Big Smoke, she just waves her hand vaguely and says, 'Grand."

'Stop it.' Nora's never-ending patience was finally fraying, and, sensing this, Noelle's tiny arms flailed as she began to wail.

Maudie was instantly contrite. 'I'm sorry.' All she wanted was to hold her niece close and comfort her. Although it was likely it would be the other way round, she thought, instinctively holding her arms out.

It wasn't often Nora was cross with her, and she was uncertain whether Noelle would be placed in them, but she needn't have worried.

She blew softly on her niece's face. 'There, there.' The milky scent was intoxicating and the solid warmth she cradled reassuring, calming the surging rush of emotion.

'You've a way with her, all right.' Nora smiled, but her eyes were sad with so many unspoken truths of what lay ahead for her sister. 'I don't know how to help you, Maudie, but Mam will. Sure, you're not the first girl in history to find herself in the family way out of wedlock, and you won't be the last.'

What Nora didn't say was what they both knew. What happened to fallen women like herself. As with Sheelagh McDonagh, they went away. And sometimes, even if the Mrs McDonaghs of the world did insist their daughters were grand, they never came back.

15

'I'm going to be sick,' Maudie warned Nora, as they reached the same thicket at the top of the lane where Ronan used to watch and wait for her to go inside the cottage.

Her sister rubbed her back until she'd brought the dinner she'd made short work of earlier up. 'I'll be there with you. It'll be all right.'

'I must look a state.' Maudie wiped her mouth with the back of her hand.

'You're always a beauty.' Nora wiped her sister's sweaty brow with her hanky.

Life was carrying on down the lane. Caitie, Joe, and Fionn were making the most of having finished their chores by playing hopscotch. Joe was still young enough to do his sister's bidding, and they could hear her telling him what was what as they approached. Fionn looked on with a sulky expression – he was at an awkward age, not old enough to join his brothers in the pub and too old for games.

"Da's working on the boat, and Jimmy and Shane are in the pub. But Mam's about," Caitie said, barely paying them any attention as she hopped across the chalked grid to where she'd tossed the stone.

There was a brief exchange, but Maudie barely noticed it, her head racing. Nora all but dragged her inside the cottage.

'Mam,' Nora called out, seeing no sign of her.

There was no reply, and Maudie felt a moment's reprieve.

'She'll be out the back fetching peat in.'

Maudie followed her sister's gaze to where the creel was missing from its hearthside spot.

'C'mon.'

'I'm going to be sick again.'

'No you're not.'

Nora herded her out the back door to where Jocelyn was bent over under the lean-to, filling the basket with peat bricks. She straightened upon seeing her eldest daughters standing in the doorway, and placed a hand in the crook of her back, appraising them slowly.

'And to what do I owe this honour?' Her eyes were flinty.

Maudie was trembling so badly Nora had to take hold of her elbow to steady her.

'Maudie's something she has to tell you.'

This was when she was supposed to speak up, but she couldn't find her voice for the lump wedged in her throat.

'Maudie,' Nora prompted.

Once the words were spoken aloud to her mam, there'd be no going back. What happened to her and this babe would be taken out of her hands, but what choice did she have?

'Cat got your tongue, Maudie?'

She already knows, Maudie thought. *She knew before I did.* Of course she did because nothing missed their mam's shrewd gaze.

Risking a glance from under her lashes, she saw the hard set of her mam's mouth, which told her there'd be no platitudes. No warm bosom to sink into while whispers that everything would be all right soothed her. Her mam wanted to hear her speak her shame out loud.

A spark ignited deep in her soul then. She wasn't ashamed of loving Ronan Quinn, but she was ashamed of what had been done to her. Somehow, though, she found the courage to raise her trembling chin and meet her mam's cold stare unflinchingly.

'I'm with child.'

'You're bad so you are, a fallen woman. 'Tis shameful, shameful!'

The slap sent Maudie reeling, and she clutched her hand to her cheek, terrified as to what would happen next.

16

When the knock came at the door on a murky Sunday afternoon a week later, the air inside the cottage was thick. All the unspoken things between Maudie and her parents hovered as her da faffed with his pipe and Maudie and her mam tidied the dinner things away in silence. The rest of the O'Connors had been driven out the door after a solemn meal by their mam's flapping apron.

'Don't be hanging about now. Off you go, all of you, and you're not to show your faces again until dark. Caitie and Fionn, you're to take Joe to Nora's.'

For once in her short little life, Caitie didn't answer her mam back, shooting her sister a bewildered glance as she was bustled out the door. Poor Caitlin didn't understand the dark cloud that had settled over the O'Connor family's cottage.

To Maudie's ears, the sharp rap of knuckles on the door sounded like a gavel falling. Jocelyn O'Connor tossed her cloth down and took her pinny off, pausing only to hang it up before hurrying to answer it.

'Hello, Father.' She ushered him in swiftly before the neighbours could see him and wonder what had brought him to the O'Connors' door.

Paudie abandoned his pipe to acknowledge the priest, who'd brought a faint odour of frankincense and soap with him.

'Father.' Maudie's voice was barely louder than a whisper as she tried to keep the tremor from it. The priest she'd known all her life stood there, glowering at her beneath a hedgerow of eyebrow, with a Bible tucked under his arm.

Jocelyn, meanwhile, rushed to make their caller comfortable, sweeping him over to the table, and once he was seated, she produced a tumbler filled with ruby-red port, along with a generous wedge of seed cake.

'Thank you, Jocelyn. Will you join me, Paudie?' Father Doyle raised his tipple questioningly to where Maudie's da still sat.

'I will, Father.'

Jocelyn was already seeing to a drink for her husband, and Maudie suspected she'd have liked to knock one back herself but would abstain in front of the father. Her stance was awkward as she waited to be told where to put herself, while Paudie tamped his pipe. All the sounds in the cottage – the drip of the tap, the hiss of the fire, the creak of the chair as Paudie O'Connor stood up and heaved a sigh better suited to someone nearer the grave than him – seemed amplified. Her da joined Father Doyle and his wife at the table, and then their eyes swung to her. She took a step back. The door was only a few strides away.

'Come and sit down, Maude.' This from Father Doyle.

She hesitated, aware that the trapdoor would open any moment. Her hand twitched by her side; she wanted to bolt out the door and run, to keep running until she was safe. Only there was nowhere to run to, so Maudie dragged her feet to the table and sat like a wooden marionette with her head dipped, hands clasped in her lap and the sweet, spicy aroma of port in her nostrils.

Father Doyle wasted no time. 'You'll have to leave, Maude.' Then, affixing his gaze on her mam and then da, he added in sombre tones, 'She's morally contagious.'

'I can't go. Ronan Quinn's coming back to marry me.'

'Maude!' Her mam's voice was like a slap. 'You're not to speak unless spoken to.'

'But where? Where will I go?' she cried, as hot tears burned. Maudie studied the table as the conversation about her continued as though she weren't sitting there with them.

'There's a place in Dublin where she can go to have the child, and the sooner she leaves, the better. I'll deliver her myself tomorrow night. A priest won't be questioned as to what his business is if he's stopped on the road.'

Maudie couldn't stifle her gasp upon hearing this. Tomorrow night. It was too soon. She wasn't ready. Ronan would return and she'd be gone. She cast about desperately for reasons to stay. 'But my job?'

'Tuberculosis,' Father Doyle supplied. 'You said yourself, Jocelyn, the girl's had a cough she can't shake. People, including Mrs Hughes, will be told she's been sent to a sanatorium.'

The good father had thought of everything. Maudie clenched her hands into fists under the table, wanting to pummel him for his pious ways. Mrs Hughes would be too concerned as to whether her health had been put at risk to question the story, and another girl would soon be found to fill her position.

'So I'm to disappear like Sheelagh McDonagh,' Maudie said quietly.

'I wouldn't know about that,' Father Doyle replied, making short work of his cake.

'And after, with the baby, what then?' She expected to be

shouted down by her mam, but Father Doyle answered before she could be reprimanded.

'The sisters will see to the child. The Daughters of Charity are doing good work there in Pelletstown.'

Pelletstown! Maudie's tightly held composure left her then, and she couldn't stop herself from crying out. Everybody knew of Pelletstown. It was a terrible place, one only the most desperate souls entered. 'Mam, Da, no! You can't send me to the workhouse.' Her hands had unfurled now to wrap protectively around her stomach. 'I could stay here, hide away like, and then when the baby comes, we could pass her off as a cousin whose mammy had too many mouths to feed.'

Paudie banged his fist down, and they all jumped. 'There'll be no bastard reared under this roof, and you won't darken our door again. You're dead to me, girl.'

'Da, please.' This couldn't be her softly spoken father whose feet she'd sat at of an evening as a child. But he was unmoved, and she swung her wild-eyed gaze on her mam. 'What will I do?'

'If you lay down with dogs, you get fleas.'

Her mam's words cut her to the bone. She didn't recognise these people she'd been born to. Her tears wouldn't stop, and no matter how many times Maudie wiped them away, fresh ones rolled down to take their place.

'Calm yourself, child.' Father Doyle dabbed at the crumbs on his plate with his finger. 'It's not a workhouse you'll be going to. It's a home – a mother and baby home called St Patrick's.'

IRELAND, 1985

The salty wind as the car's passenger door was opened brought with it a rush of memories that clogged Maudie's throat. She didn't move from the seat, needing a moment to sail along with all the clamouring images in her head because there was no avoiding the tidal pull from the past. Besides, she'd come back to face it, not hide. Her hands were clasped in her lap, and her eyes were closed, her head resting back as she breathed in slowly.

The sea smelled different here, although seagulls were seagulls wherever you were in the world, she thought as they squalled overhead.

'Are you all right?' her travelling companion asked, her forehead creased with concern as she reached out her hand.

Maudie shooed away the offer of help. 'I can manage.' And hauling herself from the car, she stood seeing not the Quinns' farmhouse and the rambling outbuildings but the scattered remains of field stone foundations. A cloak of sadness engulfed her at the vividness of the events that had razed the Quinns' home to the ground. Then, turning slowly round to gaze down at the town where she'd laughed, cried and loved, she spotted St Maur's spire immediately. They'd just come from its small churchyard, where they'd laid flowers on Nora's and Martin's graves. Her sister and brother-in-law had not made old bones. This vista hadn't changed, and it comforted her to see the coast still wrapped itself around Rush in a warm embrace.

She remembered the girl with the fiery hair whose freedom had been torn from her; who'd been spirited away from that town in the night. Taken from the cottage where she'd lived with her family by Father Doyle, her ma and da complicit, to a place that still gave her nightmares all these years later.

PART TWO
ST PATRICK'S MOTHER AND BABY HOME

17

The door to St Patrick's Mother and Baby Home, where Father Doyle had carted Maudie on a rattling journey under the cover of darkness, was immediately flung open when the father knocked. An apparition with an enormous white cornette, akin to white wings protruding from either side of its head, emerged, swinging an oil lamp. Maudie stared, frozen, at the spectral face, at the shadowed hollows under its eyes and mouth, as the lamp was raised.

Father Doyle said, 'Good evening, Sister,' as he made to forcibly move Maudie toward the apparition.

The light bobbed toward her until it was her face bathed in the glow, no doubt looking eerily back at the sister.

'Maude. I'm Sister Louise.'

A soft hand reached for hers, and Maudie lifted her gaze and looked into brown button eyes that matched the round face in which they were set. Sister Louise didn't look much older than she was and had a country accent. There was nothing ghostly about her diminutive form at all; the smile creasing her face was kind.

'Come in from the cold. I expect you're frozen and ready for your bed after that journey.' A light danced in those brown eyes. 'As for me, I'm a night owl, which serves me well when I'm on night duty.'

Maudie *was* cold, her face numbed from it, but she was warmed by Sister Louise's cheerfulness. Her company was certainly preferable to that of Father Doyle, so without further fuss, she stepped forward, dragging her case behind her. The sister prompted her to thank Father Doyle for making the journey before telling him she'd see to things from here.

'May God and Mary be with you, Maude O'Connor,' Father Doyle said, not waiting to see her inside the building as he got back into the driver's seat of his trap and told the pony to trot on.

Maudie was swept inside. The doors felt like a gaping mouth that had swallowed her up as they shut behind her. Before she could dwell on her new surroundings, however, Sister Louise asked her if she was fit and well.

'I am.' Maudie kept her voice low and hushed like the sister's, but still it seemed to echo and bounce off the walls.

'Good, good.' Sister Louise swooped to take Maudie's case. 'You won't be needing that.'

'But—'

'I'll fetch your uniform and things – I have it all ready for you.'

She disappeared through a door to the left, leaving Maudie standing in darkness. She'd seen enough to know she was in an entrance foyer with corridors running off it and stairs behind her. A shiver passed through her as she breathed in the mix of stewed food, disinfectant and overall decay. She could hear Sister Louise rustling about, and a low groan saw goosebumps form all up Maudie's arms.

'Sister, what's that noise?' Maudie asked as soon as she reappeared, a bundle tucked under her arm so she could keep hold of the lamp.

'Don't be worrying about that now. It's the pipes is all. Here we are.'

The bundle was pressed into Maudie's arms.

'There's a nightdress in there for you to put on. What else should I be telling you?' Sister Louise frowned. 'Oh yes. The Reverend Mother will see to your admission properly in the morning. And the doctor will check you over. He'll be able to tell you when your baby's due. For now, though, I think it's best I show you straight to your bed. Sleep's a cure for most things I always find. Especially homesickness.'

Maudie nodded. She was suddenly desperate to lie down and close her eyes as the events of the last few days hit her.

'You're to be in St Mary's dormitory, and you've a new name to use while you're here,' Sister Louise whispered, the yellow light swinging this way and that as she padded over to the stairs.

'A new name?'

'Yes. While you're with us at St Patrick's, you're to use the house name of Theresa.' Sister Louise's step didn't falter, and with her free hand, she hitched up the hem of her habit.

'But why?' Maudie hoped that hadn't sounded impertinent, not wanting to get offside with her.

'It's for the good of all you. It's better to have a fresh start when you leave and put all of this' – she swept her hand generally about the place – 'behind you. That's why we don't encourage you girls talking with one another when you're working. It doesn't do any good to form attachments here.'

Sister Louise's generous backside swayed to the left and then the right with each step she climbed. By the time they reached the landing, she was puffing and paused to draw breath outside a communal bathroom area with a line of sinks and toilets before continuing to a door at the end of the corridor that had been left open a crack.

Maudie, a head taller than the sister, could see over her –

because with that cornette, she certainly couldn't see around her – and what she saw in the puddled light of the oil lamp filled her with unease. Row after row of identical iron-framed beds upon which slumbering shapes were huddled beneath blankets. Someone was snoring softly, and someone's breath – or was it several girls' breath – sounded snuffled with a chill, while others cried out in their sleep. It smelled of too many bodies.

Maudie wanted to run away – she didn't belong here – but Sister Louise must have sensed her urge to flee because she spun round and took hold of her charge's hand once more. It dawned on Maudie that all the new arrivals must feel this same sense of bewilderment of how they'd come to be here in a room full of strangers as they found themselves being led past huddled mounds.

Sister Louise stopped in front of an empty cot near the far wall. 'This is you. Set your things down the bottom of the bed there.'

Maudie did as she was told, waiting while the sister rifled through the pile to hold up a nightgown.

'Here we are. Now slip that on and get to bed. Goodnight, child.'

She made to leave, and this time Maudie's hand shot out to grasp her only ally in a silent plea not to be left.

'You'll soon settle in, Theresa. Just follow the other girls' lead.'

Maudie watched as she glided away then sank down onto the bed. The nightdress scratched her skin, and she was cold even with her coat spread out over the top of the thin blanket. Sleep should have come easily given her exhaustion. But it eluded her.

She stared into the darkness, breathing in foreign smells, her ears straining with each strange sound.

'What's your name?'

The voice startled her. It belonged to the girl in the bed next to hers, and Maudie hoped her fidgeting while trying to get warm hadn't woken her. 'I'm Mau— I mean, Theresa. I'm sorry if I'm keeping you awake. I can't sleep.'

'Nobody ever can on their first night – or second, third or fourth for that matter. I still can't and I'm after being here months. They called me Jillian when I arrived, but my name's Vanessa. You can call me Nessa when they're not listening.'

'And my real name's Maude, but call me Maudie.'

'Maudie it is. When we're out of earshot of the sisters, we call them the big bonnets.'

'Shush, you'll get us in trouble,' a plummy voice hissed. It was impossible to tell which bed it had come from.

'Sister Louise turns a blind eye to talking, Lady Mags,' Nessa flung back in the girl's general direction.

'Don't call me that. My name's Cecelia, and you know it.'

'*Yes, Lady Cecelia.* Don't mind her. She's a fancy piece that one who thinks she's too good for the likes of us. But we're all sinners according to God, and that's why we're here,' Nessa whispered, and this time there was no response.

It couldn't be, could it? Maudie was taken aback despite being disconcerted at finding herself here in a dormitory full of strange girls and women. This was a Catholic home, and Miss Cecelia – whom she'd seen on occasion riding through town – was part of the Altringham family of Foxbourne House. They were Protestant. How on earth had a high-born young woman like herself come to be here?

'Sister Louise is one of the good ones,' Nessa added for Maudie's benefit. 'You don't have to be frightened of her.'

Maudie had sensed that about Sister Louise and nodded, even though Nessa couldn't see her. She didn't want to think about the sisters who weren't as kind.

'You were lucky it was her on night duty and not aul' Big

Bonnet Agnes. Keep your head down when she's about. She's the devil in disguise that one.'

Maudie envisaged a pinched-face nun with a sour expression.

Noisy sobs started up close by, and she pushed herself up onto her elbow, trying to work out which bed they were coming from. Instinct made her want to comfort whomever it was.

'That's Mol. She cries herself to sleep every night. You'll get used to it. She's only thirteen and missing her mammy terribly. Poor thing. She's frightened about the birth too. So am I. Nobody ever talks about it when they come back to the dormitory after having their babies.'

Maudie must have gasped.

'It's not her fault. The blame lies with her da, but do they care? No. It's her who's the dirty girl. And the worst of it, she'll probably be back here next year. Mol had no clue she was even having a baby until her mammy brought her here.'

That poor child! Maudie pushed the blanket off, intending to seek the little girl out and comfort her as she would her sister. Revulsion as to how a father could take what was supposed to be an act of love and twist it like so with his own child saw her shudder.

'Leave her. Like I said, you'll get used to it. She'll cry herself off to sleep soon; trying to calm her only makes it worse.'

Maudie reluctantly lay back down.

'Where are you from then?'

'Rush.'

'I'm from Dublin myself. My baby's due in two months. I'm enormous, so I am. Like a great big pumpkin with a head and legs.'

There was a tenderness to the words 'my baby'. Maudie rested her hand on her own belly.

'If I decide I can trust you, I'll tell you how I came to be here, and if you decide to trust me, you can tell me your story.

We're not supposed to talk to one another, but I think that's silly. How else are we supposed to know what's what? It's late though and we've to be up early. Try to get some sleep.'

The straw mattress shifted and crinkled as Nessa rolled away, and Maudie lay back once more, waiting for sleep to finally claim her.

18

Maudie's dreams when she'd eventually slept had been peppered with nightmares, forcing her to relive the *bóthar*. She was so tired, and a bell was ringing in the distance. It took her a moment to process she wasn't soaking wet on the muddy track and that someone was telling her to get up. She wasn't home in her bed, and it wasn't Caitlin leaning over her either, rather a stranger with a long, snaking black braid coiled over her shoulder. The previous night's events crowded in on her. She was at St Patrick's, and this was Nessa, Maudie thought, blinking up at her.

Her eyes were as dark as her hair, and she was slight, her round stomach making her arms and legs look spindly and out of proportion. It was hard to guess her age, but Maudie settled for around fifteen or sixteen. She sat up and rubbed her eyes, trying to gather herself together for what lay ahead.

Nessa was staring at her, equally curious.

'Haven't you the most beautiful hair? Sure, it's like fire,' she said admiringly, reaching out to touch it as if to check it was real. Then, remembering where they were, she changed tack and dropped her hand, her dark eyes flashing. 'There's no time for sitting about daydreaming. Get your things and follow me!'

Maudie did so, still bleary-eyed as she trooped behind her new friend. She took in the rumpled beds and wondered where the babies slept. This was a mother and baby home after all.

She tagged on to the queue that snaked from the washroom all the way into the dormitory while Nessa chatted softly, filling Maudie in about what the day would bring while her sleepy brain tried to keep up and take note. Somewhere in the distance, she could hear a baby wailing, and it made her shiver in her thin nightgown.

'The routine never changes. The bell rings at half five on the dot, and we get up, have a quick wash and get dressed. Then we make our beds and head to Mass. There's no chapel. Mass and evening prayers are held in a room much like our dormitory, and I reckon I can feel the pour souls who never left the workhouse each morning in there.'

The girls shuffled forward.

'Stop filling her head with nonsense, Nessa,' the plummy voice from the night before said, spinning round to tell her off quietly.

It was her! Miss Cecelia from Foxbourne House. She was even prettier than Maudie had remembered from glimpses as she passed through town, despite the hardships she'd obviously weathered in recent times, and looked to be around her age. How had she come to be here? Not that she'd be asking outright. The way she held herself set her apart from the rest of them and told Maudie that prying into her circumstances would not be welcome.

'It's Jillian. I've one foot out the dormitory now, Lady Mags.' Nessa emphasised the 'Mags' and lifted a sock-clad foot, twirling her ankle to prove her point. She received a scowl for her troubles and sent one straight back. Then to Maudie she said, 'That's our rule. Never answer to or use your real name outside the dorm, but Lady Mags thinks the rules don't apply to her.' Then she dropped her voice. 'No one likes her.'

'No talking!' a shrill voice cut down the line.

Still the poor baby's cry echoed through the freezing building. Why wasn't the little one being comforted? Nessa spoke up again before Maudie could ask, dropping her voice even lower at the order.

Maudie was too busy staring at Mags – or Cecelia – wishing the plaintive wail would stop because that would mean someone was tending to the baby. Empathy for the little one's cries flooded through her. There was sympathy too for this girl who lived so close to her own cottage yet a world away in the big house on the outskirts of Rush. Mind, it should be revulsion she felt for her, given Miss Cecelia and her family stood for all that she hated about British rule and the class system. How could she though when she'd wound up here at St Patrick's just like Maudie? They weren't so different after all.

Clearly, Cecelia hadn't managed to endear herself to any of the others here. How lonely she must be. She was still facing them, and Maudie stared at her nightdress. It was sodden around her breasts, and it dawned on her that Cecelia was leaking milk.

'One can always tell one's breeding by one's manners, and it's rude to stare, don't you know?' Cecelia hissed. There were hollows under her light blue eyes, and her short hair hung lank about her shoulders, but there was a boldness in the squaring of her shoulders, as though she could read Maudie's mind.

Maudie's lips tightened, and her nose curled as she realised what she'd been able to smell last night. Sour milk. The compassion she'd felt for the other girl over what it must be like to fall from such lofty heights dissipated at her superior attitude.

'Pay her no heed.' Nessa dropped her voice so Maudie had to strain to hear her. 'For all her high and mighty ways, she's no better than us. Lady Mags had a baby girl two weeks back. She's not named her baby yet either. The girls with little ones go to the nursery to feed them after breakfast. They've big bonnets who see to the night feeds.'

So the babies were in a nursery then. Maudie recalled her mam nursing her younger siblings through the night and the beatific look on her face as she'd cradled them. But she steeled herself against any emotions where Cecelia was concerned. She'd save it for the other girls, dressed in washed-out grey smocks that might once have been blue with cardigans worn over top. They were like sheep blending in with one another as they waddled past back to the dormitory, some with hands resting in the crook of their backs to ease the extra weight in their front. Maudie was struck by how defeated they all looked. She wrapped her arms around her middle and made a silent promise there and then to stay strong for her baby. She wouldn't allow St Patrick's to beat her.

'Don't speak unless you're spoken to and do as you're told is all you need to know,' Nessa said, nudging her along.

Cecelia moved up the line a few paces. She was limping, Maudie realised, surprised because she'd only seen her from afar or on horseback before. Did Nessa know the story behind what had brought her here? Was it Cecelia's baby crying? Was that why she was leaking, or did it belong to one of these other girls? Some were expecting, while some looked to have had their babies already. All the girls appeared ground down, though, except Nessa, who had a spark about her. Maudie had so many questions about St Patrick's, and Cecelia, but she'd ask them later, when they were alone.

'You'll stand out enough as it is with that hair and pretty face. And you don't want aul' Big Bonnet Agnes singling you out,' Nessa was saying, swiftly marching on. 'We're to stay here at least a year after our babies are born to work off our debt to the nuns, repenting our sins all the while. And we've to be grateful to them for taking us in, but I'm not. I hate them all,'

Nessa supplied. 'Some girls stay on because they don't want to leave their babies, but when they get too big they're sent to industrial schools.'

'What are those?' Maudie was almost frightened to ask.

'They're like an orphanage and some of the little ones there are orphans.'

'And the mothers?'

'They can stay close to their children by working in the school or the laundries.'

'The babies die – they all die,' a girl with enormous seaweed-coloured eyes tinged with madness whispered over Maudie's shoulder, making her jump.

'Quiet,' a voice instructed.

Nessa ignored the order and touched the side of her head. 'Aoife's not right,' she said quietly.

'What does she mean, though, that they all die?'

'There was a sickness going round the nursery when I arrived. That's what she's talking about.'

'Oh.' Maudie placed her hands protectively around her middle.

'There's nearly fifty of us here at the moment, so you've to be quick when it's your turn on the throne and at the basin because anyone who's late for Mass forfeits their breakfast, and we don't get enough to eat as it is.'

Nessa fell silent as Sister Catherine – who Nessa had pointed out to her earlier – came into their line of sight. Po-faced was how she'd describe her if she was telling Nora about her.

'Modesty at all times, girls,' Sister Catherine trilled as Maudie hurried to the vacated basin, pondering the irony of modesty when there wasn't an inch of privacy to be had. She'd lost sight of Nessa in the washroom's general melee, and the shock of icy water hitting her face served to wake her properly.

She took the rag she'd been allocated for washing and stole a glance at the other girls, catching a glimpse of knobbly back before a smock covered it. Some of the girls looked fit to burst, tummies taut and rippled with blue veins, full of baby, while others were either carrying small or had drooping pouches, signalling they'd already given birth. Their ages varied, and Maudie was shocked by how young some of them were. They all had one thing in common, however, aside from the obvious reason that had brought them here in the first place, and that was chattering teeth. As such, she hastily washed herself, slipped the smock over her head, finished her ablutions and then, being sure to keep her head down, hurried back to the dormitory, where Nessa was already smoothing the blanket, her nightgown folded neatly under the pillow. Maudie copied her.

'If the bed's not made properly, there's extra chores assigned. Make sure there's not so much as a ripple.'

Maudie did so, noting the black mould creeping up the walls behind her bed as she fluffed the blanket, and then the two girls joined the horde of smock-clad girls silently moving down the freezing corridor. She was one of them now. A smock girl with a stolen identity.

They ventured down the stairs and round the corner, filing in to take their place in an expansive room with not a single ounce of beauty in it.

'Can you feel them?'

The ghosts Nessa had mentioned. Maudie nodded. The fine hair on her arms was standing up, but this wasn't simply because of the ghosts, rather the watchful eyes of the big bonnets. Some were kindly, doing what they believe to be God's work, but some were malevolent, urging them to repent their sins. It was those ones that filled her with more fear than any spectres from the past ever could.

And still she wondered why wasn't anyone tending to the poor little mite that was still crying?

19

Maudie's stomach rumbled as she stood outside the Reverend Mother's office. It was the same room Sister Louise had ducked into last night beside the entrance.

Please let me be assigned to the nursery. Maudie sent up a half-hopeful prayer because thus far God hadn't been looking out for her. Her heart twisted as she thought of Ronan, but she swallowed hard. She had to be strong for him now and their unborn child. 'You belong to Ronan and me,' she whispered, resting her hands on her belly.

Nessa had explained as they made their way to the dining hall that the nursery was the best job because then you got to spend precious extra time with your baby, and you could share all the love pent up inside you with the other babies who sorely needed it. The kitchen, she said, was bearable, with the bonus of being able to pilfer a little extra to eat, as was working in the garden, where at least you were in the fresh air. It was the cleaning that was the worst because it didn't matter how hard you scrubbed, the place was never clean to the sisters' satisfaction. That was back-breaking work and a task usually assigned to girls who weren't at St Patrick's for the first time. As for

Nessa, she spent her days toiling in the laundry and had held out red-raw hands as evidence.

Maudie had made her mind up there and then – no matter what work she was tasked with, she'd get on with it and keep her head down. Her time at St Patrick's would be used to plan how she would walk out those same iron gates Father Doyle had brought her through, with her baby in her arms. Somehow, she'd make a new life for them in Dublin.

'Come in, child.'

Maudie started at the clipped instruction, having lost track of how long she'd been standing in the foyer. She stepped inside the room – which was warmer than the cavernous foyer – and stood in front of a desk littered with paper, behind which sat the elderly Reverend Mother. Her hands were clasped in front of her, her demeanour more regal than motherly. Maudie immediately pushed her shoulders back and stood taller under the stern frown as she was slowly appraised. You could tell a lot about the make of a person by their eyes, Maudie thought, and the Reverend Mother's were bulbous like a toad's.

'Welcome, child.'

There wasn't a flicker of warmth to take the chill off her greeting or a softening of her expression, and Maudie, trying not to fidget under the unwavering gaze, was unsure whether she should reply. Silence was the safest option, she decided, breathing out only when the Reverend Mother retrieved a slip of paper from the top of one of the piles and, after pushing the bifocals she'd been peering over up the bridge of her nose, began to read what was written on it.

'Maude Jean O'Connor.'

Her name was sounded out slowly, and Maudie nodded confirmation that this was her.

'House name Theresa.'

Again she bobbed her head, even though it was a statement not a question.

Those toad eyes peered over the top of the bifocals again. 'You're now under the care of the Daughters of Charity, here at St Patrick's, where the sisters will guide you and where you will follow the rules of the house. You're to obey their instructions at all times and will work industriously in order to atone for your sins.'

The Reverend Mother paused, giving her a hard stare, and Maudie wondered if she was contemplating whether she'd be troublesome or not.

She'd never know the verdict.

'Your time here is to be used for hard work, prayer and reflection on your moral failures, and as recompense for our services, you will stay on at St Patrick's for one year after your child's born.'

Maudie knew better than to ask what would happen to her child after that year, given what Nessa had told her. No unmarried mother left St Patrick's with their baby, but she would be the exception, so she simply watched the Reverend Mother's pale lips continue to move, only focusing once more when the paper was slid toward her, along with a pen.

'What happens within these walls stays within these walls. I trust I am making myself clear to you?'

'Yes, Mother.'

'Sign your name at the bottom of the page and then wait outside my office until Sister Agnes comes to take you to the infirmary. The doctor will see you, and then you're to make your way to the kitchen, where you'll begin work.'

Maudie's heart sank upon hearing Sister Agnes's name mentioned along with her assignment to the kitchen as she picked up the pen. The page was filled with screeds of typewritten text, and she thought she should at least read it before setting her name to it, but the Reverend Mother was already clearing her throat. The pen hovered over the paper, a blob of ink beginning to form on the nib as she hesitated.

'Is there a problem?'

Maudie grinned inwardly, unable to resist asking sweetly, 'Am I to be signing it as Theresa, Mother, given I'm under St Patrick's roof?'

It was impossible to tell what the Reverend Mother was thinking, but the steely reply that Maude O'Connor would suffice was satisfying.

Maudie scribbled her name then left the office with her head held high, revelling in her small victory.

The feeling of one-upmanship left swiftly when she spotted a diminutive figure – Sister Agnes presumably – gliding toward her. However, as she drew closer and Maudie saw the heart-shaped face, sweetly pretty beneath the cornette, she thought perhaps Nessa had judged her unfairly.

The sister eyed her back, and Maudie wondered what she saw looking at her. The answer, she supposed, was simple. Another grey smock.

'Theresa?' The voice was even sweet, almost musical.

'Yes, Sister.'

'I'm Sister Agnes.'

Then to Maudie's surprise she added softly, 'You've such beautiful hair. It glows like fire.'

'Thank you, Sister.' Maudie was backfooted by the compliment, and the strange glint in the eyes of the woman, who looked to be ten or so years older than herself, left her uneasy.

Sister Agnes dragged her attention from Maudie's hair, hastily knotted at the nape of her neck in the few minutes she'd had in the washroom, and turned away. 'Follow me.'

Maudie could hear the swishing of her habit as she trailed behind her, wondering about the woman beneath it. It was hard to equate such prettiness with cruelty. Perhaps Nessa had upset her somehow. Then she remembered the glint she'd detected in her eyes and silently admonished herself for judging a book by its cover.

For a small woman, Sister Agnes's pace was brisk and Maudie hurried to keep up.

They passed a girl on all fours in the corridor Maudie found herself scurrying down. She had a scrubbing brush in her hand and a bucket of soap-scummed water next to her. Maudie breathed in the medicinal tinge of carbolic soap and coughed.

'Put your elbow into it, girl,' Sister Agnes instructed, her melodic voice at odds with her order.

The girl scrubbed harder, glancing up at Maudie with red-rimmed, resigned eyes, causing her step to fumble.

'Keep up, girl.'

It was then a door opened a little way down the corridor and the unmistakable sound of babies crying drifted toward them. It was a sound that ate into your soul, Maudie thought. A sister exited what had to be the nursery, and as the door closed, the sound was cut off, like a hand slapped over a mouth. The cries she'd heard weren't from hungry or tired babies. They'd a heartbreaking apathy to them that told Maudie all the little ones wanted was to be held.

The sisters passed one another, dipping their heads in acknowledgement, and Maudie stole a glance through the glass panel at the top of the nursery door. Cots were lined up much like the beds in her dormitory. All were full, and her eyes fell upon a baby red in the face from sobbing, little fists curled and flailing. These babies were tiny, fed by their mams when a bell rang, not played with or cuddled for longer than it took to feed them. Maudie knew this from Nessa, who'd told her the older children who weren't boarded out were moved to a different wing once they began eating solid food. Too many, Nessa had said, were buried in Glasnevin Cemetery nearby. Maudie had shuddered trying to imagine a life spent inside these walls. However, Nessa's sage words that it was better for the babies to be taken when they were small because then at least they had a chance of thriving had sent a cold chill rippling through her.

The infirmary was at the end of the corridor, and the odour of disinfectant stung Maudie's eyes as she sought out the source of the guttural groaning she could now hear. A girl was lying on a cot with her back to the door. Her smock was soaked, and it was at that moment Sister Agnes revealed her true colours.

'Stop that noise this instant.'

'Please, Sister, something for the pain.' A head twisted to reveal anguished eyes.

Maudie stifled a sob and took two steps toward the girl to offer comfort, but Sister Agnes's arm blocked her path.

'You're suffering because of the devil's work, girl. Pain's God's punishment for not keeping your legs shut.'

Maudie gasped, not believing what she'd heard.

'And have you something to say?' Sister Agnes turned on her then, eyebrow arched.

Over the sister's shoulder, Maudie saw the girl on the bed give a small pleading shake of her head and knew she'd only make things worse for her as well as mark her own card.

'No, Sister.' She clasped her hands in front of her and lowered her gaze.

Sister Agnes continued to eye her as though getting her measure and then swept to the door at the far end of the room and rapped sharply. Maudie tried to offer comfort with her eyes to the poor girl, silent now, but she'd turned away.

'Enter,' a male voice replied.

'Come – don't dawdle, girl.' Sister Agnes stood in the doorway, and Maudie had to brush past her into a smaller room, as stark as the one she'd left.

She took in a high window that made her think of the barracks' jail. A cot, identical to the one the labouring girl was lying on, was pushed hard against the wall, and a man with a shock of white hair that matched his coat stood before her, a clipboard in his hand. He barely looked at her as she was instructed to remove her underwear and get on the cot. Maudie shuddered but did as she was told, trying to quell the memories of the Tan that this strange doctor had brought to the fore.

Sister Agnes might be a cold-hearted woman despite having a face like an angel, but as she closed the door, leaving Maudie alone with the doctor, Maudie would have given anything for her to stay.

20

Her baby was to be born in the middle of winter, which worried Maudie given St Patrick's cold, damp conditions.

Maudie had grown used to being chilled to the bone and hungry all the time. The days were long, each one rolling into another in the same servient routine as the one before. There wasn't much chance for chatting with the other girls because they were never left unsupervised during the day – not that she wanted to talk to Cecelia, who was also on kitchen duties and had made it clear she didn't need friends. It had also quickly become apparent to Maudie that Cecelia had never done a day's work in her life.

Maudie had gleaned enough from Nessa to know Lady Mags, as she insisted on calling her, had been brought here by a priest just as most of them had, but that was all. 'She's a cold fish is our Lady Mags. Sure, she's not even named her poor baby.'

Maudie suspected she was frightened of getting attached to the child only for her to be snatched away, but she kept that thought to herself.

Maudie's path had yet to cross Sister Agnes's again thankfully. She'd seen Sister Louise on several occasions, though, and was grateful for the kindly smile she offered. She wasn't like the others. There was a softness to her that hinted at compassion. When she was on duty, a blind eye was turned to the bread squirrelled away in Maudie's smock pocket.

'Here,' she whispered into the silence of the dormitory now, holding out a hunk to Nessa, who snatched at it. She didn't need to thank her. It went without saying she was grateful for the little extra snuck her way.

Nearby, Molly was crying into her pillow again, and Maudie silently eased herself off the cot – still unused to her ever-expanding belly – and, despite knowing she'd be in trouble if she was caught out of bed, tiptoed over to her.

Maudie could never hide more than enough bread for herself and one or two of the girls. It was like playing God, a role she'd had no wish to take on but she'd determined to do what little she could. Nessa had been good to her, and as for Molly, that child deserved a little kindness in her short life, so she slipped her a portion. The only reward she needed was hearing the younger girl's sobs stop as she took the bread and ate it so quickly she'd be sure to give herself the hiccups.

She didn't know why guilt plucked at her like fingers on harp strings where Cecelia was concerned, but as she made her way back to her cot, Maudie hesitated. 'I feel I should I offer her this,' she said to Nessa, eyeing the bread in her hand before dipping her head toward the mound lying with her back to them in the next row. 'She's feeding her baby, after all.'

'Don't you dare! She thinks she's one of quality that one, with her high and mighty ways. I bet she's never gone hungry in her life before now. Well, I have. Plenty of times, and I don't doubt you know what it's like to go short, so either you have it or I will,' Nessa bossed.

True that might be, but Maudie was thinking of Cecelia's

child. Ignoring Nessa, she padded over and prodded the lump in the nearby bed.

'What?' Cecelia glanced over her shoulder and, seeing Maudie's outstretched offering, turned her nose up as though she'd catch something nasty were she to accept the bread before turning away. Maudie felt as if she'd been slapped and wished she'd listened to Nessa.

Nessa giggled. 'I told you so.'

'Don't.' She didn't want the bread herself now, so she passed the small hunk to Nessa, who broke it in half and shared it with Molly.

As Nessa brushed crumbs from her mattress, Maudie lay down and pulled the blanket over herself, fully expecting her friend to go to sleep now she had a little extra in her belly. Instead, she propped herself up on her elbow.

'I've decided I trust you,' she whispered in that matter-of-fact manner of hers, and Maudie, suddenly wide awake, mirrored Nessa's pose.

'About time.'

Nessa began to talk, and Maudie strained to listen, not wanting to miss anything.

'As soon as I was of an age, I left home to begin work as a live-in housemaid for a factory owner and his family over in Clontarf. I was lucky to get the job, I thought.'

The area meant nothing to Maudie, but she listened raptly to Nessa's description.

'You want to have seen the house. I'd never seen the likes before. It was huge and seemed to float above the sea; there were fresh flowers in every room along with airs and graces I'd no clue about. The children were seen not heard and had a governess, and the missus floated about in pretty dresses never seeming to do much of anything. I went home each Sunday afternoon, but I was terribly homesick in between times, even though home was nothing special. It was noisy, though, and I could melt into the background, unlike in that house. It was so quiet. So different to what I was used to. Do you see?'

Maudie could. Nessa painted a picture with her words – she was a natural storyteller.

'The mister, now he was kind and showed an interest in me when no one else was about. I was nothing special in my family, one of eight mouths to feed, so nobody had ever been interested in what I thought or had to say until him. I didn't care that he was old enough to be me da because I liked the way he made me feel worth listening to and not so alone.'

Maudie reached out then and grasped Nessa's hand, sensing the way the rest would pan out.

'I wanted to make him happy, Maudie – that was all. The way he made me happy, and I didn't want him to stop being interested because I liked it. I thought I loved him, but now I'm not sure I even know what love is. He can't have loved me, though, or I wouldn't have been sent here. I don't know where I'll go when I leave here either because my family doesn't want to know me.'

Nessa lapsed into silence. Maudie was trying to visualise the sort of man who could prey on a young girl's vulnerabilities like so, and then she realised Nessa was waiting for her to speak up. It was her turn to talk, and her voice choked up thinking of the cruelty of how she'd come to be at St Patrick's, but somehow she whispered her story, the moon going behind the clouds as she glossed over what had happened that terrible afternoon along the *bóthar* because the walls had ears.

Even then, Maudie was crying. Her determination not to feel sorry for herself for all that had befallen her had deserted her the moment she'd begun to confide in Nessa everything she'd been holding inside.

'You don't know who the father is then?' Nessa asked quietly.

'No.' That was the truth of the matter and one she'd not

spoken aloud until now. She could wish with all her heart to be carrying Ronan's child, but she didn't *know*. Not for certain.

'And Ronan?'

'He'll come for me when he can.' Maudie knew she wasn't the only girl to hold on to this hope, but she knew Ronan would never willingly leave her. 'He's the husband of my heart.'

Nessa squeezed her hand tightly but stayed silent, and Maudie was grateful she understood the pointlessness of platitudes. It was an unspoken truth that neither girl knew what the future held for them or their babies here at St Patrick's, but there was reassurance in human touch, and they continued to hold hands until they fell asleep.

Maudie dreamed of JP. His face haunted her as much as the Tan's because it was his betrayal that had led to the Quinn brothers' disappearance. It had to have been him who'd reported them, despite what he'd said. He'd all but told her he would. Even in sleep, however, her mind refused to wander into a world where her baby was born with cruel eyes and pale lashes.

Nessa's baby came in the hours before dawn.

21

Maudie lay there trying to get her bearings, wondering what had woken her but grateful simultaneously to leave her nightmares behind. Then she heard the whimpering. 'Nessa?'

'It hurts, Maudie.'

Maudie sat up, wide awake. 'Should I fetch the sister?'

'No! Don't leave me.'

'What's happening?' was whispered into the dark. Then Cecelia's distinctive voice was backed up by others.

'Nessa's baby,' Maudie replied a moment later, hearing prayers being uttered as she got up and padded around the other side of the bed, kneeling to rub Nessa's back as she'd seen the midwife who'd helped her mam deliver do.

'I'm frightened.' Nessa's voice was tiny and engulfed with pain, almost childlike.

Maudie injected a soothing conviction into her voice. 'Listen to me now, Nessa. You'll be grand, and your baby will be born before you know it.'

'I didn't think it would hurt this bad. Rub harder, Maudie, please.'

Maudie did so, grimacing with each stifled cry as Nessa,

hand fisted in her mouth, cried silently. She kneaded her friend's back like she did the bread dough, until her hand began aching. She was aware Nessa needed help, but each time she broached someone going to find it, she only grew more distressed. When the bell rang, Maudie's hand was numb, and she'd no idea how long her friend had been labouring. Her whimpers were turning into shrieks that echoed off the dormitory walls. Even if she'd wanted to hide what was happening, it was no longer possible to do so. Maudie ordered a wide-eyed little Molly to fetch the sister on duty.

'Quick as you can now, Mol!' For Nessa's sake, Maudie hoped it would be Sister Louise's round, beaming face that would appear, full of gentle reassurance that all would be well.

God was busy that morning, however, because it was Sister Agnes that bore down on them a few minutes later. The only mercy was that Nessa, now writhing in agony, was oblivious.

Maudie abandoned her post and stood up, ensuring Nessa couldn't hear what she had to say. 'I'm worried for her, Sister. Something's not right.'

Sister Agnes's lip curled back as she pushed Maudie aside and grabbed Nessa, shaking her hard. 'Pull yourself together, girl. You're making a spectacle of yourself.'

'For God's sake, Sister, have some pity!' The words flew from Maudie's mouth as she squared up to the nun.

A stillness settled over the dormitory, and then a whip-like crack sounded as Sister Agnes's hand connected with Maudie's jaw. Maudie's head snapped back and she stumbled, her hand to her face, unaware of anything except her, the nun and the need to get help for Nessa. There was a maniacal glitter in the sister's eyes which Maudie ignored, taking it upon herself to help Nessa to sitting.

'Go with Sister Agnes, Nessa, for the sake of your baby. Go.'

Momentarily, Nessa's pain-wracked eyes settled on Maudie's, seeking reassurance.

Maudie nodded. 'You can do this.'

It was only as her friend stumbled off, hunched forward and screaming with each step, hands clasping her belly that Maudie allowed herself to cry.

It wasn't just for herself.

She wept for Nessa. For all the other girls who'd shuffled into line for the bathroom, terrified.

They'd all seen what their own futures held.

22

Where was Nessa?

It was the not knowing that was the worst of it, or so Maudie thought. The days had turned to weeks, then a month had passed, and now it had been over two months since her friend had locked eyes with Maudie so trustingly.

The weather was turning colder as they edged toward the coldest days of winter and ever closer to her own baby's arrival. She was terrified of what was to come and what would happen afterward. Robust kicks that should have filled her with joy were tempered with worry for her friend. Why wasn't there news of her or the baby? Maudie swung from wild hope she'd run away with her child and was forging a new life somewhere and fear of what might have happened. She might not be a midwife, but she'd picked up that all was not well with poor Nessa and her babe.

She'd pressed the girls who trooped to the nursery to feed their babies whenever the bell rang for information, but they'd not seen or heard so much as a whisper of her friend since the morning she'd stumbled from the dormitory under the cruel watch of Sister Agnes. Her worry hadn't been eased by the fact the nun had made it her business ever since to be wherever Maudie was. A viper waiting for an excuse to strike.

Nessa's bed had been filled not long after she'd left the dormitory for the last time. It was as if she'd been erased when a sunken-eyed and lank-haired woman had placed a nightgown under the pillow then made the sign of the cross, eyeing her distastefully. She wasn't a fallen woman, she'd been quick to inform Maudie. Her husband had hit upon hard times was all and, as such, she'd be keeping herself to herself for the duration of her stay. It wasn't the only thing he'd hit upon, Maudie had thought, noting the woman's bruised cheek. But she was too numb to care.

Girls came then went, and Maudie barely noticed. But Mol, of course, was different.

The day she didn't show up for evening prayer, last seen clutching her back and crying that the baby was coming, she'd prayed hard for a safe delivery of the youngster's child. Terrified she'd vanish too.

But her prayers were answered because Molly returned to St Patrick's a week later. She was years from becoming a woman, but she was a mother now and no longer cried herself to sleep, frightened of the unknown. The first chance she got, Mol excitedly relayed that the birthing was painful, yes, but it was quick. Then there he was, a baby boy born with a fine set of lungs and a thick head of black hair. She gushed over having named him after a local lad from her village who had nice eyes.

'The sisters call him Brendan, but he's Connor to me.'

The child's naivety that one day she might marry the lad made Maudie want to cry. And when Molly told her she'd be going home to the farm soon because she was needed, she did.

Mol misinterpreted her tears. 'Don't cry, Maudie. I'll be grand. There's always plenty to eat at home, and I think me da will leave me be now he knows what can happen. Do you think me ma might let me bring Connor home with me too?'

Maudie dried her tears and plastered a cheery smile to her face. 'Perhaps she will.' What was the point in telling the truth? Hope was all any of them had in here.

And while Nessa's face haunted her, Mol's innocent belief that all would be well lit a smouldering fire in Maudie. If she didn't take matters into her own hands and try to get to the truth, she would go mad.

Her chance came when Sister Agnes ventured outside to see what was taking Cecelia, who was carting the buckets of peelings to the pigs, so long. Ignoring the wide eyes and hissed warnings of the other girls, she let the knife clatter to the worktop and hurried from the kitchen. No one stopped her as she made her way determinedly along the corridor to the foyer.

She finally came to a standstill outside the Reverend Mother's office and tapped lightly on the door. 'I'm doing this for you, Nessa,' she whispered.

'Enter.'

Maudie pushed the door open a little wider and stepped inside the room to stand in front of the Reverend Mother's desk.

'What is it, child?' Her toad-like eyes bored into what felt like Maudie's very soul overtop of her spectacles, and her face grew hot under the all-seeing gaze.

'I'm sorry to intrude, Mother, but please would you tell me where Nessa, the girl you call Jillian, has gone? I've been terribly worried about her.' She hadn't any idea what her friend's last name was, but the Reverend Mother had to know who she was because during Maudie's time here at St Patrick's, Nessa was the only one who'd left to give birth and not come back.

A furrow embedded itself between wiry swirls of brow. 'That's of no concern to you. Who sent you?'

'No one, Mother.' Maudie was talking too fast as she clasped and unclasped her hands in front of her huge belly.

'Did I not explain the rules of St Patrick's, girl?' the Reverend Mother thundered. She seemed to grow taller as indignation swelled her chest, making her look ever more like a toad.

Maudie focused on the network of spidery veins decorating her cheeks as she edged toward the door, aware this had been a terrible mistake. The Reverend Mother could tell her where Nessa was, but she wouldn't, and all she'd achieved in trying to find answers was bring trouble down upon herself. She felt sick.

'Who's overseeing you in the kitchen?'

'Sister Agnes, Mother, but—'

A hand slapped down on the desk. 'You will return to the kitchen and tell Sister Agnes I wish to see her immediately.'

'Please Mother, I only wanted to know about Nessa.' Maudie tried to keep the desperation from her voice, knowing that if Sister Agnes was reprimanded, it would be her who'd pay dearly – but then the Reverend Mother must surely know that.

'Enough of your impudence, girl!'

Maudie fled then, her feet turning toward the entrance. She wanted nothing more than to run and never look back. The door wasn't locked; there was nothing to stop her, but where would she go? To leave would put her baby at risk, and she wouldn't do that. There was nothing for it but to do as she'd been told.

The silence Sister Agnes appraised her with as she returned to the kitchen to convey the Reverend Mother's summons was more terrifying than any slap she could wield. And with a shaking hand, Maudie returned to her task of peeling the mountain of potatoes.

'You're for it now, you stupid girl. Sister Agnes doesn't forget. Keeping yourself to yourself is the only way to survive this place,' Cecelia murmured, her hand going to her cheek. It was the first time she'd spoken to Maudie since she'd refused the morsel of bread.

There was a haunted look in her blue eyes, and Maudie wondered if she was remembering damage Sister Agnes's hands had dealt in the past, and shivered at the chill the sister's name had conjured.

23

The afternoon that followed Sister Agnes's return to the kitchen was the longest of Maudie's life. There was a smell about the nun that was almost feral, and Maudie nicked herself more than once, aware that the odour was anger. Malevolent eyes watched her, and when that day, then the next, passed with no repercussions, she understood Sister Agnes had decided to bide her time. This was torture, and she didn't dare try to smuggle any bread from the kitchen.

On the third day, Maudie's shoulders unknotted a little and she eyed the chunks of bread ready to be placed on plates, thinking about Mol feeding little Connor. Her hand twitched, but still she was wary. By the fourth day, however, she concluded Sister Agnes must have, by some miracle, decided to let Maudie's insubordination go. She could only hope the reprimand from the Reverend Mother had chastened the nun into keeping a low profile.

A new mother needed sustenance, she told herself, glancing about the kitchen. Sister Agnes was chastising Cecelia for being too slow in her work, so she hastily shoved a portion in her pocket. Mol would sleep all the better for having a little extra in her stomach.

Later that evening, as Maudie left the kitchen for evening Mass, a hand slapped down on her shoulder.

'You've been helping yourself to extra bread, Theresa.'

Maudie froze. She'd been so stupid thinking there wouldn't be a reprisal from Sister Agnes. What frightened her most was the way in which the nun had spoken. Her voice had held the usual sing-song quality that belied her true nature, but Maudie had also detected a note of glee. She'd been biding her time, waiting for an opportunity to pull her up.

The other girls hurried past, eyes downcast, wanting no part in whatever was about to happen. But Cecelia, to Maudie's surprise, had paused, torn between fear over intervening and knowing right from wrong. Maudie gave an imperceptible shake of her head. It would do no good for them both to bear the brunt of Sister Agnes's wrath, but she didn't move.

'You've been taking bread from the kitchen.' A statement not a question.

Her gut reaction was to lie. 'No, Sister. You're mistaken. I haven't.'

'Empty your pockets.' The crooning voice had been replaced by a sharp bark.

Maudie gritted her teeth, and her eyes flashed with challenge.

'Are you deaf, girl?'

She could flee, but Sister Agnes, perhaps sensing her panic, stepped in front of her, blocking her path, and before Maudie knew what was happening, the nun had lunged forward, thrusting her hand into Maudie's pocket before holding the bread aloft triumphantly.

'I didn't take that.' The second lie tumbled forth because this wasn't about Maudie's self-preservation; it was about her baby's.

'Insolence!'

The slap, a thunderclap, saw Maudie's head snap back, and she stumbled backward, losing her balance.

'Leave her be!' Cecelia shouted, having drawn herself up to her full height.

For a whisper of a second, Sister Agnes hesitated, but then her rosary beads materialised seemingly from thin air, hitting Cecelia's face with a crack and cutting through the flesh of her cheek.

Maudie watched in horror as blood trickled from the wound, the sight of which saw Cecelia's face bleach white before she collapsed in a heap. Maudie knew she should try to get up and run for help, but she was frozen – and then Sister Agnes was on her, dragging her deeper inside the kitchen by her hair while her feet scrabbled for traction.

Ice-cold fear as to what would happen next coursed through Maudie, and she tried to cover her belly. To fight back would make things worse, but she would if this evil woman tried to harm the baby.

She was pushed onto her knees, and she hunched forward protectively when she heard a drawer opening. Her head was so close to the linoleum floor, the detergent used to clean it burned her nose and eyes.

Risking a glance up, she saw Sister Agnes had scissors in her hand, the look in her eyes akin to the rabid dog Maudie had seen in town once. It had bitten a small child and been shot shortly after.

If she'd had a gun, Maudie wouldn't have hesitated to use it – she'd done it before to save herself. She heard someone whimper then realised it was her, crying out as her hair was yanked loose from its knot.

A rebellious glimmer kindled within her. 'What happened to you?' Maudie angled her head to see blind fury in the young sister's face as she began hacking her hair off. Red-gold tresses tumbled down around her.

The sister ignored her question. 'You wanted to know what happened to that girl? The one you call Nessa,' Sister Agnes panted as she continued to cut. 'Her and that creature got what they deserved. God decided they weren't fit for this world.'

Maudie cried out. It couldn't be true. Nessa and her baby couldn't be dead!

'They died in a pool of blood.'

The fight left Maudie then, and all the air seeped from her body. She knew the sisters and the doctors wouldn't have fought hard to save either of them.

She barely registered the remainder of the attack, only coming back to herself when she was finally yanked to her feet and marched from the kitchen.

Nessa was one of many fallen women. Neither she nor her baby had mattered to the world they inhabited, and Maudie didn't either. *We mattered to each other though,* was Maudie's last thought as she stumbled into evening prayers, ignoring the other girls' shocked gasps. Nothing mattered anymore.

Sister Agnes had won. She'd extinguished the chink of hope that somehow Maudie and her baby would stay together.

She understood now what an impossible dream that was.

24

Maudie was one of St Patrick's girls proper now, with her hunched shoulders and bowed head, accepting of her lot here at the home. The only difference between her and the other women was her hacked hair. One of the girls she worked alongside in the kitchen had tidied up the worst of it, but even still, it was a constant reminder of who was all powerful. Which, after all, had been Sister Agnes's intention.

Since that terrible afternoon, Maudie moved through her days, working hard and avoiding Sister Agnes's gaze in the kitchen, praying and giving no one cause for complaint. At night, though, the tears came. Her heart was full of sorrow for the cruel world she would soon bring a child into. She hadn't thought it was possible for anything to hurt as badly as what the Tan had done to her on the *bóthar*, but she'd been wrong.

Now, it was only young Molly and Cecelia, whom she'd misjudged, who broke through her determination to remain aloof since Sister Agnes had done her worse. They tried to comfort Maudie to sleep in their dormitory to no avail. Cecelia, saying she'd learned about herbal healing in her old life, would massage rosemary leaves pilfered from the kitchen garden into her tender scalp to help it heal and had taken to placing a sprig of lavender under her pillow each night. All the while, Maudie's tears flowed for Nessa and the other women, including herself; for Cecelia, who would bear a permanent reminder of the cruelty of this place in the form of a jagged scar across her cheek, for Mol, and all the lost little babies.

She barely heard Cecelia when she tiptoed over to her bed one night and said, 'I've named her, my little girl. She's to be called Vanessa. Nessa for short. She won't be forgotten.'

It barely penetrated the fog Maudie was engulfed in, and she scarcely registered Cecelia taking her hand and holding it in hers.

The kicks from her baby grew stronger day by day, but she couldn't summon the strength to wonder over them because she understood now that she didn't control her future or that of her child. The Reverend Mother and sisters here at St Patrick's would decide her fate, as they had so many others before her. In her darkest moments, she wished to go to sleep and never wake up.

Then, one evening, as Maudie's time drew near, Sister Louise paused alongside her in the dining room, resting a hand on her shoulder as she bent down to whisper close to her ear. 'Your friend Nessa's buried up the road in the Glasnevin Cemetery, as is her baby. The little one's in the Angels' Plot. I pray over the babies' and their mothers' graves. I don't forget them. Nor does God.'

Those whispered words and that small touch conveying kindness meant everything. Someone cared, and it was enough for Maudie to shake off her malaise. She mattered! Her baby mattered!

She thought about how hard Ronan and others like him were fighting for what they – she – believed in and knew he'd expect her to be strong. Not just for her but for their child because this baby had to be his. She remembered the girl she'd been in the dunes, full of spirit and determination to free Ireland. That girl still existed. She was still Maudie O'Connor.

This was what she held on to when, in the middle of the night, the pains came.

'Mol, Cecelia.' Her whispered voice shook with terror in the darkened dormitory. 'I think the baby's coming.'

25

Maudie would have given anything to have Nora by her side, holding her hand and telling her everything would be all right. Above her head, affixed to the wall, she spotted a wooden crucifix as she arced back in a spasm of agony like nothing she'd ever felt. The sister assisting with the birth was clutching rosary beads and praying, for all the good *that* was doing. There was to be no relief though. This, now, was her penance.

Another sister, peering between her legs, was barking instructions, and near the door a familiar face offered her comfort. Sister Louise! As the pain, far worse than Mol and Cecelia had promised it would be, ripped through her, she held on to those kindly brown eyes, drawing strength from them.

Time had no meaning, and as the pain grew, there was only her and this primal force. She cried out, clawing at the sheet beneath her, all rationality gone. Then at last, when she thought she would surely go out of her mind, it came – an all-consuming need to push.

Maudie didn't need to be told what to do and clenched her teeth, bearing down with all her might.

There was a slithering, burning sensation followed by a

robust cry, and she sank back on her elbows, sobbing as she caught her first glimpse of a tiny, squalling face before the flailing bundle was whisked away.

Half delirious, Maudie caught the words, 'A girl.'

As the sister with the rosary beads pocketed them and busied herself with cleaning up the aftermath of the blood-soaked birth, whisking the sheet and towels away, Sister Louise told the other sister she'd take over and stepped forward, wiping the baby down before swaddling her tightly. She was shrieking her indignation at finding herself in such a stark place, and Maudie didn't blame her one bit.

'Please.' She held her arms out, wanting to comfort her. 'Let me hold her.'

The sisters who'd assisted with the birth left the room with the dirty linen, and when the door closed behind them, Sister Louise hurried toward the table where Maudie lay. 'Just for a moment, and then she's to go to the nursery.'

Maudie's smile was weary with gratitude as the weight of her baby settled into her arms. 'Emer,' she breathed, staring down at the little miracle she was holding. She'd named her for the wife of the warrior chief of legends, Cú Chulainn, whose Emer was said to have been both fierce and wise.

'The name when given means *beautiful queen*.' Sister Louise smiled, not explaining how she knew this.

'And you are that, Emer. My beautiful little queen. I'll never let you down, my love. Never.'

If Sister Louise heard her, she pretended not to.

Emer's face was screwed up tight, an angry red, but Maudie was filled with a love she'd never known before and a need to protect her daughter at all costs. All her fears and doubts as to how this child had come to be were extinguished. Emer was hers – that was all that mattered. Still, seeing the three small port-wine petals reminiscent of a shamrock on the side of her neck was enough to tell her Emer was unconditionally Ronan's too.

She watched the little girl's face relax as she continued to coo to her, and then her eyes blinked open, fixing on Maudie. They were so full of trust, her heart nearly burst with love, and it swept the memory of the agonising hours she'd endured away as nature intended.

She cradled her daughter close, inhaling her smell and smiling as her tiny hand worked free of her swaddling to flail about in a show of spirited determination. Ronan would love this child too because she was part of her, and one day the three of them would be together. A proper family. Elation mingled with exhaustion, but Maudie knew for certain now she could endure anything for the sake of her child.

All too soon, footsteps sounded in the corridor outside the room, and Sister Louise hurried over to pluck Emer from her arms.

Maudie held her baby tightly. 'Please, please, don't take her from me.'

'I'm sorry, but she's to go to the nursery now.' Sister Louise's panicked gaze turned to the door as it opened, and the nun who'd clasped her rosary beads throughout Maudie's labour appeared, her arms empty of washing now. Her glance was sharp and questioning upon seeing Maudie clutching her baby to her chest.

'Is everything all right?'

'I was just about to take baby to the nursery.' Sister Louise shot Maudie a pleading look.

She'd no choice but to let Emer go, seeing it hurt the good sister to take her almost as much as it hurt Maudie to relinquish her.

Emer's cries echoed down the corridor, tugging at Maudie as though they were still bound to one another by an umbilical cord. She swallowed hysteria down, aware she would do herself and Emer no favours by lashing out, and allowed the remaining nun to help her wash before tugging the clean nightdress over her head. She was to go back to the dormitory now, but tomorrow she would be expected to report to the kitchen for work.

All she wanted to do was run to the nursery, fetch her baby and leave this place, but where could she go? There would be no warm welcome for her and Emer in Rush. For now, she had no choice but to bide her time, regain her strength and focus on putting a plan together for her and Emer's future. Still, the instinct to go to her daughter threatened to overrule common sense, and she squeezed her eyes shut in a silent plea for Ronan to come back from wherever he was and rescue them from this nightmare.

'I'll get to feed her, though, won't I?' Maudie hated the pleading tone in her voice as she was led back to the dormitory.

'For a time, child, but you'd be wise not to allow yourself to grow attached to the baby. It will only make things harder for you in the long run.'

Maudie rubbed at the goosebumps that covered her arms – not from what the sister had said but what she hadn't.

That there would be a time, all too soon, when little Emer would no longer be hers.

26

The months passed in a blur of routine which saw Maudie feel as if she was finally putting that terrible afternoon on the *bóthar* and all it had unleashed behind her. Thoughts of Ronan and where he was still consumed her, but she clung to the belief that he'd come for her. What other choice did she have? Because she was a mother now and had to be strong not for herself but for Emer.

She lived to hear the bell that signalled it was time to make her way to the nursery to feed little Emer, even as she resented the lack of nourishment she and the other mothers received. She knew the nuns ate well with fresh eggs, portions of meat and fish along with the vegetables the girls – or inmates as they saw themselves – had grown over the summer. How were the babies to thrive if their mothers' milk was of such poor quality?

Still, she was grateful Emer was a fighter whom Mol and Cecelia said was beginning to resemble her mother more and more with each passing day. Emer was more robust and better able to stave off illness than some of the little ones whose hungry cries filled the space. Cecelia fretted because her little Nessa was small and didn't appear to be thriving. Maudie's heart broke for her and all the other babies born into life here, but she couldn't save them all. One day she'd find a way to help though, she resolved.

Then one evening, Sister Louise again came to her rescue. 'Look under your bed,' she whispered out of earshot of her fellow sisters.

A parcel of food had been squirrelled away, which Maudie doled out as best she could. And the food kept coming night after night. It was a miracle.

Sister Louise's small kindness helped, as did those precious minutes holding Emer, which were blissful even if she wasn't allowed to interact with her. Bonding with the babies was actively discouraged, and the mothers who'd filed into the nursery, summoned by the bell, were never left alone with them. There was never a second when there wasn't a watchful eye on them. Maudie felt certain, however, that words weren't needed to convey her love. Surely Emer could feel it in the tender way her mother held her.

A new energy had infused her in the months since she'd given birth, despite most of the nuns' best efforts. The tears she'd shed after learning of Nessa and her baby's death had dried up because they wouldn't help her or Emer. That didn't mean she'd ever forget her friend and her little one – she would carry their loss with her always. She owed it to them to make the most of the precious gift she'd been given and find a way to make her way in the world as a mother. So when silence fell on the dormitory and the girls slumbered, Maudie no longer cried but plotted how to get herself and Emer far away from St Patrick's. She wouldn't accept her lot – to do so would be to let Ronan down, and now a plan was finally shoring up in her mind.

27

It wouldn't be long now. Another few weeks and Emer would be three months old and, Maudie hoped, better able to withstand the journey they were going to make. It was going to be the longest of Maudie's life because she'd decided their only option was to leave Ireland. It would break her heart, but she'd already withstood worse. Somehow, she'd make her way back to Rush, even if she had to do so on foot. Then Nora would help her to secure passage to America as she and Ronan had planned, only now she'd be sailing there without him. Unless, by some miracle, he was able to escape with them. If not, once she was settled, she would write and tell Nora where she was so he could join them when it was safe.

In America, she felt sure she and Emer could start a new life. She'd leave behind the stigma and shame the church insisted upon here and live as a respectable widowed woman with her baby daughter. Ronan would be so proud of her when he managed to come for them. It was a dream Maudie clung to, telling no one of her plans – not even Mol or Cecelia, who'd finally confided how she'd come to be here. And what a story that was! They'd formed a strong and unlikely friendship. They might have grown up near one another, but their backgrounds were so different. Motherhood, however, had bridged that gap. She'd no choice but to do right by Emer. Her daughter would not be raised in an orphanage because she wasn't an orphan.

Fate, however, had other plans.

28

'Where's my baby? Maudie cried, seeing the empty cot still indented with Emer's shape. She scanned the nursery, her gaze coming to rest on several bare-bottomed babies being changed. Emer wasn't one of them. And her heart began to beat faster on a second sweep of the nursery because she wasn't there.

Sister Joan, a kindly nun who'd a way with the more unsettled babies, rustled forward, frowning. 'What are you doing here, Theresa? I told Sister Agnes to tell you not to come this morning.'

Maudie stared at the nun, perplexed. 'She didn't pass that on. Why shouldn't I come?' *She's my baby.*

'Oh dear.' Sister Joan wrung her hands together.

'Where's Emer, Sister Joan?' Maudie wasn't supposed to call her baby by the name she'd given her, but she didn't care. Something wasn't right – she could feel it, and cold panic prickled her skin.

'I'll deal with this, Sister,' a sing-song voice said behind her. 'I told her she was no longer needed in the nursery, but she ran off before I could stop her.'

No longer needed? Maudie spun round to face Sister Agnes. 'I don't understand.'

'Your little girl is one of the fortunate ones, Theresa. You should be grateful. Remember that.'

'Sister Agnes,' Sister Joan interjected, softening her tone as she turned to Maudie. ''Tis for the best she's gone, child. You'll be able to move on with your life once your time here at St Patrick's is done.'

The floor seemed to tilt beneath her feet, and Maudie clutched the end of the cot to support herself. There was a roaring in her ears, and she shouted over it. 'Gone where?' Her mind had gone blank, and all she could think of was that Emer would be hungry and she needed to go to her. Her daughter needed her mam.

The room suddenly seemed airless, and her throat began constricting because while Sister Agnes had a crowing look about her, Sister Joan appeared sympathetic, but still neither nun had replied to her question.

'For the love of God answer me!'

Sister Agnes's eyes flashed dangerously. 'Don't raise your voice to me or Sister Joan, girl, and it's not for either of us to say where the baby's gone.'

Around them, life in the nursery continued with mothers nursing their babes. Maudie's breasts ached, hot and heavy with the need to feed her daughter.

'Sister Joan will bind you, and then you'll get back to work.' Sister Agnes's distaste at the wet patch on Maudie's smock was evident in the curl of her lip.

''Tis best to keep busy, child,' Sister Joan said soothingly, but this only served to alarm Maude further.

Maudie shook her head. It didn't make sense. None of this made sense. She could see a challenge flickering in Sister Agnes's eyes. She wanted her to push further. By challenging her, she'd give her an excuse to hurt her again. The woman was evil hiding under a nun's habit. Well, she wasn't afraid of her.

'I think it best you leave me to explain things to the child, Sister Agnes.'

Sister Agnes, however, didn't move, and Sister Joan stepped forward, reaching out to Maudie to offer comfort, but Maudie stepped back, feeling like a caged animal.

'The little one has gone to a very good home. It's a stroke of good fortune. She'll be well loved and want for nothing, Theresa,' Sister Joan said softly.

'My name's Maude, and she'll be wanting her mother. She'll be crying for me.'

Sister Joan looked stricken. 'It's God's will.'

'God doesn't steal babies!'

'The child is better off without you.'

The cruelty lacing Sister Agnes's words saw something deep inside Maudie snap. She lunged for the nun and tore at her bonnet, wanting to scratch her eyes out. Sister Agnes fell to the floor with a cry, covering her head, but Maudie was a woman whose child had been stolen, and she wasn't giving up. All the pain and rage inside her spilled forth as she hit out at Sister Agnes.

Around her, the other women clutched their babies to their chests, wide-eyed, while Sister Joan, recovering from her initial shock over Maudie's sudden attack, tried frantically to pull her off her fellow sister.

'Don't just stand there,' she shouted to the girls watching on. 'Help me, one of you. She'll kill her. You there, go fetch the doctor. Run!'

Sister Joan was right. She would kill her, and she wouldn't be sorry, just like she wasn't sorry for the Tan. She'd save all the girls who'd come after her from this cruel woman. First, though, she needed answers.

'Tell me who took her,' she shouted, but there was no sound

from Sister Agnes other than cowardly whimpers. 'Tell me!' Maudie bellowed, continuing to lash out.

She didn't see the doctor approaching with a needle until it was too late. Her body was rendered useless, and then darkness engulfed her.

29

Her daughter was gone. Emer had been given away! Maudie moaned, overwhelmed with a pain that was as much physical as emotional.

She opened her eyes and blinked several times, trying to clear her focus before propping herself up on her elbows. Her eyes settled on the crumpled fabric of her smock, and fragmented pieces of memory swirled around her head.

She was in the nursery, Sister Joan was there, she couldn't find Emer then... Oh dear God, there was Sister Agnes, no, no, no! Maudie shook her head, wanting it not to be true. She tugged at the neck of her smock and looked down at her bound breasts, then the last piece of the puzzle slotted into place and the full, horrific picture played out.

She sat up properly, a second moan escaping her lips as her head took a second longer to catch up with her body. Weak light spilled in through the dormitory windows high above the empty beds lining the length of the room, suggesting it was evening. She fought off the fogginess determined to send her back to sleep and rubbed her temples.

Maudie had thought she could endure anything after Emer was born, but she was wrong because she couldn't endure the pain of losing her. She wrapped her arms around her knees and began to rock, keening softly, unable to stop the tears falling. It was too much.

A featherlight touch brushed her shoulder, and a voice like a breath of wind whispered, 'You must be strong, Maudie. Emer needs you. Don't give up.'

'Nessa?' Maudie's head snapped up. Had the nuns lied to her?

There was no one there, but that didn't mean Nessa wasn't with her. She wasn't alone after all; her friend was watching over her, willing her on.

This certainty saw her swiping her cheeks dry with the backs of her hand. Then, like the sea after a storm, a calm stole over her because she would find out where Emer had gone and fetch her back. For now, though, there was nothing to be done except wait.

Hearing the footfall that signalled evening prayers were finished, Maudie lay back down and closed her eyes, pretending to be asleep. She'd didn't stir, not even when Mol came to stand beside her bed briefly. The younger girl would be worried about her. Word about what had happened was sure to have spread in that mysterious way it did despite the sisters' best efforts that the girls not converse with one another, but she couldn't afford to confide her plan in anyone, not even Mol, who'd likely try and stop her.

Time seemed to crawl by as she lay there counting the seconds, waiting until the sounds of settling in the dormitory gave way to slow, even breathing. As quietly as she could, she slipped from her bed. The boards beneath her feet creaked as she bent to fetch her shoes.

'Maudie?' Molly's voice whispered sleepily.

'It's all right, Mol. Shush now and go back to sleep. I'm only going to the bathroom.'

The fib did the trick because Molly laid her head back down, and Maudie padded past the other beds toward the door.

The corridor was in darkness, and the click as she closed the door behind her seemed to echo overly loudly in the empty expanse ahead of her. Maudie took a few steps but then paused outside the bathroom, waiting for her eyes to adjust to the windowless light. Aside from the steady dripping of a tap, all was quiet, and staying close to the wall, she scurried silently down the corridor like one of the many rodents that roamed the halls of St Patrick's nightly.

Soft footfall sounded behind her, and Maudie spun round, holding her breath. There was nowhere for her to hide and no good reason for her to be roaming the corridors.

A second later, she exhaled, seeing Cecelia limping toward her. When she reached her, she grabbed Maudie by her wrists, holding tight and nearly causing her to drop her shoes. For a split second, Maudie felt the Tan's fingers digging into her wrists as he pinned her arms over her head, and she opened her mouth in a silent scream.

'Shush now, Maudie, and come back to bed. You're not right.'

'Oh, but I am, Cecelia – my head's clearer than it's been since the night I arrived here.'

'Please come with me.' Cecelia's whisper was urgent given the deep trouble they'd find themselves in if they were caught out of bed.

'You still have Nessa. Mol has Connor. I have to find my girl.'

'Then Nessa and I will help you if you'll let us. It's only a matter of time until I lose her – you know that.'

Maudie could see she meant it. If she agreed, Cecelia would

run to the nursery, snatch Nessa and flee with Maudie. She was touched once more by her bravery, but they'd be stopped before they'd even reached the main door if Cecelia was to do that.

'I never thanked you for standing up to Sister Agnes for me. I misjudged you, and I'm sorry for that. I'm glad we became friends. But I have to do this on my own for Emer. Besides, Mol needs you.'

Cecelia eyes were glistening. 'Don't forget us, will you?'

'Never. How could I? I'll come back for you one day, I promise.'

They both knew Mol would never leave here because she firmly believed one day she could return to her family farm with Connor and all would be right in her world.

'I believe you will.'

The two young women clung to one another for a moment, their friendship unlikely but cemented through circumstance.

Maudie wasn't sure how or when she'd fetch Cecelia and Nessa, but she would. She didn't know what the future held, but for the present, all she could think of was finding Emer. Only then could she help her friend.

A cough sounded somewhere in the distance, and Cecelia released her. 'Go,' she urged.

Maudie did, hurrying to the stairs and staring down at the deserted foyer below. It was illuminated a ghostly yellow by the moonlight streaming in through the windows that framed the main doors, which were bolted. She began to creep down them with the Reverend Mother's office in her line of sight. The door was open, and a triangle of light shone on the floor outside the room.

Maudie's bravado seeped away from her then, and her legs buckled. She sat down on the stairs because whoever was on night duty wouldn't allow Maudie to storm into the office and begin rifling through the records until she found the paperwork telling her where Emer had gone. Her mind was still addled with the sedative she'd been given earlier, making her foolish. What she should have done – would still do, she decided – was have Mol pretend to be taken ill. This would give her an excuse to fetch the sister on duty, thus luring her away from the Reverend Mother's office and leaving her free to search for information on Emer.

She'd reached for the railing to pull herself upright, intent on sneaking back to the dormitory and waking Mol, when the door below opened fully and Sister Louise emerged, oil lamp held before her. She spotted Maudie on the stairs, immediately trapping her in the lamplight.

'Is that you, Theresa?'

Maudie didn't answer. She thought about fleeing, but it was too late for that because the nun had already reached the foot of the stairs.

'I thought I heard someone moving about. Come on now, child, what are you doing wandering about?'

'My baby,' Maudie said, her voice cracking, as she sank back down onto the step.

'Now, now, child, come. I'll take you back to the dormitory. It's rest you're needing. Things won't look so bleak in the morning. Sure, they never do.' Sister Louise's voice was overly cheery as she advanced up the stairs toward her.

Maudie remembered the strength Nessa's presence in the dormitory earlier had given her. She wouldn't back down and be led meekly back to bed. She owed it to her friend and her baby to leave this place with her head held high, but most of all she owed it to Emer to go and find her.

'My name's Maude, Sister Louise – you know that.' She stood up, her legs trembling as she clutched the bannister rail. 'And how can I rest when my baby's been stolen from me?' Her eyes darted past the rotund nun to the open door of the office. The information she sought was tantalisingly close.

'It was for the best, child.' Sister Louise was standing in front of her now, her girth blocking Maudie's view of the main doors. 'You won't agree now, but in time you'll see I'm right. Sure, what sort of a life could you give her?'

This wasn't said unkindly; rather it was trotted out as though the sister had said it one hundred times, so many times she almost believed what she was saying. Almost.

'I could give her a mother's love – that counts for an awful lot.'

'I don't doubt that you loved your child. But it's not up to us to question God's will.'

'It wasn't God's will, Sister. You know it as well as I do. It was the Reverend Mother's. Please, Sister Louise, do you know who took her?'

'All I know is it was an American gentleman and his wife. They were well-to-do. Your little one will have a good life. She'll want for nothing, Maude.'

'Except me.' Maudie grappled with what she'd been told. She needed more. She needed a name, an address at the very least. 'Let me take a look at the paperwork? Please, Sister Louise, at least grant me the peace of knowing where she's gone.'

'She'll be going to America. Imagine that. She'll have the sort of life most of the girls in here would give anything for their babies to have.' There was something childlike about Sister Louise, and Maudie could see the girl she'd been before she'd had her calling.

'Please, Sister, I'm begging you. How can I ever have peace always wondering where she is?'

Sister Louise's eyes were gentle and filled with empathy, and for a fleeting moment Maudie thought she'd waver, but then her lips tightened.

'It won't serve any purpose for you to know anything further, Theresa. The paperwork's done. The baby's not yours anymore. You need to put her out of your mind now. Work hard and do your penance. Then, when your time comes, you'll leave here and go back to your family.'

'Emer is my family.' She shoved her feet into her shoes.

Sister Louise moved to take Maudie's arm and steer her up the stairs, but Maudie wrested the lamp from her and left her blustering as she darted down the stairs. She was in the office with the door locked behind her before the nun knew what was happening.

Maudie expected to hear her shout and raise the alarm, but there was only silence.

Moving around the expanse of desk, she perched in the Reverend Mother's chair and began opening drawers, rifling through the contents for the paperwork that would tell her who had taken Emer and where they were from.

She found what she was looking for on top of a sheaf of papers in the bottom drawer. The neat handwritten notes were brief with barely a mention of her other than to say the mother had come to St Patrick's from Rush, County Dublin. It didn't matter though. What mattered was she had a name and location for the couple who had her daughter.

Mr and Mrs Declan Kinsella of Savannah, Georgia, United States of America.

Maudie thought fleetingly of Ronan and their plans to visit America as she stared at the address. She could never have imagined the last time they were together all that was going to unfold and that she would be going to America with or without him. She had no choice because America was where their baby was.

Maudie didn't dare risk unlocking the Reverend Mother's office door; instead, she wrestled with the window, wrenching it up and clambering out. The night air was cool as her shoes touched the gravel, and she began to run down the drive toward the gates. They were half open as they had been the night she'd arrived.

She turned for one last look at St Patrick's, thinking of all the poor souls slumbering within those walls, some of whom might never leave. One day she'd help them, she vowed, but for now all she could focus on was Emer, so she stepped through the gates and disappeared into the night.

30

The eerie glow of the gas lights along the deserted Dublin streets were behind her now as Maudie reached the outskirts of the city. She was intent on putting as many miles as she could between herself and St Patrick's because she wouldn't go back there, no matter what. Nothing would stop her getting to Emer.

Her head was light from the after-effects of the sedative and lack of food, but she didn't dare allow herself to rest for fear of not getting up again. She had to get to Nora and find out if Ronan had sent word. What she would do if he hadn't wasn't something she could allow herself to think about.

Her mind drifted into hazy thoughts of the journey to America as she walked along the deserted stretch of road with fields either side. She knew nothing of the practicalities this would involve, but her frown was wiped from her face as a thunderclap echoed through the night air. It was swiftly followed by an ear-splitting scream, and Maudie's gaze was wild-eyed, her heart banging in her chest. A spilt-second silence ensued, but then she heard the unmistakable sound of horse's hooves in the distance. Instinct took over, and she stumbled off the road and flattened herself into the gully, praying the moon would stay behind the clouds.

The hooves grew louder and louder until they were upon her, and she squeezed her eyes shut and clenched her fists in readiness. She wouldn't go back!

A short while later, she realised the thundering hooves had receded, and her fists slowly unfurled. They'd passed her by. Still, she lay with the damp earth soaking through her smock. She was so tired, and all she wanted to do was drift away.

A second scream shattered the night, jolting her from her stupor. She pulled herself upright as the sky lit up in the distance. Gunfire and foxes!

She forced herself to stand and focused on putting one foot in front of the other until every part of her body ached. The thought of Emer spurred her on, and eventually the terrain grew hilly, the fresh, salty air from the coast below a balm after St Patrick's. It helped banish the stink of carbolic soap and boiled cabbage from her nostrils.

The route she was picking her way over led her down into Skerries, so she'd need to be extra vigilant. She'd her wits about her enough to head for the railway line. It would be safer to take that path rather than pass through the village.

Just as she'd hoped, no one from the quiet fishing village bothered her as she followed the tracks, and it wasn't long before she was surrounded by farmland.

The sky had begun lightening, with birdsong filling the air, when Maudie caught sight of St Maur's spire with her hometown nestling around it. She stopped as a rush of mixed emotions swept over her. She was almost there!

Maudie hobbled forth, breathing in the heady mix of animals and sea. The scent of home. Only it wasn't home anymore. Her mam had made it clear she wouldn't be welcomed back, and besides, her home now was wherever her daughter and Ronan were.

Be strong Maudie, be strong, the wind seemed to whisper. *You're nearly there.* It gave her the strength to stagger the final quarter mile to the cottage.

She pushed open the unlocked door and stumbled inside. Nora had her back to her, washing dishes at the sink, while Noelle, at her mother's feet, chewed on a chunk of stale bread. Seeing Maudie, she dropped the crust and stared up at her wide-eyed, bottom lip trembling.

'Nora,' Maudie ventured, and now she was there, her body sagged, spent.

Nora spun round sharply, dropping the dish she was drying, which narrowly missed Noelle. The little girl lost interest in the aunt she barely knew, more interested in the plate rolling around on the ground.

'Jesus wept, Maudie! It can't be.'

'It's me all right,' were Maudie's last words before she slumped forward.

Nora was quick off the mark, lunging forward to catch her then leading her to a chair at the table. 'Here, sit down. You look half starved – and your hair! What did they do to you?'

The angst in Nora's voice saw Noelle raise her gaze to her mammy.

Exhaustion overcame Maudie, and as sobs wracked her body, she leaned forward, resting her elbows on the table and placing her head in her hands. All she wanted to do was sleep, but first she needed answers to burning questions, and between hiccups and tears she asked, 'Have you word from Ronan?'

Nora shook her head, speaking over Noelle, who had joined in on the sobbing, 'Not Ronan. No one's heard a thing. But we received a delivery for you. It was left on the stoop overnight.'

Nora scooped her plump tot up and sat in the chair next to her sister, bouncing Noelle on her knee while gently rubbing Maudie's back, well used to multitasking. 'Shush, now. You're safe, Maudie. I've got you.'

Maudie was too tired to ponder the mystery package, instead allowing her sister's hand to soothe her. Gradually, the shuddering sobs stopped. 'I'm sorry, Nora. I wouldn't have come, but I'd nowhere else to go, and I need your help.'

'I'm your sister – of course you should have come to me. We'll talk more once you've eaten and had a chance to rest. Here.' She thrust her baby daughter at her, and the two of them stared at one another curiously, then Maudie, recalling the song she'd sung to her niece as a newborn, began to croon softly. Noelle soon relaxed and jammed her fist in her mouth. Meanwhile, Nora had busied herself at the stove, and when a pat of butter started sizzling in the pan, she began cracking eggs into it. Maudie's empty stomach churned.

Soon she was sipping sweetened tea and forcing down the heartiest breakfast she'd seen in a good while. How many mornings had she dreamed of a meal like this in the dining hall of St Patrick's? But that was before she'd lost Emer.

Nora, who'd set Noelle down on the floor so her sister could eat in peace, kept one eye on her as she crawled about and the other on Maudie, all the while chatting lightly and filling her in on the family news. Life had carried on as normal in her absence, and it seemed impossible to Maudie that so much had happened to her this last while and yet nothing had changed here in Rush. She picked up on her sister's change of tone as she spoke about their mam, glad of an excuse to put her fork down to listen.

'She's not been well, Maudie. Not since Father Doyle took you away. I think it's guilt making her sick.'

Maudie picked up her fork once more and began to shovel in what was left on her plate. She could feel Nora watching her and wasn't sure what she wanted her to say, but she couldn't conjure sympathy for their mam. She was a mother now herself, and no matter what society decreed was right or wrong, her daughter's well-being would always come first. It was as if she were dead inside where her mam and da were concerned, and she didn't think that would ever change. Certainly not until she was holding Emer once more.

Nora pushed back from the table and disappeared before returning with the tin bath, which she set down beside the hearth. 'Will you watch her for me while I fill this?'

Maudie carried her plate to the sink and then slipped her shoes off, feeling a sweet release as she pulled her holey stockings off and sat down on the floor next to her niece while Nora warmed water over the ticking fire. 'She's a beauty already, Nora.' Her mind turned to the sickly pallor of the tots at the home. The contrast between her bonny niece and Cecelia's little Nessa was stark.

Nora smiled over. 'She takes after her aunt Maude.'

Maudie's hand went to her hair.

'I'll trim that for you. Sure, you'll look like you should be in the pictures by the time I've finished.'

Maudie smiled her gratitude then tried to ignore the pain in her heart as she played with and cuddled Noelle because with every breath she took, Emer was slipping further away from her.

'There now.' Nora emptied the last pot of warm water into the tub. 'Martin's a creature of habit. He won't be back until his stomach tells him it's time for his dinner and the children are at school. And as for you,' she said, scooping up her daughter, 'it's time for you to catch forty winks.'

When Nora returned, closing the door on her protesting child, Maudie was slipping the smock over her head. She gasped upon seeing the milk-soaked binding. Her hand covered her mouth as she muttered something about God and Jesus and *what did they do to you?* Then, ever practical, she stepped forward and gently helped unwind the sodden material, bundling it up along with the smock and underwear.

'These are only fit for burning.'

Maudie, unselfconscious in front of her sister, stepped into the water then crouched into a seated position with her knees bent. The water soothed her grazes, blisters and bruises, and the feel of Nora's fingers massaging her scalp clean saw her close her eyes. For one blissful moment, she forgot about everything, but then as her hair was rubbed dry and Nora combed it through in readiness to snip off the ends, Maudie began to talk. She told her sister all that had happened since the fateful night Father Doyle had delivered her to St Patrick's. Nora didn't interrupt, not once. When Maudie had finished talking, her freshly trimmed hair was nearly dry, and the water had cooled.

'Come on – you'll catch a chill if you sit in there any longer.' Nora held a towel out.

Maudie held on to the edges of the tub and pulled herself up, drying off before stepping out of the water. While Nora tore an old sheet into strips to use for binding, she allowed herself to enjoy the sensation of being properly clean for the first time since she'd arrived at St Patrick's. She'd finally washed the cruelty of the place from her hair and body.

Once the strips of fabric were tucked into place, and Maudie had climbed into fresh undergarments and a borrowed dress from her sister, she sat in Martin's chair. Her eyes were beginning to flutter closed, but they opened as Nora, having seen to the tub, pressed a parcel wrapped in brown paper into her hands.

Maudie's eyes were bleary, but despite this she was aware the handwriting, which simply said *For Miss Maude O'Connor*, wasn't familiar. It wasn't from Ronan. Her heart sank as she tore the paper off.

Inside was a tea caddy; Maudie opened it then stared at its contents. Money. Where had it come from?

She tipped it into her lap, hearing Nora gasp at the sight of so much money. A slip of paper nestled amidst the notes, and she felt her blood roaring in her ears. Surely this was a message from Ronan?

She unfolded it, devouring the words she thought had been scribbled in panicked haste. *For America, Maudie, with all my love, Ronan.* This was the money he'd been putting aside. He wanted her to go on ahead without him.

'What will you do with the money, Maudie?'

'I'm going to America to fetch Emer. It's what Ronan wants.'

'Ah no, you can't, not on your own. I don't believe that's what he wants, and he doesn't even know you've a daughter.'

'It is – the note says so. Sure, you know yourself people leave this country every single day seeking a new life. That's what I want. A new life with my child. I'm going to fetch Emer. No one will look down upon a widow and her child in America because that's what I am, for all intents and purposes. Ronan will come for us when he can.'

Nora wasn't convinced.

'What would you do if it was one of your three stolen from you?' Maudie asked her sister.

'I'd go to the ends of the earth to bring them back,' Nora sighed, her voice gentle. 'But, Maudie she's not yours anymore, at least not legally. She's been adopted.'

'It can't be legal if she was stolen from me. If I had no say in it. She's mine and Ronan's, not some strange American couple's.'

'But how will you support yourself, let alone a child? I presume you've enough money for your passage and to get by for a short while in that lot there.' Nora pointed to the money still nestled in Maudie's lap. 'But what then? How will you work and mind a child with no family to help you?'

Maudie didn't want to hear any of it. Her mind was made up.

Nora studied her sister a few moments longer, recognising the set of her jaw. There was no point arguing further.

Maudie stuffed the money back into the cannister, along with the note, and began to raise herself from the chair.

'Where do you think you're going?'

'I'm going to ask young Liam Lynch to take me back to Dublin in the pony and trap. His mam will be grateful for the extra money.' She had it planned in her mind. She'd purchase a case to travel with and buy only the necessities to fill it with when she reached the city. Tonight would be spent in a lodging house, and then she'd catch the first train to Cork in the morning, where she'd book her passage to America.

'Maudie, you're not in your right mind, and you've certainly not thought things through properly. You're going to need a passport, and then there's the paperwork the customs men will demand upon your arrival to America. So listen to me now. Martin knows people.'

Everybody knew somebody in these troubled times, Maudie thought dully, because Nora was right. She'd been foolish and so intent on getting to Emer, she hadn't taken the practicalities of the journey she'd have to make into account.

'So you'll lie low here with us until he can get what you're going to need sorted, and I'll hear no more about it.'

'I didn't know if you'd want Martin and the children to see me.' Maudie's voice shook.

'Listen to me, Maudie O'Connor. I want you to always remember this. You've nothing to be ashamed of. Nothing. Do you hear me?'

'I killed a man, Nora. I took a life. Do you think all that's happened since is God's punishment?'

'No! That man was evil. You put him from your mind!'

Maudie nodded slowly.

'No one deserves to go through what you have. Sure, those sisters treated you like an animal. It's them who should be ashamed, punished. You hold your head up and walk tall from this moment on, do you hear me?'

Maudie raised her chin. 'I hear you.'

31

'If we leave now, Maudie, you'll make the train to Cork.' Martin's voice drifted in through the open cottage door, finding its way into the bedroom where the sisters were finishing packing. In the corner of the room, Noelle slept soundly in her cot.

Maudie felt like a different woman to the one who'd fallen in through her sister's door a few months ago, frightening the life out of Nora. Her restoration was thanks to the things she'd once taken for granted but doubted she ever would again. Good food, baths and clean clothes had rebuilt her strength for the journey that lay ahead.

Nora had shaken her awake from where she was cuddling in next to Damian and Rose before the rooster began crowing, saying they would need to be on their way and that Martin was readying the pony and trap. The youngsters, who'd been delighted if a little bewildered initially by their aunt's reappearance, had taken it all in their stride, including being sworn to secrecy as to her staying with them.

As for Martin, Maudie's opinion of Nora's husband was firmly embedded. He was a good man. The best kind of man. He'd not questioned her sudden appearance, her boyish hair or the urgency with which she needed to go back to Dublin, and she'd never know how, but it was thanks to him she had a passport and the documents to ensure she wasn't turned away when the ship docked in America.

Now, Nora was standing in a puddle of lamplight, bending over her bed. She closed the small case with a snap. 'There.' The linens she'd had stored inside it under the bed had been turfed aside, and she'd generously filled the case with a nightdress, undergarments and dress.

'You're sure you can spare them?' Maudie was dubious. 'I'd planned to buy the necessities I'll need for the trip when I arrive in Cork.'

'Of course I can. I'll not have any sister of mine setting off travelling without a fresh change of clothes,' Nora replied brusquely, picking up her favourite hat, the one she wore to church, from the top of the dresser and setting it down firmly on Maudie's head.

Maudie's instinct told her she was fibbing, but she recognised the same determined set to her sister's jaw she herself was prone to when she'd made her mind up. There was no point arguing with her over the clothes, but the hat was a different matter. 'Ah no, not your best hat.'

'Would you stop giving out?' Nora said to her, ignoring her husband's instructions as she took a moment to fiddle with the pieces of hair visible beneath the hat. 'I'm almost used to it now.' Then, stepping back to admire her handiwork, she said, 'It curls quite becomingly under your ears – you look like a little faerie, and your hair always grew like wildfire. Sure, it will be long again before you know it.'

Maudie moved toward the dresser and picked up the mirror to take a peek for herself. It startled her to see the gauntness of her face, but Nora was right about her hair. 'You've worked wonders with those scissors, thank you.' She'd no longer stand out, marked by her experiences.

The only thing her sister hadn't been able to wave her magic wand over was her shoes. Maudie knew Nora would gladly go barefoot for her if it came to it, but given her feet were a size smaller than Maudie's, it hadn't been an option. She hadn't wanted to buy a new pair in town either because nobody knew she was back, so she'd have to put up with the worn soles and hole in the toe until she reached Cork.

Tracking Maudie's gaze, Nora tutted over the state of her footwear as she picked up the case.

'I promise you I'll buy a new pair when I reach Cork.'

Satisfied, Nora said, 'Grand,' before instructing Maudie to scoop up Noelle. 'And I shall treat myself to a new coat and hat in the city. 'Tis a good excuse.'

'What do you mean in the city, and why am I to pick up Noelle?'

Nora smiled. 'You didn't think I'd let you go to Dublin without me and the children tagging along for the ride, did you?'

Maudie's eyes filled because she'd forgotten what kindness was. She turned away before Nora could see and scooped her niece up, holding her breath as she stirred. She cradled her close, relieved when she gave a contented sigh and settled back into sleep.

The room dipped into darkness as Nora snuffed the lamp, and then Martin called out, galvanising them both.

'Right. I'll put your case on the back of the pony and trap then see to the children,' Nora instructed. 'I've food packed for the journey.'

Her sister was a marvel, and Maudie was profoundly grateful to her as she navigated the short distance from the room outside the farm cottage, where the first hints of a new day were lightening the sky.

Martin had beaten Nora to it with the children and was

hefting a sleepy Rose into the trap, depositing her next to her brother.

'They'll be delighted with the adventure of it all,' Nora said, emerging alongside Maudie and giving the two little ones something to nibble on.

With her children sorted, she closed the farmhouse door and clambered up next to Martin, who'd now taken the reins. Maudie passed Noelle into her mother's waiting arms and climbed up alongside them. Then, with a flick of the reins, they were off.

A mist hovered over the fields as Maudie twisted round to look back toward Rush. She longed to see Caitie and her younger brothers. It was simply too much to think she'd never see them again, and she'd have liked to have said goodbye at the very least. There wasn't time, however; nor would her presence at the cottage where she'd once lived have been welcomed.

The journey into the city had passed without incident, and they arrived at bustling Kingsbridge Station in good time to purchase her ticket for the train. Maudie did her best not to dwell on Cecelia, Nessa, Mol and Connor, hidden from the world at St Patrick's, focusing instead on the children. They were clinging to their mam's sides, overwhelmed by all the comings and goings of folk and the shrill whistle of a train chugging out.

'We've time for a cup of tea,' Nora said with a glance at the station clock, as Maudie stashed her ticket away, safely keeping a tight hold of her suitcase.

That sounded like music to Maudie's ears, and Martin agreed he was parched, so Nora led the way to the nearby tearoom. They found a table, and Martin ordered tea with scones served with jam and cream, which the children were quick to reach for when they were presented. As Nora played mother with the tea, Martin reached into his coat's breast pocket. 'This is for you, Maudie.'

Maudie frowned, hesitating – Martin and Nora had already done so much for her.

He slid the small package across the table toward her. 'You're to take it. I know you think you've plenty, but you'll soon chew through it. So there's a little extra for your journey in there and an address. Me da's late brother and his wife emigrated to America when they were first married and made a new life in Savannah. When he died some years back, Aunt Annie wrote to say she'd decided the house was too big to rattle around in on her own and that she'd run it as a boarding house. Me da reckons his brother was a spendthrift and it was more likely Annie had no choice but to begin renting the rooms out if she didn't want to sell the place. We'll send a telegram today letting her know she's to expect you, and Nora will write with more detail.'

Nora nodded, affirming that this was the plan.

Maudie covered her mouth with her hands, momentarily speechless, but then she found her voice, 'Thank you, Martin, Nora, for everything.'

She hadn't thought further than getting to America, and to have somewhere to stay when she reached Savannah was a comfort. Although how she'd even get there from New York she didn't as yet know. She would have to figure things out as she went along. 'Martin, I can leave with a clear conscience knowing you're looking after Nora and the children.'

A humble man, he shifted in his seat, muttering that he'd only done what anyone would do given the circumstances, which they both knew wasn't true.

Nora reached across the table then and took her sister's hand in hers, giving it a quick squeeze. She didn't see Rose give Noelle a piece of jammy scone until it was too late, and everyone's mood was lightened by the sight of the little girl with a blob of jam and cream on her nose, grinning her two-tooth smile at them all.

Martin kept an eye on the time, and once cups had rattled back into their saucers, he announced the train would be pulling in any minute.

This was the moment she'd been dreading, Maudie thought, as they navigated the busy platform. Saying goodbye. She didn't want to drag it out, but at the same time she wanted to grab hold of each of them and never let them go.

As passengers began to board the train around them, Nora's eyes filled for the first time. 'I promised myself I wouldn't cry.'

'Me too.'

'I love you, Maudie. I hope you find her and can get on with your life.'

'I will.' Maudie had to believe the nightmares would stop, and that those pale-lashed eyes wouldn't follow her to America. 'And when it's safe for Ronan to come and find me, you'll tell him where Emer and I are, won't you?'

'Of course. And don't forget to buy shoes when you get to Cork.' Nora's grin was watery.

'I won't.' Maudie managed a smile back before the breath was squeezed from her by her sister.

'I didn't want to give this to you before now.' Nora released her and fetched an envelope from her bag.

Maudie recognised her younger sister's writing.

'A letter from Caitie?' Maudie asked, her eyes lighting up as she recognised the messy handwriting she refused to practise because she was far too busy getting into mischief.

'It is. Maudie, listen to me now. I want you to promise me you won't open it until you're on the ship and Ireland's behind you.'

'Why? Do you know what it says?'

'Please, will you promise me?'

After everything Nora had done for her, it was the least she could do, and she swore to forget about what her younger sister wanted to say to her until she was at sea, tucking the envelope away in her bag. Tears threatened as it hit her then that this was it. It was time to say goodbye.

Rose, picking up on the serious expressions of the adults, began to cry, and Maudie gave the little girl a cuddle. 'I'll tell Mammy to be sure to get you an ice cream before you go home. How does that sound?'

Rose's tears dried up like magic, and Damian, dancing around the group, said, 'And me too.'

'Of course you too.' Maudie caught hold of him and gave him a hug, laughing as he tried to wriggle free. Then it was Noelle's turn, and she placed a soft kiss on her niece's chubby cheek.

Martin gruffly pulled her to him. 'I'm very sorry for all the troubles that befell you, Maudie. Go well.'

Maudie embraced Nora one last time, then the train whistle sounded, so she picked up her case and hurried on board. She didn't dare look back because she didn't want her tears to be the last memory Nora and her family had of her.

She was oblivious to her fellow passengers as she settled herself into her seat. This was only the first step in her journey. There were so many obstacles lying between her and Emer, the biggest of all being that her daughter was no longer legally hers.

Her head ached with all that she was going to have to overcome. Still, she resolved as the train chugged slowly from the station, no customs officials or paperwork would stand in her way. Come what may, she *would* be reunited with Emer.

32

Maudie was wedged in with her fellow passengers, all vying for space along the promenade deck of the SS *Baltic*. She covered her mouth and coughed from the cloying mix of close bodies, coal smoke, seaweed and the faint whiff of the livestock the ship was also transporting. They were all smells she'd be used to after a day or two, she supposed, pinching herself over having made it this far. Soon, she'd be on her way to America – and to Emer.

Overhead, the sky was clear and blue. It was a good day to set sail, and beneath her feet, the engines rumbled to life. The mournful blast of the ship's horn soon followed, and clusters of passengers linked arms and began to sing. Tears pricked at Maudie's eyes. The words were full of lament for the country most of them making this journey would never see again, along with prayers for a safe journey and bright future. Shouts of farewell and weeping all around her were drowned out, and she wished Ronan was there by her side, his hand encasing hers. If he was, she wouldn't be frightened by the journey in front of her.

Ronan! Her heart cried out for him because this was a

voyage she'd once dreamed of making with him, full of hope for their future. Instead, she was making it alone out of the need to find their baby, stolen from her by those charged with her care. She swallowed down the bitterness because it would serve no purpose, and it dawned on her properly then that she might never see Nora, Martin, her nieces, nephews or siblings again. There would be no sharing in the day-to-day highs and lows of life amongst her family or watching the young ones grow. But she'd be with Emer, and Ronan would find her. Suddenly, the pull to America was stronger than the tug of homesickness, and it stopped the threatened tears in their tracks.

Maudie blinked hard then leaned over the bulwark. The water below them was churning, and she resolved to look only to the future because they were moving!

'It's terribly sad but awfully exciting too, don't you think?' a girl squeezing in next to her said, summing up what Maudie had been thinking perfectly. She was small with dark hair tucked under her hat and eyes to match. Her dimples as she beamed up at Maudie were endearing, and Maudie swept aside her pensive mood and smiled back. It was all the encouragement the girl needed.

'I'm Sheila from Dublin, and I'm travelling to New York on my own. I've nannying work lined up for a la-di-da family in Gramercy Park. They're in shipping. My cousin is employed as a housemaid, and she put a word in for me because she's been awfully homesick. I've nine younger brothers and sisters I've been helping me mam raise, and the Williamses only have four children. So it's going to be like a holiday.' She laughed; it sounded like a bell tinkling. 'Sorry! I'm always being told off for talking far too much. What's your name and what's taking you to America?' She flashed her dimples once more. 'I won't be offended if you tell me to mind my own business. I'm always being told if there's work in the bed, I'd sleep on the floor, just to see who's doing it too.'

Maudie wasn't offended at all, despite feeling quite dizzy from the barrage of conversation. For the last three days, she'd kept herself to herself at the guesthouse she'd stayed at in Cobh, waiting for the SS *Baltic* to depart. It had been strange sleeping in a room all by herself for the first time in her life, but she supposed she'd have to get used to that when she got to America. She'd be all alone then.

Her only outing while in Cobh had been to buy shoes, and she glanced down at them, wishing she could tell Nora she'd kept her promise. She'd bought three dresses to match the new persona she'd assume from hereon in as well. That of a respectable young lady who'd lost her fiancé in the fight for freedom. It was a far cry from the fallen woman the nuns had decreed her to be. She would never be that girl again.

Maudie had bought a few more practical items too but had been careful not to overspend because she didn't know how long the money Ronan had carefully put aside or the little extra Martin had pressed upon her would stretch once she arrived in America. New York to be precise, and from there, somehow, she'd have to find her way to Savannah. It was a city she hadn't even known was located in the southern states of America until Martin had told her.

Was it madness what she was doing? she wondered, digesting Sheila's plans almost enviously because she had it all worked out. Sheila having a place to live and work lined up almost certainly guaranteed her entry into America, whereas all she had was her determination to find her daughter and an address where she planned to stay while she tracked her down.

Sheila was eyeing her curiously, so Maudie introduced herself, keeping her story close to the truth but pared back, telling Sheila her name and that she was going to Savannah, Georgia to stay with her brother-in-law's aunt in her boarding house in the hope of finding nannying work. It all sounded airy and vague, but her past and the truth behind this journey she was embarking on had to remain a secret.

Maudie was relieved the whitewashed story was enough for Sheila, who dimpled up at her. Hopefully it would satisfy the authorities waiting on Ellis Island too.

'I adore your hair by the way. It's so modern. Mam would have gone mad at me if I'd come home with a cut like that, but I'm going to get mine snipped off as soon as I get to New York.'

Maudie was grateful for the other girl's company and felt less alone as they watched the colourful terraced houses lining the streets of Queenstown grow smaller and smaller while those around them continued waving frantically to the loved ones they were leaving behind. There was nobody for Maudie to wave to, and she wasn't sure how she felt saying goodbye to Ireland's emerald shores. It was a country she'd loved with a passion and wanted to free from British tyranny with all her heart, just as Ronan did, but she'd never thought the Eire she knew and loved could turn on her and her child like so, or that Ronan would have no choice but to vanish without word.

As the ship glided past the lighthouse at the mouth of the harbour, passengers' tears were replaced with excitement at being on their way, and Maudie smiled at Sheila, who was still chattering on. There'd be no more tears on her part either, she vowed. The past was behind her now.

Only later, having kept her promise not to read Caitie's letter until Ireland was behind her, did Maudie realise the past wasn't done with her yet. And as she ventured back up on deck to crumple the pages into a small ball she tossed into the stiff winds, she didn't know if it ever would be.

Maudie's steerage-class quarters weren't all that dissimilar to the dormitory at St Patrick's, but aboard the SS *Baltic*, her days were her own. Martin and Nora had wanted her to travel cabin class, but Maudie had been adamant that if she could survive St Patrick's, then eight days in the bowels of a ship would be a doddle. Besides, it was only for sleeping in she'd told them.

She was lying in the middle berth of the three-high bunks barely wider than she was with her hands clasped under her head, having discovered it helped to ward off the nausea. She'd found her sea legs during the day, but at night, with the stifling air and constant rocking and rolling of the ship, her stomach would begin to lurch threateningly. If she fixed her gaze on the slats above her, though, she could keep the sickness at bay. Overhead, Sheila's straw mat rustled, and the bunk's frame squeaked as she fidgeted.

Her new friend had swapped her assigned berth with a widow travelling to see her sister in New York so she could be close to Maudie, and she was comforted by her presence. Nighttime was hard because with nothing to distract her from her yearning for Emer, her mind would travel to dark places. She'd relive the horror of what the Tan had done to her, and how she'd pulled the gun's trigger, the disbelief on his face as he'd realised he was going to die. Worse than that, though, was the memory of waking at St Patrick's to find her baby gone. Inside, she felt as empty as her aching arms.

They were five days into the crossing, and the pain of being parted from Emer was always there. Maudie tried to hone in on the glimmers of hope that helped to soften it and ease her off to sleep. Moments like her return to Rush, where Nora and Martin hadn't judged her, instead choosing to help her. Then there was Sheila, whose natural exuberance helped her fend off the malaise that constantly hovered, waiting to take hold, as she dragged her about the ship in search of fun. Tonight, though, Sheila's presence didn't help because all she wanted was to hold her daughter and rock her to sleep as the ship would eventually her.

A barking child's cough in the bunk below her made

Maudie wince. It was followed by a plaintiff, 'Ma.' There were three little ones squeezed in next to each other on the bottom bunk while their mam's was adjacent. Mrs O'Brien shared hers with her ten-month-old baby whilst her two slightly older children slept above her. The Cork woman was on her way to meet her husband in America to begin a new life, and Maudie heard her bunk creak as she rolled off it to see to the child coughing. It was no wonder her youngest had picked up a cold in these cramped conditions.

Someone further down the line began to pray quietly, while outside, footsteps passed down the corridor. All the while, the ship groaned against the weight of its passengers as it ploughed through the ocean toward America.

The next day was crisp and clear, and the shadows of a sleepless night were chased away by fresh air and a game of shuffleboard. Maudie and Sheila were entertaining Mrs O'Brien's older two, as they'd taken to doing. The motherly woman had swept both girls under her wing the moment she'd learned they were travelling on their own, and Maudie and Sheila were only too pleased to help her keep an eye on her brood of six. It made the days pass quicker.

In the sheltered alcove nearby, two men squatted, engaged in a card game. Snatches of what they were saying drifted down to where Maudie waited her turn. 'Detained at Ellis Island... Board of Inquiry... Second try to get into America.'

Maudie put the overheard snippets from her mind as she took the cue the gap-toothed, freckle-faced little lad was holding out to her.

'I don't know what I'd have done without you and Sheila's help. You've both such a way with children,' Mrs O'Brien said to

Maudie one dinner time as their journey neared its end. Maudie was plopping a dollop of mash on each of the older women's little plates, and it was then she was seized with an idea.

'Mrs O'Brien, would you write me a reference before we disembark to say I'm of good character and good with children? I'm hoping to find a nannying position when I reach Savannah, you see.'

It had occurred to Maudie that if she were charged with looking after wee ones, it could enable her to inadvertently bump into Mrs Kinsella with Emer, or indeed her nanny. It was a long shot, but then that was all she had, and at least it gave her a direction to go in when she arrived in Savannah. Shop work would be of no use to her.

'Of course I will, child. Like I said, I'd not be making it through this journey unscathed without you and Sheila helping me. One of them would have gone overboard for certain.'

They both looked to the ringleader in her merry crew, little Charlie, who'd an innate curiosity for things he'd no business investigating and who'd been frogmarched up from the engine room by an irate crew member before the ship had even fully got out to sea.

'I know I can speak for Sheila too, Mrs O'Brien.' Her friend was overseeing the two older children as they carried their plates to the table in the dining hall. We've both grown very fond of your children, and this sailing would have felt like it was taking forever if not for them keeping us on our toes.'

The two women exchanged a smile before Maudie's eyes flitted to the map of America pinned to the mess hall's wall. She'd had no idea how vast it was or that it comprised fifty states until she'd seen the map and counted them before trying to trace a route to Savannah. A person could vanish in a country that big; indeed, anything could happen to a young, single woman travelling on her own...

33

IRELAND, 1985

The sky was sullen, and the lonely sound of a crow cawing made Maudie shiver as they passed through the wrought-iron gates of Glasnevin Cemetery.

Maudie's legs betrayed her, unsteady now she was here. Not because of her age, as the woman whose hand reached out to help her assumed, but because of the bricks of grief weighing on her shoulders.

She swatted her travelling companion's concerned hand away and trotted out her stock reply – one she always used when someone pointed out that she'd grown old. 'Stop fussing. I'm fine.' And she carried on. If her companion had questions as to why she'd brought them here, she didn't ask. Instead, she simply said, 'This place is like a who's who of Irish history. It's the largest cemetery in the country.'

Maudie made no comment, continuing in the direction of a round tower that loomed large amongst the sea of simplistic and fussy headstones, Celtic crosses and Victorian mausoleums that stretched as far as she could see.

The map was flapped. 'That over there is O'Connell Tower, in honour of Daniel O'Connell.'

Maudie hadn't come here for a monologue on who patronised the cemetery, and she pushed on until, with a few more twists and turns, there it was. A large grass area with the cemetery's high walls in the background, marked by a single memorial stone flanked by two angel statues. Her throat squeezed when she spotted the bunch of fresh white daisies that had been laid by the memorial stone, along with a battered teddy bear that was forlornly keeping watch over all the babies buried in the Angels' Plot.

In her hand was the posy of forget-me-nots they'd stopped off to buy on their way back from Rush, and Maudie clutched it tightly. Those bricks on her shoulders grew heavier as she recalled the words Sister Agnes had spat. Then she remembered how Sister Louise had softened the ugliness of finding out about Nessa and her baby's death by telling her where her friend and her babe were buried, and how she'd come to Glasnevin and prayed for them.

The sisters had been yin and yang, light and darkness.

Nessa's grave would likely be a pauper's, given she'd been disowned by her family, and as such unmarked, but still Maudie could feel her friend, who'd never grown old, spurring her on toward a spot on the grass, and this was where she set the flowers down.

Maudie's life had been full of goodbyes both big and small. The biggest of all being to her family and country, but now here she was back on Irish soil, finally able to say the goodbye she'd waited a lifetime for.

PART THREE

AMERICA

34

Beneath an indecisive sky, a cheer that was anything but erupted on the deck of the SS *Baltic*. Ahead was the colossal statue that symbolised the gateway to their new lives in America. The Statue of Liberty. Tears flowed freely from the passengers over their hopes for the future in a new land. A land that would bring Maudie one step closer to finding Emer. She was so close now yet still so far.

What if she was turned away like the fella she'd overheard the two men talking about? She was an unmarried mother – *and a murderer*. She quickly banished the rogue thought. The authorities didn't know any of that. However, not having work lined up, or family waiting for her, could be grounds to turn her away. She could be detained and put on the next ship back to Ireland.

Meanwhile, Sheila's excitement was palpable as she gripped Maudie's arm, oblivious to the swooping seagulls who'd come to join them, hungry for the ship's scraps.

'Isn't she magnificent? And look there at the skyline. Have you ever seen the likes of it?' Sheila's eyes were enormous as she pointed across the swirling muddy-toned waters to where tall buildings arrogantly decorated the horizon. 'Manhattan,' she breathed reverently. The vista was so foreign to anything either of them had seen before. 'The tallest one there, that's the Woolworth Building.'

Maudie's own eyes were bright, and she was aware of the smell of coal smoke from a passing steamer and Sheila yammering on about the tug boat come to guide them into the harbour as she soaked in the moment she'd dreamed of sharing with Ronan. She was so close now. She thought she could hear Emer crying for her on the wind, and clutching hold of her hat as that same boisterous wind threatened to whip it off, her eyes cut back to the statue and the imposing Ellis Island immigration station. A red-brick blockade which she'd have to pass through before she was allowed to set foot on American soil.

Maudie, with Sheila beside her, and Mrs O'Brien ushering her brood, joined the tide of weary passengers dragging suitcases and clutching restless children, as they were herded toward the smaller boat that would take them to Ellis Island – where their fate hung in the balance. Beneath their feet, the gangplank moaned and the shouts of deckhands echoed, while closer by, stories began to fly about what they could expect next.

'My cousin told me there's all sorts of special medical exams, for tuberculosis, eye diseases, disability and problems up here.'

Maudie glanced to her left in time to see the lad, who reminded her a little of her older brother Jimmy, tapping the side of his head, but he wasn't finished yet.

'If they suspect any of those, they'll mark you with chalk and hold you in detention, like.'

The very thought of being somewhere against her will once more sent a shiver racing up Maudie's spine as she shuffled forward, until she was standing on another deck slick with sea-spray.

Other voices clamoured to be heard as the packed boat chugged them toward the island, where a single stamp could decide whether she was to be allowed to stay or forced to go.

'If you haven't got a sponsor, you'll be sent back.'

'It's harder for single women, so it is. My brother said it's because they don't want us becoming a public charge.'

Acutely aware she didn't have a sponsor, Maudie whispered, 'What's a public charge?' to Sheila, who always seemed to know everything.

'A charity case. But sure, we'll be grand. I've an offer of employment, and you'll be going to your brother-in-law's aunt there in Savannah, and you've a glowing reference from Mrs O'Brien.'

Maudie wished she had the same strength of conviction as Sheila, but all too soon it was time to say goodbye to the kindly Mrs O'Brien and her children. She wasn't prepared for the emotion of yet another parting, even though they'd already exchanged addresses and promises to write. Tears streamed down her face as she watched the matronly figure, with children hanging off her arms and clinging to her skirt, make her way through the crowds to the processing line for families. Soon, she'd have to say goodbye to Sheila too.

If Maudie were to have closed her eyes against the sights, sounds and smells of the immigration station she was queued in, panic might have filled her boots. The combination of barked instructions from officials, ominous footsteps on wooden floors, crying babies and children combined with an underlying whiff of boiling vegetables wasn't dissimilar to St Patrick's. She kept her eyes wide open, however, aware that here at least there was hope.

As it happened, the fears that had plagued her since leaving Ireland and catching pieces of overheard conversation, exacerbated by the scaremongering as they disembarked the SS *Baltic*, were unfounded. Martin had done her proud with the documentation he'd sourced, as had her sister with her insistence on nursing her back to full health. Maudie was cleared within hours, having passed the extensive medical tests and numerous questions as to who she was, where she was going and what she would do for employment. It had saddened her deeply to see a young girl from Limerick with whom she'd chatted on occasion during the Atlantic crossing sobbing and being led away whilst her own passport was stamped.

'It was her eyes that let her down. Poor eyesight,' an older woman behind Maudie who reeked of onions informed anyone close enough to hear.

That poor lass wouldn't be the only one, Maudie thought as she boarded the free ferry that would take her and Sheila to Manhattan, where they'd go their separate ways. She owed it to them and all the others who'd made this journey only to be met with heartbreak to grasp her good fortune with both hands.

Hope shone in her soul as the ferry ploughed toward a shoreline where the skyline soared with promise. She had passed muster. She'd made it to America. And soon she'd be on her way to Savannah, to Emer. This moment right now marked the start of a new beginning, and one day soon, Ronan would be part of it too.

35

The heat swamped her as she stepped out of Union Station, but Maudie didn't mind because at last she was here. Savannah! The city where she'd be reunited with her baby.

Armed with directions to the boarding house owned by Martin's aunt, Mrs Callaghan, she set off, but it wasn't long before she regretted her decision to walk to River Street instead of taking the trolley. The stickiness of the heavy air made her feel like she was wading through water.

The thought of Emer spurred her on though, and at last she reached the bustling port where longshoremen and dockworkers shouted to one another and the smell of industry was all around. Bales of what she guessed to be cotton were stacked high along the dock, ready for shipping, amongst a myriad of other crates.

This was as good a spot as any to catch her breath – just for a moment, mind, because somewhere nearby Emer was waiting for her.

She turned her face toward the river to try and catch a whisper of breeze off the wide brown expanse. The swift-flowing water teemed with tug boats, cargo and steamships, but it was the proud paddle steamer carrying its passengers lazily across the river that held her attention. She watched its enormous wheel churning through the water and thought it ever so graceful.

'Oh!' Maudie stumbled, shaken from her contemplation as a young lad knocked into her.

'Sorry, Miss!' A cheeky-faced lad peered over the box he was carrying, and Maudie was reminded of young Liam Lynch from home. Or rather her *old* home. Home was wherever her daughter was, and for now that was here in Savannah.

This boy was around the same age as Liam, with the same determination given he was carting a box almost bigger than he was.

'No harm done, young man.' Maudie helped him straighten his weighty parcel.

'Thanks, Miss.'

'Try and watch where you're going.' Maudie smiled as she watched him race off, bowed by the box's weight and paying no heed whatsoever to her words. Then, mindful of wasting time, she set off too.

Once the oncoming horse and carts laden with goods had rattled past, she crossed the cobbled street. Her nose twitched when she caught the tantalising whiff of something buttery and sweet beneath the pervasive tang of the port, and she decided to ask Mrs Callaghan what it was once she'd found Emer and settled into the boarding house. How exactly all of that would work she'd yet to figure out, but somehow it would. She had to believe that.

As she wandered up the subtle rise away from the river, she was hit by a tug of emotion so strong she felt winded, and her steps turned to a stagger. She had made it to Savannah despite everything. Emer was so close.

'Are you all right, Miss?' a well-dressed man stopped to ask in a slow Southern drawl.

Maudie blinked, registering a craggy but kindly face beneath a panama hat. 'I've not long arrived here. It's the heat, I think. I'm not used to it.'

'Ah, you're not the first Irish person to arrive in the South to say that.' He gave her a warm smile. 'Welcome to Savannah, and I can assure you: in a few weeks, you'll be fully acclimatised.'

Maudie couldn't believe she'd ever get used to this stickiness.

'There's a seat a short distance up the road in a square where you might find some respite. Perhaps if you catch your breath in the shade before continuing on your way?'

'Yes,' Maudie said gratefully. 'I'm sure I'll be fine if I can sit down for a moment.'

'In that case, follow me.' The older gent took her case and trotted off, and sure enough, a few minutes later, Maudie sank onto a park bench in the blessed shade.

'You've been most kind. Thank you. I'll be grand now,' she reassured her saviour, as he placed her suitcase down.

'You're quite sure?'

'I am, thank you.'

The gentleman doffed his hat and wished her good luck in Savannah, then went on his way, leaving Maudie to regroup.

The noisy birdsong – like a whistling tea kettle – was unfamiliar, and the trees providing her with a leafy arbour weren't like Irish trees. Did Emer watch those grey-green cascades dangling from their boughs and swaying whimsically as she drifted off in her pram?

She got to her feet. She was torn between beginning her search for Emer and the Kinsellas immediately, desperate for a glimpse of her child, and reaching Mrs Callaghan's boarding house so she could collapse into bed because it had been a long journey south. The way her stomach was protesting, she could do with something to eat too, and her throat was parched. She needed to be clever, though, in order to get her daughter back, and she'd be no good to her if she wasn't fit and able for the fight. So, recounting the directions she'd committed to memory, she set off once more.

The distant sounds of the port faded altogether, replaced by the clickety-clack of a trolley car and the parp of a motor-car horn. A horse's whinny as it waited impatiently by the side of the street, attached to a carriage, startled her, and she watched a delivery boy whizz past on his bicycle. As for the pavement she was making her way along, it too was busy, and Maudie's eyes hungrily appraised the scene when she spotted a young woman, a nanny judging by her uniform, pushing a perambulator. She blocked her path in the hope the baby might be Emer, but she was too tiny, and the nanny quickly excused herself and hurried on her way. Numbly, Maudie walked on, passing dapperly dressed men, interspersed with giggling young women arm in arm, and wished Ronan was by her side.

She felt so removed from them all. They were simply going about their daily business, while she had travelled thousands of miles to this strange city to take her daughter back. Was her desperation visible? she wondered, avoiding an older woman's gaze. She was carrying a parasol and wore an expression Maudie thought said that in these parts, manners were next to godliness. Well, they needn't worry – they were where she came from too!

Reaching an intersection, she paused to peer up at the street sign before veering left, satisfied she was on the right track. Her feet throbbed by the time she reached the sleepier, tree-lined street in which she hoped to find Mrs Callaghan's boarding house. She meandered down it, scanning the numbers, before coming to a halt outside a smart house in a row of identical brick residences. All were well kept, which boded well, with steps mirroring one another up to twin front doors. A myriad of windows stared down at her as she set her suitcase by her feet, feeling as though her arm was hanging disproportionately long. She shook it out then fetched the address Martin had pressed upon her.

Yes, she thought, rereading his handwritten note and squinting up at the brass plaque alongside the door, this was the right place.

Maudie climbed the stairs then picked up the brass knocker and rapped sharply. The sooner she was shown to her room, where she could wash and change, the sooner she could begin her search for Emer.

36

A larger-than-life woman filled the frame. Her eyes were crinkled and her smile welcoming, with only the slightest tinge of her Irish roots audible in her greeting. 'Hello there.'

The words gushed forth. 'Hello, I'm Maudie O'Connor. I believe my sister, Nora Gallagher – she's married to your nephew, Martin – wrote to tell you I was coming.'

'Maudie O'Conner.' The woman clapped her hands delightedly. 'She did indeed write, and my goodness, child, you're a waif, so you are. Well, we'll soon fix that. Welcome, welcome. Come on in.'

Maudie silently thanked her sister, knowing she'd never have let her down, and decided she liked the woman on the spot. As such, she was happy to be swept inside an entrance that was considerably cooler than outside. She registered sweet-smelling flowers in a vase and an expanse of polished timber floors before she was herded up the stairs with a swish of Mrs Callaghan's skirts. They made a pit stop along the way to inspect the bathroom on the second-floor landing, which was perfectly clean, and then the older woman opened a door at the end of the hall and stood aside to let Maudie look.

'I trust you'll find the room satisfactory. You've a grand view over the square.'

Maudie made a quick inventory of the simply furnished room, which smelled of furniture polish. A bed, dressing table, writing desk and chair along with a jug of water and a glass, but best of all there was a fan. What more could a girl need?

She deposited her suitcase at the foot of the bed and stared longingly at the crisp covers before walking across creaking boards to the window. It was open a crack to allow airflow, and she saw that the view was indeed gorgeous. She could picture herself sitting in the chair provided, watching the goings-on in the shady square below between penning letters home and to her new friends, Sheila and Mrs O'Brien, while plotting how to get Emer back.

'It's perfect, Mrs Callaghan.'

It really was, but that thought triggered a frisson of fear that the room rate in this gem of a boarding house would be unsustainable for more than a week or so, and she chewed her bottom lip. After all, she had no idea how long she'd be staying, and no plan of action for that matter as to what steps she'd take to get Emer back now she was here. Nor what she'd do to survive with a baby daughter when she did.

As if reading her mind, Mrs Callaghan said, 'Now listen. We're family, you and I, so there's to be none of this Mrs Callaghan business. You're to call me Aunt Annie, do you hear me?'

Maudie hesitated then smiled. 'Yes, Aunt Annie.'

'Grand. Now we can sort out payment later, and given you're family, I think we can come to an arrangement you'll find agreeable for the duration of your stay.'

'Thank you, Mrs— er, Aunt Annie.' Maudie gushed her gratitude not simply to the motherly figure in the doorway but to Martin and Nora, to whom she owed so much.

'I expect you're hungry, thirsty and worn out after your journey. Even the locals struggle here when it's as hot as this.'

So much for the gentleman in the panama hat assuring her she'd soon acclimatise, Maudie thought.

'Now what I suggest is you freshen up and unpack while I rustle something up to put some meat back on your bones and roses in those cheeks. Shall we give it, say, half an hour?'

'I don't want to put you to any trouble.' Although the truth was Maudie was famished.

Aunt Annie flapped her hand. 'It's not a bother.'

She bustled to the door and hesitated, tucking a stray silver strand behind her ear. 'Maudie, it's lovely to have someone here not only from the homeland but from my own family, and I look forward to hearing all the news from home, along with what's brought you here.'

Maudie gave a weak smile in return as Aunt Annie left her to make the room her temporary home. She poured a glass of water and drank it greedily. She liked the warm, big-hearted woman whose roof she'd be staying under, and not being honest with her as to why she'd come to Savannah didn't sit well, but if she knew the truth... She refused to imagine herself homeless here in a strange city. Nobody would ever know her reasons for being here, Maudie resolved, setting the glass down.

'Hello, Aunt Annie?' Maudie stood in the foyer of the boarding house, unsure which way to go. She felt so much better having had a wash and tidied her hair, and was eager to venture out to begin looking for Emer.

'In here, pet,' a voice sang out, and Maudie headed toward it, stepping into a kitchen that could've fitted her family's entire cottage. Well, almost. It still had a homely feel to it thanks to the china on display in the Welsh dresser, the dried herbs hanging from the wooden rack and the delicious aroma of home cooking impregnated in the walls.

'I thought it would be cosier to chat in here, although I serve breakfast in the dining room at the front of the house. I like my guests to feel at home here, but it's important to have boundaries. I've three other lodgers staying with me at the moment, all gentlemen in Savannah on business, and they've no business poking their noses in my kitchen. There's plenty of time to show you around the house though. It can wait. For now, sit down and sample a Southern staple. Iced tea. The locals call it the house wine of the South, and you'll be a convert in no time.'

Aunt Annie's eyes twinkled as she reached for a jug of amber liquid with ice cubes and slices of lemon floating in it.

Iced tea? Maudie had never heard of such a thing, but she was eager to embrace all things new to her and so accepted the glass, waiting for Aunt Annie's encouraging nod before taking a sip.

She savoured the cool drink for a moment. It was sweeter than she was used to and lemony. Her verdict? 'That's lovely and refreshing,' she declared, making the older woman smile, and despite herself, Maudie's eyes strayed to the plate of sandwiches and cake on the table.

'If I'd known you were arriving today, I'd have whipped up a welcome pie,' Aunt Annie announced, sliding the sandwiches toward Maudie. 'I'm afraid these will have to do.'

Maudie was torn between politely declining the spread by saying she'd somewhere to be and tucking in. 'Oh, really, there'd have been no need, and this looks wonderful. Thank you.'

'Don't be shy. Dig in, child.'

Maudie didn't need to be asked twice and was soon biting into a tangy cheese sandwich which Aunt Annie informed her also contained pimento.

She was on her second sandwich when her new landlady

picked up a knife. 'I'll cut you a wedge of apple cake, shall I? It was my grandmother's recipe, and it's a taste of home.'

Her mouth full, Maudie nodded, hoping to convey a 'yes, please'. She might want to put her life in Ireland behind her, but that didn't mean she'd forgotten how much she loved apple cake! Besides, what use to Emer would a mother fainting from hunger be?

A scruffy dog mooched into the kitchen then, its tail slowly flicking left to right. It flopped down at Maudie's feet and stared up her with imploring, liquid brown eyes.

'You're to ignore Tucker, Maudie. He's the biggest con artist in Savannah. He'll try to convince you he's half-starved when in fact he's the most well-fed dog in all of Georgia.'

Maudie laughed as Annie told her how the dog, getting on in years, had a daily routine of making his way round to the back entrances of her neighbours' homes and affixing whomever happened to open the door to him with a woebegone gaze until he was tossed a tasty titbit. Nevertheless, at the first opportunity, Maudie slipped a sandwich under the table.

Once satisfied Maudie was well fed, Aunt Annie pressed her for news of the family – even though Maudie was certain Nora would have filled her in when she'd written – and Ireland.

Maudie, resigned to not making a quick escape, decided she looked like an inquisitive, well-fed bird, listening with her head cocked to one side as she obliged her with stories of her nephew's life with Nora and the children on their farm. She touched briefly on the ongoing troubles she'd once been so passionate about but no longer had the stomach for because all that mattered to her now was Emer and Ronan. By the time she'd finished talking, her throat was dry, and she accepted a second glass of the iced tea gratefully.

'Nora explained in her letter you were seeking a new life here in Savannah.' There was a knowingness in the older woman's eyes that made Maudie blush, but it was true.

'I am, yes.'

'Well, you've come to the right place for that, Maudie. We all come here for one reason or another, and a fresh start is one of them,' Aunt Annie said as she reached across the table and patted Maudie's hand. She didn't press her to reveal *why* she wanted to make a new life for herself far away from Ireland. Instead, she twittered on about what to expect in Savannah.

Maudie listened intently, deciding that some things were similar to Ireland, church being the cornerstone of life for example. She would be expected to attend with Annie while she was staying at the boarding house. And as for the segregation she'd yet to witness but had been informed of, Ireland had different versions of it based on religion. Then there were anomalies like prohibition. There'd be riots if that were to be enforced in a country with a pub on every corner! Finally, Aunt Annie told her that as a young lady here in the South, she would need to be mindful of social etiquette and remember her station. She should be modest and ladylike at all times, and if she knew what was good for her, then she'd stay well away from jazz halls and steer clear of the flapper fashion too. Aunt Annie's stern tone as she mentioned the latter saw Maudie bite her lip to stop a small smile. Frivolity was the last thing on her mind. There was only one thing she'd come to Savannah to do.

The conversation moved on to the late Mr Callaghan and his widow's widespread offspring and then, barely pausing to draw breath, Aunt Annie gave her hand a second pat. 'Everything will be new and strange to you at first, Maudie, but you'll soon settle into our way of life here in Savannah.'

Maudie's smile was tremulous because everything did feel exactly like that, and when she paused to think about it, it was overwhelming. In an attempt not to dwell on how she would need to find her feet quickly for Emer's sake, she remembered the sweet smell near the port earlier and enquired as to what it was.

Aunt Annie beamed. 'Why, that would be taffy, dear. You must have passed by a confectioner's. It's a soft, chewy sweet made with butter, sugar and corn syrup, and it's one treat most newcomers to the South take to like a duck to water.'

Maudie thought she'd like to try it, but she'd more pressing matters to see to than sampling local sweets. 'I'll need to find work smartly. I'm hoping for a live-in nanny position. I've a grand reference.'

'And I'm sure you'll have no bother finding a good family to employ you, but while you're looking for your new home, I'd be much obliged if you'd help me with the chores around this place.' Aunt Annie waved her hand vaguely. 'It's rather a lot to manage on my own, and in exchange for your help, you'll receive full board, of course. I'll make sure you still have plenty of time for your job-hunting. Now then, does that sound an agreeable arrangement?'

Maudie couldn't believe her luck. 'Oh it does, thank you!'

Fate was finally smiling upon her.

37

The reality of how Maudie would go about what she had come to Savannah determined to do sank in after a few days at Mrs Callaghan's. She couldn't very well go around staring into perambulators in the hope one of them contained Emer. A lurking fear she didn't want to acknowledge whispered that she might not even know her own child. She'd have grown and changed in the months that had passed since she'd been stolen. And even if she did find her, what then? If she were to snatch her back, where would she go? Somehow, she needed to track down the Kinsellas' address and take the time to think; she was aware there'd only be one chance at getting Emer back.

There were practicalities to think about too. The most pressing of which was finding work. She needed to be earning money if she was to make a home for them both in the near future.

So Maudie forged a routine at the boarding house, stumbling out of bed disoriented the first few mornings after sleeping badly, her mind always whirring, full of Emer. She'd grown used to being lulled to sleep by waves and then the rattling of a train carriage. Now, for the time being at least, she needed to get used to the various cracks and creaks of the old house as she lay in her bed wide-eyed. Aunt Annie had told her the noises were down to the heat as the timber floors and rafters shrank and expanded, and not a chain-rattling ghost as some guests who'd heard stories of the infamously haunted city suspected. It was the first Maudie had heard about Savannah ghosts. By the third night, however, she put all notions of spectres making their presence known out of her head and, for the first time since Emer had been snatched from her, slept soundly without a single nightmare.

Her day would begin when she rose early to help cook breakfast for the guests. There were three men currently staying at the boarding house, all of whom were in Savannah on business and liked to be away bright and early. On her first morning of rolling her sleeves up to pitch in, Aunt Annie had informed her she served a hearty Southern-style breakfast, as was expected in the city known not only for ghosts but for its hospitality too. However, she insisted on adding a touch of Ireland to the laden plates with a thick slab of black pudding sourced at a local butcher. He was from the home country and did her proud. Maudie had swiftly learned the art of making grits and biscuits, which, like the iced tea, were Southern staples. They weren't dissimilar to porridge and scones, and she'd developed a taste for all three.

When the rush of the breakfast service was over and their male guests had assured them they were fuller than a tick, she and the woman who was rapidly becoming a mother figure would sit companionably at the kitchen table and enjoy their own meal at a leisurely pace. Then Maudie would begin clearing the dining-room tables, being careful not to trip over Tucker, who had a habit of flopping down in the most inconvenient spots. She'd set to washing up, plunging her hands into the cast-iron sink, while Aunt Annie lumbered upstairs to ensure all was spick and span. Only when the last of the dishes had been dried and put away did Maudie sit back down at the table and commandeer the newspaper the guests had first dibs on to scan the 'Help Needed' section.

Yesterday, under Aunt Annie's guidance, she'd made her way to a boutique employment agency in the heart of the town. To her relief, the heat hadn't been as oppressive as the day of her arrival – either that or she was getting to used to it. She'd eagerly absorbed the sights and sounds of people going about their daily business in the heart of what she was beginning to see as a rather splendid city with its beautiful squares and grand buildings.

The lure of a sweet shop – or candy store as she'd learned the Americans called it – had seen her pause along the way to gaze in the window. Her mouth had watered at the sight of the handmade confections, the pulled taffy in particular, and she'd promised herself that one day she'd be standing here with her daughter, allowing her to pick a treat. Right there and then, though, she couldn't be splurging on sweets, not when she was unsure when she'd secure work. She needed to make each penny count.

The agency hadn't been difficult to find, perched above a lively coffee shop filled with young, arty types putting the world to rights. It had seemed to Maudie that those that had spilled forth from the café, arms linked and laughing, had looked right through her. She'd felt insignificant and provincial, dressed as she was in her best dress, which couldn't compete with the fashions she'd seen on show here in Savannah. She was sure who she was and where she'd come from was stamped on her forehead. Still, the point of signing on at the agency was to find work, not a modelling assignment, she'd told herself and squared her shoulders, determined to put her best foot forward.

Half an hour later, Maudie had left the agency, doing her best not to be disheartened by Mr Sutton's disparaging glance over her handwritten reference or the way he'd sniffed as he'd eyed her through a haze of bluish-grey smoke upon hearing that she was seeking a nannying position.

'Your letter of reference ain't worth a hill of beans in Savannah, young lady. Positions like that are filled through word of mouth, with the girls having come highly recommended from other families. Perhaps you might do better to consider shop work as per your previous employment in Ireland.'

Maudie had nodded mutely. It wasn't what she'd wanted to hear.

It was on her fourth day at the boarding house, as she sat flicking through the paper, that a name jumped out of the newsprint at her. Kinsella! Her hand began to shake as she stared at the photograph above the brief byline about Mr and Mrs Declan Kinsella at Thursday evening's hospital charity ball.

She tried to remain calm because surely Kinsella wasn't an uncommon name. It certainly wasn't in Ireland. She mustn't get ahead of herself because this glamorous couple might not be the same people who'd come to Ireland and left with her child. Still, she scanned every detail of their photograph hungrily, disappointed that the text below didn't tell her much, then flopped back in her seat with a sigh.

Aunt Annie's voice over her shoulder made her jump; she hadn't heard her come back downstairs.

'Any luck today, Maudie?'

'I hadn't got that far yet, I'm afraid.' Maudie felt her cheeks pinken at getting caught perusing the society pages of the paper instead of scanning the jobs section. 'I was admiring the fashions.'

Aunt Annie pulled out the chair next to her and sank down heavily. 'Ooh, my gout's troubling me something terrible today. Let's have a look then. The who's who of Savannah might take my mind off my cursed toe.' She pulled her glasses from her blouse pocket and slipped them on as Maudie slid the paper across to her.

'Oh, I say, aren't those gowns beautiful?' There was a dreamy quality to Aunt Annie's voice.

'They are. I've never seen any so pretty, especially hers.' Maudie pointed to Mrs Kinsella.

Aunt Annie lifted the paper so as to inspect the picture closely. 'That's Caroline Kinsella née Millard. She has impeccable taste, and with that willowy figure of hers, she's a couture dressmaker's dream.' A gossipy, conspiratorial gleam lit the older woman's eyes as she leaned in close to Maudie. 'Mr Kinsella – handsome, isn't he?'

Maudie nodded.

'Well, he made his fortune in banking, but Caroline Kinsella comes from old monied Savannah. The Millards. Her parents both died a few years ago of Spanish flu.' She crossed herself and carried on. 'Terrible sad it was. The Kinsellas moved into the family home on Chatham Square – Millard House – soon after their passing. And they've been the talk of the town these last months.'

'Have they?' Maudie was all ears but wary of appearing too interested. She needn't have worried though – Aunt Annie was in her applecart as she gave her a sage nod, as if she was privy to all of the goings-on in Savannah's high society.

'They've not long returned from a trip to Ireland. Mr Kinsella has Irish roots, and given the loss his wife had suffered, he thought time away from Savannah might do her good.'

Maudie felt as if every nerve ending in her body was on fire as she waited to hear what she instinctively knew was coming next.

'There's nothing unusual in a trip to see the home country, but what took everybody by surprise was that the couple returned with a baby girl.' Aunt Annie paused for dramatic effect.

It took all Maudie's strength not to give the game away and continue to feign naivety. 'Was Mrs Kinsella pregnant when she left Ireland then?'

'If she was, then the couple hadn't breathed a word of it, and she was slender as a whippet at the time. Still is – you can see that for yourself.' Aunt Annie jabbed at the newspaper. 'And that's other thing. The timing. I'm afraid you don't have to be a mathematician to know the dates were off. There's a rumour they've not been able to squash that the child was adopted in Ireland. Although, I'm not one to gossip you understand, Maudie.'

'Of course not, Aunt Annie.' Maudie's ears were ringing with all she'd learned, and adrenaline coursed through her veins.

Her first instinct was to run there now, to Millard House on Chatham Square, and take her daughter back. But she was no longer legally Emer's mother, and the Kinsellas wouldn't relinquish the child they'd adopted to a young woman who'd tracked them down from Ireland and claimed to be her mother.

So what could she do? But Maudie already knew the answer. She would do whatever was necessary to be with Emer again.

38

The seat in the charmingly laid out square from which Maudie kept vigil was partially hidden by shrubbery and the overhanging branches of trees. She'd told Aunt Annie another white lie in an ever-growing list of fibs that once her chores around the boarding house were done, she spent her days familiarising herself with the streets of her new home, keeping an eye out for 'help wanted' signs in shop windows, and knocking on doors in the hope of finding work.

'Mr Sutton made it clear I shouldn't hold out much hope for a nannying position, Aunt Annie, but I had my heart set on it, and you never know your luck. It will help take my mind off missing the young ones back home.'

When what she was doing, in fact, was whiling away the hours here on a bench seat in Chatham Square. It gave her a bird's-eye view of Millard House.

Maudie could feel pearls of perspiration along her hairline, and if not for the close proximity of her daughter and the hope that today she would finally catch a glimpse of her, she'd yearn for the fierce wind off the Atlantic that could cut you in half on a winter's day.

Millard House's cheerful blue front door was flanked on either side by gas lamps and sat at the top of steps framed by iron railings. But the door remained stubbornly closed, and the only comings and goings had been various deliveries taken down the adjacent side alley – presumably to the kitchen – around the back of the house, along with a gardener who'd materialised to trim the side alley's greenery.

She was beginning to wonder if the Kinsellas had gone away, leaving a skeleton staff, but she could feel Emer was nearby, and so fanning herself with the newspaper she'd brought to make it look as if she'd a benign purpose for sitting on the bench, she continued to wait across the road from the house she could describe with her eyes closed.

Millard House was a mellow, three-storey brick home and every bit as grand as she'd imagined it to be. Maudie had counted twelve tall shuttered windows, plus three at basement level. It was located on a sleepy street woken only by the odd passer-by, delivery man, errand boy or vehicle puttering past. The people who passed through the square were well dressed and did so at a strolling pace, in no particular hurry to get to their destination, seeing but not really seeing the Irish girl sitting there. It was lunchtime before things burst into life.

There was a school across the way, and the children would tumble forth, eager to get to their playground, the square, and run off their pent-up energy after a morning spent inside a stuffy classroom. That was when the square became a magical place, their shouts and laughter replacing the occasional whine of a hungry mosquito. Maudie would feel less adrift in a strange land because while her surroundings might be foreign, children were the same no matter where in the world you were.

You could set your watch by the schoolchildren, Maudie thought, as they began spilling across the street under the mindful gaze of a teacher to fill the square with their boisterousness. She unwrapped the sandwich Aunt Annie insisted on pressing upon her – along with a thermos of iced tea – before she left the house, saying their arrangement was full board.

It was then the door to Millard House opened.

Maudie dropped her sandwich in her lap and straightened, alert like a prairie animal being hunted – only she was the one doing the hunting.

A black woman whose age was hard to guess from where she sat appeared. She was dressed in a smart uniform of high-necked navy cotton dress with linen cuffs and collar, and a long white apron knotted about her waist, but it was the keys hanging from a chatelaine around her waist that told Maudie this woman was the housekeeper.

Her breath came in hot, fast bursts when she saw what the woman held. It was the hooded end of a perambulator. This was it. The moment she'd been waiting for. Her chance to see Emer!

She was staring so hard her eyes were burning, and she expected the housekeeper to spin round under her gaze, but of course she didn't. Instead, she hesitated before taking a cautious step down in her black patent-leather shoes. Her head twisted to keep an eye on where her feet were falling – and on the perambulator she was holding aloft at the same time.

Then a girl with her mousy brown hair neatly pinned up emerged. She looked to be several years younger than Maudie, and from her pinny and plain grey dress, which had similar white cuffs to the senior woman's, Maudie guessed she was the maid. The young girl looked anxious and was clutching the handlebar end of the perambulator with a white-knuckled grip visible even from this distance. Between them, the pair manoeuvred their way gingerly down the steps.

Maudie was watching them so intently she was surprised to see a third figure had materialised on the steps. The woman's face was hidden by her hat, but her immaculate dress and whippet-like figure told Maudie that this was the woman she'd seen in the newspaper – Mrs Kinsella. She stood watching the tableau, only moving down the steps once the perambulator was set down.

Maudie's breath steadied as Mrs Kinsella said something to her housekeeper and the maid before they were swallowed up by the doorway, leaving the lady of the house to take a stroll with Maudie's child.

It was then the cries of an unhappy baby drifted toward her, and her insides felt like a cloth being wrung out because she couldn't run across the street to Emer and snatch her from the perambulator. What good would she be to her daughter tossed in a jail cell? She had to bide her time, wait for the right moment and be smart, though she still had no clue what she was actually going to do.

Quickly, she packed her lunch things away and picked up her bag, then hurried across the cobbles to follow Mrs Kinsella and Emer at a sufficient distance not to cause consternation.

'You're simply out for an afternoon walk, Maudie,' she whispered.

As it happened, she needn't have worried about being spotted and confronted as to why she was on their trail. Mrs Kinsella was too intent on trying to soothe the distressed baby. When the woman paused, wracked by a sudden coughing fit, Maudie wanted to charge up to the perambulator and demand the woman hand over her baby, but common sense somehow prevailed.

Maudie thought they'd been walking around ten minutes when Mrs Kinsella looped back and bounced the perambulator into the now deserted Chatham Square, then sat down in the very seat Maudie had been holding vigil from. She was half hidden by shrubbery when she observed Mrs Kinsella place her head in her hands. The woman's body was shuddering, and dark tendrils of hair had escaped her hat and plastered themselves to the side of her face. Without thinking, Maudie made her way along the path to her.

Hearing footfall approaching, Mrs Kinsella hastily raised her head and swiped tear-stained cheeks, while Emer continued to howl.

Maudie opened her mouth, unsure of what was going to come out, and what did took them both by surprise. 'It's awfully hot, isn't it?'

Once she'd recovered herself, Mrs Kinsella gave Maudie a watery smile. 'It's hotter than blue blazes, and I thought the heat might make my daughter drowsy, but it's only made her madder than a wet hen, I'm afraid. You're Irish.' The latter was a statement, not a question. She reached out and took hold of the perambulator's handlebars, rocking it gently, but the wails remained at a heart-rending level.

'I am. I've not long arrived in Savannah. My name's Maudie. Maudie O'Connor.' She had no qualms in giving her real name because the nuns wouldn't have told the affluent American couple anything about her except that she was a poor unfortunate, a fallen woman. Aside from the Reverend Mother and Sister Louise, she wasn't sure the other nuns even knew her real name wasn't Theresa.

Maudie wondered whether Mrs Kinsella found this everyday conversation bizarre given the crying child between them. She gave no sign of it if she did, though, nodding politely at Maudie's response before introducing herself.

'Mrs Caroline Kinsella. Pleased to make your acquaintance.'

They smiled at one another.

'What's your baby's name?'

'Juniper, but more often than not Junebug.'

Maudie liked the nickname and rolled Juniper around in her head, trying it on for size. Again, words blurted forth. 'I used to help my mammy with the little ones. She always said I had a way with them, so perhaps I might be able to help. Would you mind?'

She gestured to the perambulator, her arms physically aching with the need to hold Emer – or Juniper, as she was now called. All her nerve endings felt like they were on fire, and her body filled with an adrenaline surge as she wondered what she'd do if Mrs Kinsella suddenly eyed her warily and hurried away with the child she'd named Juniper. But she didn't.

She simply dipped her head wearily as though to say *be my guest*. Tears sprang forth once more in eyes the same greyish-green as the trees' strange, spidery fronds overhead as she said, 'I was an only child, and Juniper's my first baby, so I've not had much experience.'

Her voice dropped to a whisper Maudie strained to catch. 'I've not found motherhood easy, and I've tried everything to get her to sleep. So's my housekeeper and maid, but' – her dainty shoulders rose and fell in a shrug – 'well, you can see for yourself she's plumb worn out.' Her striking face, with its angular cheekbones, crumpled. 'If you can soothe her, I'd be eternally grateful because I can't seem to get a thing right.'

Despite herself, Maudie felt sympathy swell for the distraught, desperate and clearly exhausted woman. Her need for her daughter overrode any sympathetic notions, however, as she moved in front of the perambulator, not wanting Mrs Kinsella to see her face because she knew it would give her away. She could feel it had reddened as she forced her heart – which had risen into her throat and threatened to choke her with the pain of those lost months – down. Instead, she focused on drinking in her first glimpse of the daughter who'd been there one minute, gone the next, as though she'd never existed in the first place.

She'd changed so much at nearly seven months. She was bonnie now, with a shock of hair as black as Ronan's. Her little face was screwed up, red and angry, her fists clenched and flailing while her chubby legs were pulled up to her belly.

Maudie reached into the perambulator and plucked her

roly-poly daughter up, savouring the remembered smell of her as she held her to her chest, rubbed her back and began to sing the song she recalled singing to her siblings when Mam was at her wits' end. This moment, she thought, holding the part of her that had been missing these last months, made everything that had happened since running away from Pelletstown worthwhile.

The little girl's body began to unfurl, and her enraged cries turned to sporadic sobs as Mrs Kinsella watched on in wonder.

'You've got the magic touch.'

Maudie continued to rock her child, and Mrs Kinsella made no attempt to take her from the other woman.

Did Emer know her – instinctively? Perhaps she remembered her mother's smell. Maudie suspected her unsettledness and distress were a combination of teething and a reaction to Mrs Kinsella's anxiety as a new mother.

Even as she thought this, something twisted inside her. This woman wasn't Emer's mother. She was!

She realised Mrs Kinsella was speaking to her.

'Juniper was born in Ireland.'

Juniper – she was Juniper now, not Emer, and Maudie tried to feign surprise. 'Was she?'

'Yes. My husband, he has Irish blood, and we were touring there for several months.' She hesitated but didn't elaborate further as she began to cough. 'I'm sorry. It's an annoyance I've had since our return from the Emerald Isle,' Mrs Kinsella explained once she'd recovered.

'Juniper's a lovely name.' Perhaps if she said it out loud enough, she'd get used to it.

The Southern belle smiled, and this time it reached her eyes. 'Thank you. It's a long-held favourite of mine. I always said if I was lucky enough to be blessed with a daughter one day, she'd be called Juniper. Now I have been. Only I don't think Juniper's feeling blessed with me as her momma.'

'Oh, I'm sure that's not the case. What a pretty name you have, Juniper.' Maudie, who was jiggling her daughter around to her hip, could afford to be generous.

Juniper hiccupped.

'Oh, and what was that?' Maudie jiggled her again, and the two women laughed as the child bestowed them with a gummy grin. Juniper had forgotten, in that magical way of small children, that she'd been upset in the first place, and in that instant Maudie had seen the shadow of her father in her smile and her eyes, the same shade of clear-skied blue as Ronan's.

Juniper opened her mouth again, but this time it was to give an enormous yawn.

'I think someone needs a little sleep,' Maudie said, laughing, her heart lighter than it had been for the longest while. She gulped her daughter's scent in before reluctantly placing her down in the perambulator, waiting a beat to see if she'd holler her indignation at no longer being held, but she didn't make a peep. Her eyes lingered on the three port wine marks on her neck, and she wished Ronan was by her side now, drinking in the sight of their daughter.

Dragging her gaze away, she recalled her mam settling the wee ones under the rustling leaves of a nearby rowan tree, and so Maudie positioned the perambulator directly under an oak laden with swaying Spanish moss. Juniper gazed up, mesmerised, her hand reaching up and then flopping to her side. Her lids began to droop, and when they fluttered shut, Maudie sent a silent message.

I've got her, Ronan. I've found our daughter, and I promise you, I won't let her go.

Maudie wanted to take her daughter and flee back to Ireland with her, but there was no chance of her even leaving the state of Georgia with Juniper before she was arrested. Ronan would have to come to them, so all she could do was wait.

39

'Oh, please won't you say yes, Maudie? It's the least I can do to thank you for saving my sanity!' Caroline Kinsella implored, her shoulders having visibly relaxed in the ensuing quiet as Juniper slept.

'I'd like that very much, thank you.' Maudie leaped at Mrs Kinsella's invitation to return to Millard House with her and the still sleeping Juniper for refreshments.

The tiredness Maudie had seen reflected in Mrs Kinsella's eyes had disappeared, replaced with a dancing light, but then she raised her hand to her mouth and coughed.

'Excuse me.' She swallowed several times before continuing. 'Winnie, my housekeeper, will want to meet you too. I mentioned being an only child, but I don't feel like one. Winnie's like a sister to me. She'll be sure to say you've got the magic touch when she hears you got Junebug off to sleep. I guarantee it.' Caroline appeared giddy with her daughter's sudden silence as she got to her feet.

Maudie couldn't help admiring how well she wore her clothes. There wasn't a spare pound on her.

She stood up, also eager for the off. 'I can push the perambulator if you like?'

Caroline Kinsella gestured to it with a smile, and the two women set off down the path, Maudie pinching herself at her good fortune as she gazed down at the rosy cheeks of her sleeping child. Her heart was full of so much love she was fit to burst!

'If you wait here with Juniper, I'll fetch Birdie to help with the perambulator. I'd do it myself, you understand, but with my cough, I'm not supposed to strain myself. Which means I'm not allowed to do anything other than take a gentle stroll until I shake it off. Doctor's orders, I'm afraid.' She made a tutting sound, one hand reaching for the iron rail. 'Life would be so much easier if Winnie didn't forbid me from coming and going through the back entrance. We could store the perambulator in her kitchen if she'd let me and not have to suffer this ridiculous carry-on every time I want to take Junebug for a walk.'

She climbed the steps, then pushed open an unlocked front door and disappeared inside.

It dawned on Maudie that there was nothing to stop her snatching Juniper right now and running away with her. Her heart began to thump as she imagined fleeing, and she took a step but then faltered. Where would they run to? Aunt Annie wouldn't turn her away, not if she told her the truth of her story, but it would only be a matter of time before Maudie was found and Juniper returned to the Kinsellas as her legal parents. She'd be arrested for kidnapping, and Aunt Annie would be led away too for aiding and abetting. That couldn't happen, and besides, she'd lose all hope of ever getting close to Juniper again.

It was too late anyway because the young maid Maudie had seen earlier was skipping down the stairs, a deep set of dimples brightening her otherwise nondescript face as Maudie angled the perambulator in her direction. There were no introductions as they proceeded up the steps with their precious cargo, carefully setting it down where Mrs Kinsella waited inside the entrance.

'Thank you, Birdie.' The lady of the house closed the door behind them. 'Would you mind seeing to some afternoon refreshments for myself and Miz O'Connor?'

Birdie dipped her head. 'Yes, ma'am. My real name's Bridget, but everybody calls me Birdie, even my own mama.' She dimpled again for Maudie's benefit.

Mrs Kinsella smiled indulgently. 'That we do, Birdie, and would you ask Winnie to join us in the parlour, please? I'd like her to meet Miz O'Connor.'

'Of course, ma'am.' The young girl scuttled off toward the back of the house and disappeared through a side door.

'Birdie's parents were from Ireland, but she's as Southern as I am.'

The exchange had given Maudie a chance to take stock of the grand hallway with its high ceiling and wall sconces. She inhaled fresh, sweet-smelling flowers that added a splash of colour from the vase on a console table with claw-and-ball feet. Then her gaze tracked the Persian runner – from under which parquet flooring peeked – to the staircase: a spiralling mahogany affair leading to the second floor. Her first impression was that the inside of Millard House was every bit as splendid as the outside had hinted it would be.

It was a far cry from her own humble beginnings, Maudie thought, as Mrs Kinsella led her into the parlour. She was ushered over to a damask-covered sofa and perched on the edge of the seat, doing her best not to be overawed by her surroundings.

'What a beautiful room this is,' Maudie said, craning her neck this way and that. Her gaze landed on a window framed by heavy velvet drapes, in front of which was a roll-top writing desk. She pictured herself sitting there writing to Nora and occasionally pausing to watch the activity on the street outside and the square beyond. An enormous Persian rug covered the floor, whilst overhead a chandelier dripped from the ceiling. A gilded mirror hung above the fireplace and a glass-fronted cabinet displayed the family china. Various portraits punctuated the bird-scene wallpaper depicting the faces, Maudie assumed, of the Millard family's ancestors. She rubbed at her arms, gone goosy under their reproachful gazes. Potted ferns and palms adorned empty spaces, while a phonograph sat upon a cabinet in keeping with the rest of the furnishings, inside which their records would no doubt be tucked away. Maudie was lost in thought, wondering what music the Kinsellas would listen to when they relaxed of an evening, when she realised Mrs Kinsella was speaking to her.

'Thank you, Maudie. The house has been in my family for several generations, and it's the only home I've ever known apart from a brief spell living elsewhere when Declan and I were first married.'

Maudie half listened as she began to talk about the history of the house and who was who in the frames glaring down at them, but her mind had drifted back to her family cottage in Rush. Millard House was worlds away from where she'd come from. The thought unsettled her because she could see that under this roof, Juniper would never want for anything – except her real mother's love, she reminded herself, and a connection with her homeland. But that same homeland had stolen her from her mother.

She clasped her hands then unclasped them, along with her ankles, wishing there wasn't a gentle vulnerability to Mrs Kinsella, despite her wealth and glamour. The latter seemed quite unaware of the traitorous feelings of the young woman sitting opposite her. It was these qualities that made the genteel Southern woman instantly likeable, and Maudie didn't want to warm to her. Her mind had crafted the woman into an evil baby snatcher, but having met her, she could already see that wasn't the case and knew the couple whose home she was now in under false pretences had adopted Emer/Juniper in good faith. The Kinsellas weren't the evil ones. The treatment she'd received at St Patrick's was proof of that.

Her confusion was swept aside as Birdie rattled into the parlour carrying a tray with cool drinks and a selection of afternoon tea delicacies. Once she'd set it down on the table – already set with linen as though Maudie had been expected – she gave a small curtsy and hurried from the room. A split second later, there was a thud that saw Maudie glance at Mrs Kinsella to see if she should be concerned.

'Birdie?'

'I'm fine and dandy, ma'am. It was those two left feet of mine – I tripped over them again.' This was followed up by, 'Don't worry, ma'am – I didn't wake the baby.'

'Heavens to Betsy, Birdie, you will do bellowing like so.'

'Yes, ma'am.'

Mrs Kinsella shook her head, exasperated. She waited a moment before leaning over the table between them and lowering her voice. 'I do declare that child's accident prone. Birdie's only been with us a year. She replaced her sister, who left to get married, and I'm afraid she's going to hurt herself one of these days. I swear my heart stops whenever she takes to the stairs, waiting for her to come tumbling down.'

Maudie wasn't sure what to say, but as it happened, a tap at the door stopped her from having to reply.

'Come in, Winnie dearest.'

The housekeeper stepped into the room, and Maudie tried not to gawp because she had the smoothest, shiniest skin she'd ever seen. She was quite beautiful.

'Maudie O'Connor, it's my pleasure to introduce you to Winnie Jackson.'

'Pleased to make your acquaintance, Miz O'Connor. And if you don't mind me saying, your hair is purdy, ma'am.' Winnie beamed at Maudie and watched her with equal fasciation as the sun streamed in through the window, turning her hair to fire.

'Maudie's an Irish Colleen with that red hair and those emerald eyes, Winnie.' Mrs Kinsella smiled. 'And oh my stars, she's a miracle worker too.' She reached for the plate of biscuits and held them out to Maudie. 'While our Winnie here is a marvel in the kitchen. Please won't you try one of her praline cookies? They're simply the best in all of Savannah.'

'My momma's secret recipe.' Winnie's sparkling brown eyes were now curious as she looked at Maudie. 'A miracle worker you say, Miz Caroline?'

Maudie took one of the cookies, suddenly feeling shy as she wondered over the easy relationship between these two women born to very different stations in life.

'Oh yes.' Mrs Kinsella explained how Maudie had happened upon her across the street in the square.

Maudie smiled as she explained how Maudie had been drawn like a moth to a flame by Juniper's cries on account of missing her family back home dreadfully.

'We briefly introduced ourselves, and then Maudie offered her services given she'd helped her momma look after all *her* babies. Well, you can imagine, Winnie, I was desperate by then. Junebug hadn't let up since before I left the house, and without a word of a lie, within moments of Maudie picking her up, that baby girl's tears dried up and she was sound asleep.'

Winnie nodded. 'You've surely got the magic touch then.'

'I said you'd say that.' Mrs Kinsella smiled, and Winnie laughed.

Maudie flushed with pleasure and embarrassment, still intrigued over the relationship between the lady of the house and her housekeeper. Mrs Kinsella had said earlier Winnie was like a sister to her.

'Winnie and I grew up together in this very house,' Mrs Kinsella explained, having read Maudie's curious expression correctly. 'Her momma came to live here and work for my parents as their housekeeper when she was widowed suddenly while expecting Winnie, a late baby. All her other children had flown the coop by then. Winnie and I were born a month apart and grew up together. When Winnie's momma retired and went to live with her sister, Winnie took over her role. We're so blessed she stayed on to look after Mr Kinsella and myself after my parents passed away.'

'Lord only knows, Miz Caroline, you can't look after yourself, let alone yo' husband.'

Mrs Kinsella's laugh was like a tinkling bell, and she didn't appear to be offended in the least, but it morphed into a cough, and Maudie saw fear flickering in Winnie's eyes. It made her wonder if this cough was more than an annoyance and perhaps something sinister as she watched the housekeeper rush forward to fetch the glass of iced tea and held it out to Mrs Kinsella to sip. The bond between the pair was easy to see, she thought, as Mrs Kinsella regained her equilibrium with an apology. Still, though Winnie might have been as good as family, the line between employer and employee was still clearly there as she wasn't invited to sit and join them. Instead, she stood to one side of where Maudie and Mrs Kinsella were seated, her hands clasped in front of her as Mrs Kinsella encouraged Maudie to tell them a little about herself.

Maudie decided it was best to keep it simple because it would be easier to stick as close to the truth as possible and that way she couldn't get tripped up. 'I'm from a family of fishermen in Rush, County Dublin on Ireland's east coast.'

Mrs Kinsella clapped delightedly, and Winnie looked startled. 'Declan, my husband – his roots lie in Rush. Now don't you think that's a coincidence?'

Maudie tried to nod enthusiastically, but of course her being there was no coincidence.

'It surely is,' Winnie said quietly.

'Go on, Maudie,' Caroline Kinsella urged.

Maudie looked at her skirt as she continued blagging her way through her story, trying not to mumble. 'I lost my fiancé, Ronan, recently. He died fighting for his country, and after his death, well, I couldn't see much of a future for myself in Ireland any longer. My brother-in-law's aunt runs a boarding house here in Savannah, and my sister sent a letter of introduction to Mrs Callaghan to say I was coming. Mrs Callaghan – or Aunt Annie as she insisted I call her – has been wonderful to me, and I think Savannah's beginning to feel like home already.'

'I'm sorry to hear of your loss, but it's wonderful to hear our city's made you feel welcome. Isn't it, Winnie?' Mrs Kinsella's eyes glimmered with genuine warmth.

'It sure is.'

'I hope you find your fresh chance here, Maudie. Something tells me you will.'

'Thank you, Mrs Kinsella.'

The older woman smiled and took another sip of her iced tea; however, she didn't touch the biscuits. No wonder she was so thin, Maudie thought, noticing Winnie showed no signs of moving.

'Have you found employment since arriving in our fine city?'

'Not yet. I was hoping to secure a nannying position. I have a glowing reference, but the agency I signed on at told me most girls in the good families of Savannah are employed via word of mouth and I'd be better placed seeking shop work.'

'Well, that's true, yes. It's very much a case of who you know in Savannah.' Mrs Kinsella's gaze met Winnie's in silent communication.

Maudie nibbled on the cookie, which really was very good, watching the exchange from under her lashes and wondering what the pair were saying without words.

'Do you know, Maudie, I think perhaps we were meant to

meet in the square today.' Mrs Kinsella's pretty face turned to hers once more.

Maudie's stomach plummeted, and the cookie turned to sawdust in her mouth. She'd been caught out. Of course she had. How had she ever thought she could get away with pretending there was no connection between her and Juniper? It must be stamped all over her face, and she'd all but given herself away by saying she was from Rush, but how could she have known Mr Kinsella's family also hailed from there? She lowered her eyes, abandoning the cookie to the plate and smoothing her skirt anxiously, unsure of what to do.

'Because you saw for yourself I need help with Juniper.'

Winnie was frowning, but Maudie was too busy trying to make sense of what Mrs Kinsella was saying to notice.

'Declan's work and our charitable connections are so demanding on our time, and Winnie has a lot on her plate as it is.'

'I don't mind, Miz Caroline. You know I adore Miz Juniper like she's my own. She's teething is all,' Winnie protested.

'And I love you for it, Winnie, but we've been struggling since Declan and I returned from Ireland, and you know it. Junebug is a delight; she's my heart, but she's not what you'd call an easy baby. Declan and I always planned on hiring a nanny, but I haven't heard of anyone I'd feel happy entrusting with our lil darlin's care – until now. I said it's a case of who you know in Savannah, Maudie, and now you know me.'

Maudie's initial panic at having been rumbled slowly ebbed away, and she held her breath, waiting to hear what Mrs Kinsella would say next.

'I think you might have been sent to us by the angels, Maudie. And Declan – Mr Kinsella – would love Juniper's new nanny being not only Irish but from the same town his ancestors came from. Why, it's positively serendipitous.'

Maudie was on the edge of her seat, unable to believe it

could all be this easy. Was she about to be offered the chance to spend her days with her daughter? To be under the same roof as her baby in honest employment was so much more than she could have hoped for as she'd kept watch across the way, praying for a glimpse of her child. She couldn't believe her luck and wanted to dance a jig at the joy of this unexpected turn of events, but she mustn't appear too eager or she'd rouse suspicion. She had to be careful not to refer to Juniper by the name she'd given her too. As it was, Winnie was clearing her throat and fidgeting as though about to speak up. But Maudie didn't intend to give the housekeeper a chance.

'I've something to show you.' Maudie fetched Mrs O'Brien's reference from her bag and thrust it toward Mrs Kinsella with a smile.

The gentlewoman skimmed over the handwritten letter praising Maudie's way with children before passing it to Winnie, whose lips had sandwiched together. 'Like I said, Winnie, sent by angels.'

If the housekeeper was impressed by the glowing words contained within the reference, Maudie couldn't tell. She simply passed it back to Maudie with an, 'If you say so, Miz Caroline.'

'I do say so, and what say you, Maudie? Would you like to live here at Millard House employed as Juniper's nanny?'

Maudie's hand's steepled to her mouth, and her face shone as she told Mrs Kinsella how much she would love that, in between thanking her for the opportunity and promising her she wouldn't let her down. It was no lie when she added, 'I'll look after little Juniper as though she were my own.'

Mrs Kinsella smiled. 'I don't doubt it for a moment.'

Fleetingly, Maudie felt badly – Mrs Kinsella was completely unaware of the irony of her new nanny's vow.

40

Maudie's heart was singing over the prospect of making Millard House, Emer's home, hers too. Her mind clamoured over the chance to make up for the time she'd lost with her daughter. Though here she'd be Juniper's nanny, not Emer's mammy. Emer would continue to be called Juniper, or derivatives of it, and Maudie wouldn't be the one *her* baby would call mam; nor would she get to make decisions on her behalf.

'I've something needs attending to in the kitchen,' Winnie announced. 'May I be excused?'

'Of course.'

'It was a pleasure to meet you, Miz O'Connor. I'll be seeing you again soon.'

Maudie didn't know if it was her guilty conscience, but the housekeeper seemed none too pleased by the prospect of a new nanny, and determined to endear herself to her, Maudie called to the retreating figure, 'Yes you will. And it was delightful to meet you too, Miss Jackson.'

The maid's step faltered, and she half turned. 'It's Winnie.' There was no smile to accompany her words.

'Then please – I'm to be Maudie.' Her own smile didn't falter.

They nodded at one another, a wariness in both their eyes despite Maudie's curved lips, which she worried were beginning to form a grimace. Then abruptly Winnie swept from the room, leaving Mrs Kinsella and Maudie to hash out the finer details of the spontaneous arrangement they, at least, were both thoroughly pleased with. Of course, Maudie would have agreed to sleeping in the hearth like Cinderella if it meant being under the same roof as her child, so she had no qualms accepting a live-in position with a monthly salary, to be agreed upon once Mrs Kinsella had conferred with her husband.

'Mr Kinsella is in charge of our finances, but I'm sure it will be more than fair.'

'Of course, Mrs Kinsella. That all sounds most agreeable.'

The Southern woman hesitated, eyeing Maudie speculatively. 'There's something about you. I feel I can trust you. Am I right, Maudie?'

'You are, Mrs Kinsella.' A bold-faced lie.

'I feel you will understand.'

'I'll certainly do my best, ma'am.' Maudie attempted to copy Birdie's way of addressing the lady of the house, but it came out sounding more like 'marm', making Mrs Kinsella smile.

She leaned conspiratorially forward from her perch. 'This isn't common knowledge, but I know the rumour mill is rife, so I'd appreciate it if you kept what I'm about to tell you to yourself.'

'Of course.' What was she going to say? Maudie sat statue-still in anticipation.

Caroline Kinsella cleared her throat. 'I wasn't entirely honest with you in the square earlier. Our decision to travel to Ireland wasn't simply so Declan could visit the land his family came from as I said; rather, we went with the intention of adopting a child. We haven't been blessed ourselves – a source of great, ongoing sadness to both of us.'

Maudie made to utter a platitude, but Mrs Kinsella held her hand up. 'Please let me continue because I think you'll find this story has a happy ending.'

'Of course.'

'My husband has strong ties with the Catholic Church. He's a generous benefactor not only to them but to the Irish cause too. "The boys fighting back home" he calls them. You mentioned you yourself lost your fiancé in this war for independence?'

'Yes.' Maudie bowed her head, allowing herself a moment to wonder where Ronan was and hope he was safe. Was he thinking of her at this very moment as she was him? The thought that he might be was comforting. Still, she jumped when a dainty hand settled over hers.

'I didn't mean to make you jump, hon. I just wanted to tell you how sorry I am for your loss. If I were to lose my Declan, well, I—' She broke off with a shudder.

'Thank you.' Maudie blinked furiously, reminding herself Ronan wasn't dead and buried; he was waiting until it was safe for him to come out of hiding, and when he did, Nora would tell him where he could find her. In the meantime, she'd be here with their daughter, watching over her and waiting for him to come.

The warm pressure on her hand lifted as Mrs Kinsella continued to talk, pausing now and then to press her handkerchief to her mouth when she coughed.

Maudie wished she'd stop apologising and finish saying her piece.

'It was suggested that there might be another route to parenthood available to us through the Church – given our generosity, you understand.'

Maudie understood all right. Money talked. She bristled at

the injustice of it, relieved that Mrs Kinsella, intent on twisting the rings on her fingers, had missed her reaction.

'So Declan and myself travelled to Dublin, where we did pay a fleeting visit to Rush, that much is true, but as you know, your country is volatile at present, and we didn't stay long.'

Maudie tried to imagine what Mrs Kinsella would have made of Rush. Perhaps she'd called into the grocer's and been fawned all over by Mrs Hughes, who'd have delighted in a well-dressed American woman setting foot in her shop. Or maybe she'd walked past Mam and her siblings in the street. Oh, if only Nora was sitting with her now listening to this, she thought, knowing she'd tell her to stop squirming in her seat. She couldn't help it though. The idea of Mr and Mrs Kinsella being in the town where she'd been born – and forced to leave – made her feel peculiar.

'The main purpose of our visit was to meet with the Mother Superior at a Dublin mother and baby home. St Patrick's.' Mrs Kinsella shuddered a second time. 'That place was colder than a well digger's knees, and mercy me, the Mother Superior in charge... well, she was as grim as a ghost at a funeral.

Maudie bit back a smile at her colourful descriptions.

'But perhaps I'm judging her too harshly. If it wasn't for her, Declan and I wouldn't have our darlin' Junebug because upon learning of my husband's connection with the town of Rush, she told us she had a very special baby with Fingal blood coursing through her veins who she felt in her heart God wanted to be ours.'

Maudie gritted her teeth so hard she half expected to crack a tooth, and her toes curled inside her shoes as she pictured the sanctimonious Mother Superior sitting opposite the Kinsellas, resolving to give them Maudie's baby.

'As soon as I held Juniper in my arms, I knew she was right. She was meant to be ours, and we brought her home with us. And now I've met you. I think, like Junebug, it was meant to be.'

Those grey-green eyes held Maudie's emerald chips. The woman was unaware of the hot, molten fever bubbling inside Maudie as she tripped blithely on.

'Winnie knows, of course – I tell Winnie everything – but not Birdie. She's as prone to gossiping with her sisters as she is tripping over herself. She has a good heart though.' Mrs Kinsella's smile was fond, but her expression swiftly became earnest.

'We haven't told anyone Junebug's adopted because I couldn't bear the sneers from some of the less-understanding women in my circles. They're all so fixated on blood and carrying on the lineage. I don't want Juniper to ever feel she isn't ours because in my heart...' Her hand fluttered to her chest. Then she reached for Maudie's hand once more and took it in hers. 'I want you to understand, Maudie, Juniper is mine. Mine and Declan's.'

Mrs Kinsella squeezed Maudie's hand with surprising force for such a slender woman.

'Oh, I do understand, Mrs Kinsella, and don't worry – your secret's safe with me.' Maudie held the other woman's gaze unflinchingly, but her face gave nothing away.

'Good. I knew you would.'

She released Maudie's hand, and they smiled across at one another.

Juniper hadn't made a peep since they'd arrived back at Millard House, and though Maudie was reluctant to leave her daughter now she'd finally found her, she announced she had to go, as she was expected to help Mrs Callaghan with the evening meals. Before she could reply, Mrs Kinsella began coughing once more. When the fit subsided, she sank back into the armchair's cushions, looking tiny despite her height. There were blue smudges beneath her eyes Maudie hadn't noticed earlier.

'I'd get up to show you to the door, Maudie, but I'm afraid this cough, well, it wears me slap out, and what with tending to Juniper in the night...'

Before Maudie could tell her there was no need for her to be shown to the door, Caroline Kinsella had reached for the bell and given it a shake.

'But Junebug and I have you now, don't we?'

'Yes, Mrs Kinsella,' Maudie replied as Birdie appeared to see her to the door. 'You do.'

41

'Oh, Aunt Annie, you won't believe what's after happening.' Maudie knew she was red in the cheeks from having run nearly all the way back to the boarding house, but she was desperate to share her day's events with Aunt Annie, who she knew would be delighted for her.

'I might if you try me, but first of all fetch yourself a glass of water, then sit down and catch your breath. You look fit to combust, my girl.'

Maudie did so, even though she was chomping at the bit to share her news.

Once her cheeks had returned to their normal colour and she was seated opposite Aunt Annie at the kitchen table, the older woman abandoned the peas she'd been shelling.

'Right so, I'm all ears, young Maudie.'

The story – adjusted to fit Maudie's narrative – tumbled forth. '...and the Kinsellas' baby, Juniper, is the dearest wee soul, Aunt Annie,' she finished in a gush of excitement. There was no word of a lie there.

'Oh my,' Aunt Annie said, a hand resting on her shelf-like bosom and her eyes narrowing. 'It's all happened so quickly, but then I always say things have a habit of working out. Don't I, Tucker?'

Tucker made no comment from beneath the table.

'And how they have, Aunt Annie! Oh, I can't wait to write to Nora.'

'The Kinsellas of all people...' Aunt Annie appeared to swell in size. 'You couldn't find a finer family in all of Savannah. I'm so proud of you.'

Maudie wished her mam and da could hear what Aunt Annie was saying, but she'd made her bed and was dead to them.

'You've landed on your feet there, my girl. Mind, they have too. The Kinsellas will be lucky to have you. And to think it all stemmed from a chance meeting in Chatham Square. The good Lord moves in mysterious ways, so he does.' Aunt Annie was looking heavenward as she made this declaration, but again her eyes narrowed as she lowered them, examining Maudie's face.

If only you knew the truth, Maudie thought, trying not to flush under her scrutiny. There was no room in Maudie's heart for guilt over her lies, however. Her new role would give her all the time in the world to plan what she'd do when Ronan finally came for them. Now, though, there was a dinner to be made, and she pulled the dish of unshelled peas out of Aunt Annie's reach. 'There's more chance of the peas making it into the bowl if I see to the rest of these.'

'You're a bold girl,' Aunt Annie said, smiling as she heaved herself up and went to see to the collard greens waiting to be washed.

Her tone of voice took on a gossipy quality. 'Now tell me, Maudie, who did the child – Juniper you said her name is? – take after?'

Maudie's hands trembled, and she was relieved Aunt Annie was too busy at the sink to notice the pea pod she had hold of quivering like so as she told another lie. 'It's hard to say, Aunt Annie.'

Maudie was back in the corridors of St Patrick's – as an observer this time – standing barefoot outside the kitchen. Her eyes were orbs, her mouth opening in a scream when she saw Sister Agnes swooping down on Cecelia like an eagle about to snatch its prey.

'Let her go, you wicked divil!' Maudie screamed, making to lunge toward the demented nun, her hands clenched into fists, but her feet wouldn't move. She was powerless – just as she'd been when it had been her the nun was targeting. All she could do was scream, over and over again.

'Stop, Maudie, stop. Wake up! You're dreaming, child.'

Maudie's eyes fluttered open, panic filling her, but after a few blinks, she registered it was Aunt Annie standing over her, illuminated in the moonlight. She was in Savannah; she was safe. But was Cecelia? Was the nightmare an omen? Her breath was still coming in rapid bursts, and her cheeks, when she reached up to touch her face, were wet.

'Shush now. You're all right. It was a nightmare you were after having, that's all.'

'I'm sorry for waking you. I hope I haven't woken any of the lodgers.'

'Don't worry your head about that.'

'I'll be all right now,' Maudie sniffed. 'Thank you, Aunt Annie.'

The older woman didn't move. 'You know, Maudie, I believe nightmares are our demons come back to haunt us.'

'I think so too. Do you have demons, Aunt Annie?'

'I do, child, and speaking of them is the only way to banish them. I learned that a long time ago. Now bunch up because I'm in the mood for talking, and I think you need to as well.'

Maudie squished over to the far side of her bed, glad of the older woman's comforting presence as her weight sank down on the mattress beside her. She allowed Aunt Annie to smooth her hair away from her face, like a mother would a sick child, and listened as she talked about what haunted her.

'When I was growing up back in Ireland, I had an older sister, Peggy, whom I adored. I followed her just about everywhere, and then one day the priest called to the house, and the next day she was gone. My mam and da wouldn't be drawn on the matter, but us children, we pieced it together. Peggy had got herself in the family way. She'd been sent to the sisters to atone for her sins.'

Maudie stifled her gasp with a swallow. Did Aunt Annie know her story? But how? Martin surely wouldn't have breathed a word.

'When she came back, she wasn't the same girl I knew and loved. Then one day she was found floating in the nearby estuary. For the longest time, I was filled with bitterness over what Peggy had done, but when I had babes of my own, I finally understood why. My second-born was taken from the world before he even uttered his first cry. 'Tis a pain worse than dying to lose a child in any form. I couldn't help Peggy, but I might be able to help you, Maudie. If you'll let me.'

Maudie stiffened. She'd experienced so much judgment already. 'How did you know?'

'Tonight's not the first night you've cried out in your sleep like so. Peggy used to do the same, when she returned home. I wish I'd woken her and asked her to tell me what happened to her and her baby. Things might have been different if I had been willing to listen. I feel God's sent me a second chance in you, Maudie. To help your story have a happier ending than Peggy's. So I'm here now, and I'm willing to listen.'

It was hard to open up, but by stringing one stilted sentence into the next as Aunt Annie continued to smooth the hair from her face, she told her the truth of it all. By the time Maudie had unburdened herself of the reason she'd come to Savannah, the moon had gone to bed, the sky was beginning to lighten and birds were chattering about the day ahead.

'Do you hear that bird call there?' Aunt Annie asked, before smothering a yawn with her hand.

'The one that sounds like a tea kettle?'

'That's the one. It's a Carolina wren. Whenever you're frightened or feeling lost, listen out for it and let that whistle remind you you're in America now. You're free here, and by some small miracle you'll be reunited with your little girl.'

'But she won't know me as her mother.' Maudie plucked at her bedsheet.

'She'll know your love. That, my child, is going to have to be enough.'

Would it be enough? Maudie's tired mind wondered. Only time would tell.

'I'm free, but what about Cecelia?'

Aunt Annie went quiet, closing her eyes briefly, and when she reopened them, she said, 'You know, I'd like to help.'

'How?'

'I've a little money set aside. Perhaps we could secure passage for her and her little one?'

Maudie was wide awake now, and she propped herself up on her elbow. 'I could write to Sister Louise, ask her to help. It's a start at least. She had a kind heart.'

She'd promised Cecelia she wouldn't forget her, and that one day she'd be back for her. She tossed the sheets asides under Aunt Annie's bemused gaze, crossed the floor to the writing desk and picked up her pen.

'I must be going, Aunt Annie.' Maudie was keen to be on her way to her new home at Millard House and didn't want to waste time. She was standing in the entrance of the boarding house with her suitcase at her feet. Tucker was almost glued to her side as he whined up at her.

'Of course, of course. You're excited to get there, as you should be, and we can't have you being late on your first day now.' She held out her arms, and Maudie was enveloped in a floury embrace because she'd interrupted her in the midst of baking to say she'd be on her way. 'I'll see you at church?'

Maudie gave a half-baked nod, not wanting to make a promise she wasn't sure she'd keep. She still had her faith; it was what had kept her going in her darkest moments, but she'd lost faith in the Church itself because no god could condone the treatment she and all the other women at St Patrick's had suffered. Still, it was easier to go along with Aunt Annie.

As the fleshy arms released her, she added, 'You'll let me know the moment a letter arrives?'

They couldn't risk a letter from St Patrick's arriving at Millard House, so Maudie had asked Sister Louise to reply to Mrs Annie Callaghan instead.

'Of course. You'll post yours to Sister Louise on your way?'

'I will, and I promise I'll call by so often you'll be sick of the sight of me. I can't thank you enough for taking me in and helping me get on my feet, and for, well, for everything.' Visiting this dear woman, who was more of a mother to her than her own had been, was a promise she could easily keep. She could only hope that one day soon Cecelia would get her fresh start too.

Aunt Annie flapped her hand dismissively. 'It's what family does is all.'

Maudie thought about her own mam and dad but bit back her retort about that not always being the case as she hugged the woman who'd been so kind to her one more time. She'd helped restore her faith in human kindness, something Maudie had thought was gone forever.

'Maudie.' Aunt Annie's tone had taken a serious turn as she clasped hold of her hands. 'You can send your letter to this Sister Louise of yours to see if she's willing to help your friend, but her loyalty to her fellow sisters may be stronger than you think.'

'I believe in Sister Louise, Aunt Annie.'

'And I believe in you, child.'

Aunt Annie, Tucker by her side, continued to stand in the doorway, waving her off as though she was moving state and not a few blocks away.

Maudie paused on the corner of West Taylor Street and gave her one final wave, then continued the few paces to the next intersection to send the letters she'd written – not just to Sister Louise but Nora too. As she dropped the letters into the post box, she smiled, imagining Nora's incredulous face when she read how her sister had pushed fate and it had led her to the home of her daughter's adoptive parents. Then she sent a silent message to Cecelia, telling her she'd not forgotten her, before picking up her case and walking the short distance to Chatham Square.

As she took the stairs to knock on the front door of her new home, Maudie could hardly believe she would get to be with Juniper without worrying how she'd make ends meet or constantly looking over her shoulder.

42

'Oh! Excuse me.' The hand which Maudie had raised to knock flew to rest on her collarbone instead, and she took a step back. Millard House's front door had burst open as though someone had observed her ascent of the stairs and saved her the trouble of knocking. That someone being a well-heeled gentleman with a twinkle in his eye. She recognised him from newspaper photographs as the handsome Mr Declan Kinsella, but he appeared to be equally surprised to have found her standing on the doorstep, as he stared first at her then the suitcase by her feet, clearly bemused.

When Maudie recovered from the start he'd given her, she introduced herself. 'I'm Maudie O'Connor, sir, the new nanny. Mrs Kinsella is expecting me this morning.'

'Why of course you are. Excuse my manners, won't you, and come on in, Maudie.' Mr Kinsella stood aside, making a sweeping, welcoming gesture with his arm. 'I've heard so much about you from my wife. I couldn't believe my ears when she said you hailed from Rush of all places. It made me think you and Caroline meeting in the square like so was fate, and it's my pleasure to put a name to your face.'

Fate had nothing to do with it, Maudie thought, and Declan's effusive greeting was soon tempered by the frosty appearance of Winnie, who emerged from the side door at the rear of the entrance hall, seemingly drawn by their voices.

'You should have come round to the back.' Winnie flapped the dishcloth she was still holding in Maudie's direction. 'The front door's not for staff. It ain't Mr Declan's place to be opening the door to you.' Then she pointedly threw in, 'Once upon a time, we'd have had a butler for that job.'

Well that's me told, Maudie thought, determinedly keeping her smile in place. 'I'm sorry, Winnie, Mr Kinsella. It won't happen again.' Maudie had suspected Winnie thought Mrs Kinsella hasty in her offer of employment the other day. Now she could see she'd been right. She was surly and suspicious, and to be fair, she had every reason to be.

'It's modern times we're living in, Winnie; we don't need staff for everything, and it was a good shock, rest assured. If Miz Maudie had gone round the back, then I'd have missed my chance to welcome her to Millard House now, wouldn't I?'

'Yes, sir,' Winnie replied grudgingly.

And that told you, Maudie thought, and imagined sticking her tongue out at the housekeeper, even though her underhandedness was giving her guilty twinges.

'And as delightful as it surely is to make your acquaintance, Miz Maudie, I've an office to be getting to and a secretary with a worse bark than our dear Winnie here to be dealing with if I'm late.'

Maudie didn't want him to leave her alone with Winnie, but remembering her manners and her station as an employee in the household, she said, 'I'm so happy to be here, Mr Kinsella. I told Mrs Kinsella that I'll look after Juniper as though she were my own, and I can assure you I will.' She meant every word.

'I'd expect nothing less from a Fingal girl. I'm sure our

Junebug will be in the safest of hands. Winnie will show you around.'

His smile lit his eyes as he sailed out the door, and Maudie watched as it closed behind him, feeling bereft because she'd warmed to him as she had Mrs Kinsella, against her better judgment. Winnie was another matter, however, and she took her time in turning round to face the surly housekeeper.

'You heard the man. I can't be standing around here all day. I've chores waiting for me that won't get done by themselves and a housemaid that couldn't pour water out of a boot with instructions on the heel. So stop dilly-dallying.'

Maudie made to pick up her case.

'You can leave that there.'

She set it down obediently, and a whirlwind tour commenced with a glance in the doorway of the drawing room behind the parlour. It was more formal than the room where she'd sat a few afternoons ago, thanking her lucky stars that she was about to become a member of staff in the Kinsellas' household. A grand piano drew her gaze.

'Miz Caroline plays, and she entertains their guests after dinner on occasion,' Winnie stated with a hint of pride. She pulled the door to then flung open the double doors of the room to the rear of the house, revealing the formal dining room. The centre-stage table was oval, mahogany and far too big for two people to sit at.

'Miz Caroline and Mr Declan only use this room for entertaining. They take their meals in the breakfast room downstairs. We eat in the kitchen.'

Next, Maudie was picking her way down the stairs that lay on the other side of the side door through which she'd seen Winnie and Birdie coming and going. The servants' quarters where Birdie slept were here on the ground level, while the breakfast room was a charming sunlit space with French doors opening to a delightfully lush courtyard with punches of tropical colour. A small brick building lay beyond it.

'That there's the carriage house where I live, and it's out of bounds,' Winnie stated sternly.

Maudie instantly wanted to peek through the window but knew she wouldn't dare.

'And that gate there leads to an alleyway connected to Barnard Street, which will take you back on to Chatham Square.'

She moved to the door between the breakfast room and kitchen, Maudie right behind her.

The kitchen was, like the rest of the house, of generous proportions, and the remains of breakfast waited to be tidied away while the beginnings of a main meal sat ready to be prepped on the scrubbed table.

'There was a time the late Mrs Millard employed a cook – French trained no less. I might not have fancy training, but I watched and learned growing up here, and Miz Caroline and Mr Declan will tell you my food makes him want to slap his mama.'

That was a new phrase to Maudie, and she took it to mean Mr Kinsella found Winnie's food to be delicious. At least she hoped that's what it meant.

'How do you manage it all?' Maudie expected running a house this size would be a full-time job. She couldn't imagine where Winnie would find time to cook as well, and where was Birdie?

'I like to be useful, and I like to be busy. I manage, and I can assure you standards have not slipped now Mr and Mrs Millard are no longer with us.'

She moved to the wooden door and opened it, bringing in a gush of sweet-smelling air from the courtyard. 'And this is the door we come in and out of. That clear?'

'As a bell, Winnie.' Maudie's status as the nanny, an employee of the house, was being made very clear.

The other woman squinted at her then closed the door. 'It sure is some coincidence you happening to be from the same town as lil Juniper's momma came from.'

Maudie shrugged, feeling sick. Lying wasn't for the fainthearted, and from hereon in her life would become one big lie. Still, she'd done far worse than lie. Pale-lashed eyes were swiftly blinked away and the sliver of doubt over her subterfuge squashed as she thought of Juniper and smiled sweetly. 'It's a small world.'

'I reckon you got gumption, but I'll tell you what, I love Miz Caroline, Mr Declan and Miz Juniper. They're my family. I wouldn't let anybody hurt them.'

Winnie gave Maudie no chance to reply – though she didn't know what she would have said anyway – turning on her heel and striding from the room. 'Come on upstairs. Miz Caroline is waiting for you in the nursery.'

They returned to the hallway, where Winnie gestured to Maudie's case. 'Might as well take that up to your room first instead of leaving it there to clutter up the entrance.'

Maudie picked up her case and followed Winnie as she sprang up the wide sweep of stairs to the second floor, where she was shown to her small but ample room. She caught the strains of Mrs Kinsella's voice from the room next door, and her heart lifted. She was next door to the nursery!

She stepped inside and put her case down beside the dresser. It wasn't dissimilar to her room at Aunt Annie's, and along with the dresser, there was an iron bed made up with white linen and covered by a pretty lemon quilt, a washstand with a pitcher and jug, and a writing desk. The latter was positioned near the window, and Maudie, ignoring Winnie huffing in the doorway, crossed to see what view she'd been afforded. She was delighted to find a charming courtyard below. She could smell the magnolia flowers from the blooming tree, and if she were to stretch out a hand, she could pick one of its boat-like white petals.

Maudie closed her eyes and breathed in its fragrance, aware of the tinkling water from the fountain below and treasuring the sense of peace at finally being under the same roof as her child once more. Then she abandoned the view and hurried from the room, eager to see Juniper, noticing the navy skirt and high-necked blouse she'd be expected to wear in her new role hanging on the back of the door as she did.

'Miz Caroline and Mr Declan's bedroom is on the other side of the nursery to yours,' Winnie supplied, tapping on the nursery door.

Maudie felt as though every part of her was tingling because on the other side of that door was her daughter, and from hereon in, she'd get to spend each and every day with her.

As she stood cooling her heels, she became aware of Winnie's eyes on her and reminded herself to be careful. Maudie was certain the housekeeper already felt something was off about her story. She'd come this far – she couldn't risk arousing her suspicions further.

43

'Come in.' There was a smile in Mrs Kinsella's voice, and she looked toward Winnie and Maudie as they stepped into the light, airy children's room, which had pastel-coloured walls and fluttering muslin drapes. 'Welcome to Millard House, Maudie,' Mrs Kinsella said, echoing her husband.

She was sitting on a rug with her legs curled to one side. She looked girlish and frail, Maudie thought, taking in the toys strewn around her before her gaze locked on Juniper. She was sitting up and holding a book to her dribbling mouth, those blue eyes – so like her father's – staring at the newcomers.

'Thank you, Mrs Kinsella. Hello, Juniper. How are you?' Maudie crouched down. 'I met Mr Kinsella when I arrived.'

'She came to the front door, Miz Caroline.'

Again, Maudie would have liked to have poked her tongue out at the housekeeper, but if Winnie expected an outraged reaction, she didn't get one.

'Now, Winnie, I'm sure Declan was delighted to make Maudie's acquaintance.'

'I assured him I'll take the best care of Juniper, Mrs Kinsella.'

'I don't doubt it. My poor angel baby is suffering with her toothy-pegs coming through, and she was fractious in the night. It took me forever to soothe her to sleep.'

Maudie felt her insides twist at the thought of another woman comforting her baby when she woke crying in the night. Despite this, she couldn't find it in her to feel animosity for her new employer, who looked as though she could benefit from a good long rest.

'I don't mind telling you what a blessed relief it is to have you here to help, especially on those nights when this lil darlin' won't settle, which I'm afraid is most nights.'

Juniper babbled, and Maudie imagined if she could talk, she'd tell them that they wouldn't sleep either if they were cutting teeth.

'It's been a struggle. Motherhood is much more challenging than I imagined it would be.' Caroline's sigh was deep. 'I'm worn slap out.'

'Now you're not the first new momma to feel that way, Miz Caroline, and if I had my way, you'd have taken me up on my offer to sleep in Nanny Bea's ol' room so I could get up in the night with Juniper and you could get a good night's sleep.'

The casualness with which Winnie addressed Mrs Kinsella was going to take some getting used to as well, Maudie thought. Her discord of moments earlier vanished upon hearing she would be expected to see to Juniper each night. Nothing would give her more pleasure than breathing in the scent of her daughter as she cradled her close in the still of night when it was just the two of them.

'You've a short memory, Winnie. I did accept your offer, and if you cast your mind back, you had as much luck getting our lil love back to sleep as I do. And we were both snappier than a turtle on a hot rock the next morning. Besides, I've told you a child needs her momma when she's crying in the night, and failing that she needs her nanny. I should know. Nanny Bea always came running when I hollered. Maudie's got the magic touch. You'll see. She'll have Junebug sleeping all through the night in no time. Won't you, Maudie?'

'I'll certainly do my best, Mrs Kinsella.' Maudie reached out and stroked Juniper's rosy red cheek.

'If you don't mind, Miz Caroline, I've things to be getting on with,' Winnie sniffed.

'Of course, but perhaps after Maudie's had a chance to get reacquainted with Juniper, you or Birdie could give her a tour of the house?'

'I already have.' Winnie looked to Maudie, her expression unreadable. 'If you need to ask anything, you'll find me in the kitchen. I've chicken pieces that need soaking in buttermilk. Lord only knows where Birdie's at. I tasked her with changing the bed linen, and I declare she must have got lost in those sheets, she's taking that long.'

Mrs Kinsella's laughter tinkled forth. 'I'm afraid our Birdie not only has two left feet; she has a penchant for daydreaming.'

'Your momma wouldn't have stood for it, Miz Caroline. She'd have had a hissy fit, and you know it.'

Mrs Kinsella's sigh was weary. 'You're probably right.'

'I surely am.' She flounced off.

'I'm afraid dear Winnie yearns for the ol' days when we had a butler, a lady's maid, a cook, a coachman and a gardener, but Declan's modern in his thinking, and times have changed. He can't stand being waited on hand and foot. Besides, it was high time they all retired when my momma and poppa passed on. As for Winnie, Millard House is the only home she's ever known, so it was only natural she should stay on when we moved in. We employed Lizzie, Birdie's older sister, to help her out.'

She noticed Juniper was now attempting to stuff the book in her mouth, so she took it off her, amused, as she told the little girl determinedly grabbing for it, 'Books aren't for eating, Junebug; they're for Momma to read to you.'

'Momma.' The word rang in Maudie's ears.

She picked up a teddy bear lying nearby and made it do a little dance that saw her daughter's eyes light up, the book forgotten as she reached for the bear, which Maudie gave to her. The poignancy of this being the first time she'd handed her child a toy hit her, and she kept her face hidden from Mrs Kinsella.

After giving the bear to Juniper, Maudie noticed a toybox behind her, fit to burst. So many playthings, and not one of them from her. To distract herself, she took stock of the nursery.

A brush and comb set displayed on a shelf caught her attention. Until this moment, she hadn't thought about faith, but the silverware – christening gifts perhaps – saw her ponder what denomination the Kinsellas were. She'd assumed they must be Catholic given the adoption had been arranged by the Reverend Mother.

Caroline tracked her gaze. 'Juniper was baptised into the Catholic faith at the Cathedral of St John the Baptist in Lafayette Square a few weeks after we returned from Ireland. I was raised in the Baptist faith, but Declan is Catholic. We caused quite the scandal when we became engaged, and I converted to Catholicism after we married, much to my parents' consternation. But I love God and my husband. To me that's all that matters. They came round in the end. It's impossible not to love a man as good as Declan. Unfortunately, Declan's family don't feel that way about me.'

Maudie might have sympathised, given her parents' dislike of Ronan and what he stood for, but in that moment she couldn't see beyond her pain at neither of them having been at their own baby's baptism. She had no claims to this child legally; they'd been stolen from her, and right then she resented Caroline Kinsella deeply.

'Are you feeling all right, Maudie? You've gone quite pale.'

'Yes, I'm fine,' Maudie fibbed, busying herself with entertaining Juniper, whose laugh as she pulled silly faces at her eased the throb of resentment.

Until Ronan came and they made a new life somewhere just the three of them, she would have no rights where Juniper was concerned. She was an unwed mother, deemed unfit to raise a child in the eyes of the Church and society. Whereas Mrs Kinsella was more than acceptable, with her husband, grand home and money. It was as if the nine months she'd stroked her belly, whispering her hopes and dreams for the child she was carrying had been wiped away, and this both angered her and cut her to the quick. She'd been erased from her own baby's story.

Maudie couldn't change what had happened though, and she was here now, back in her daughter's life, where she belonged. She owed it to Ronan to bide her time.

'You've such a way with her,' Mrs Kinsella said, before filling her in on Juniper's current routine, which the baby girl seemed to change on a daily basis. She fetched her hanky and coughed into it, apologising in a raspy voice, then suggested Maudie go and change into her uniform so she could begin her nannying duties officially.

44
———

The tartan picnic rug was spread out on the grass, the remains of the leftover fried chicken Winnie had whipped up, along with slices of her pound cake, now packed away. Maudie had enjoyed the simple alfresco lunch but was aware that Mrs Kinsella had merely picked at hers. Still, it wasn't her place to point out that the sparrows had eaten more than her employer had.

Juniper, who'd taken to solid food like a duck to water, was also crawling these days and had no interest in sitting on the rug and playing with her toys. Her attention had been caught by a butterfly, and she was scrambling after it, getting grass stains on her plump knees. Every now and then, she'd sit back on her haunches and clap as the butterfly danced overhead, then she'd open her hands as though expecting the butterfly to be there. Maudie and Mrs Kinsella, sitting on a wooden bench, watched in amusement, and when Juniper burst into a fit of giggles for reasons known only to herself, they exchanged a glance of mutual pleasure.

'Isn't that just the best sound you ever heard, Maudie?'

'It is, Mrs Kinsella.'

'She's like a different child since you came to stay.'

'I don't know that I can take the credit for that. I think her good humour is because she finally cut those bothersome teeth.'

Juniper had slept right through two nights in a row now, and while Maudie herself felt like a new woman for a full night's sleep, she also missed those quiet moments in the dark alone with her daughter.

'You may be right, but I feel happier since you moved into Millard House.'

Maudie, surprised by the compliment, wasn't sure how to reply other than with honesty. 'Thank you, Mrs Kinsella. I couldn't be happier.' Then, thinking of Ronan, her lip trembled because she hadn't been honest after all. She could feel the other woman studying her, reading her mind.

'Tell me, Maudie how did you meet your sweetheart?'

Maudie was frightened there would come a day when she'd no longer be able to conjure Ronan's face at a whim, but he came to her then, and she could see him in her mind's eye so clearly she felt she could have reached out and touched him. Her hand shook, wanting to do just that, but stayed in her lap as she sucked in air. Why hadn't he come for her?

'I'm sorry. I don't mean to pry. I understand it must be painful for you to talk about him.'

Ronan's darkly handsome features began to fragment until there was nothing before her but Juniper, still determinedly going after her butterfly. That baby girl was everything, but still, Maudie's heart ached for Ronan.

She was torn between wanting to talk about him and guilt that when he found her, she would take the child who'd brought this woman and her husband so much joy from them. It terrified her that her happiness would come at the cost of others, and the longer it took for Ronan to make his way to her and their baby, the muddier the waters grew because how could she have her happy ever after knowing she'd broken Mrs Kinsella's heart?

'It might help to talk about him.'

Her throat was tight, and her voice didn't feel like her own as she said, 'I miss him dreadfully.'

'Those we love and lose in this life are only ever around the corner from us, dear.'

Maudie felt Mrs Kinsella's hand on hers and was touched by the gesture, the gentle warmth of it teasing the story from her. 'I can't remember a time I didn't know Ronan. Life's like that in an Irish village, but I do remember how the way I saw him changed the day he shoved JP Hennessy over in my defence. JP was an awful bully who'd taunted me one too many times about my witchy red hair and freckles for Ronan's liking.' Saying JP's name out loud after all this time made her skin prickle. 'Ronan didn't return my adoration – well, not at first. I was just the girl who'd trail after him with a lovelorn look on her face. I had to wait until I'd turned eighteen for him to see me as a young woman he could love.'

'Men can be slow on the uptake,' Caroline replied, making Maudie smile.

'He told me he fell in love with me the day I slid a tin of beans to him across the counter of the grocer's shop where I was working.'

Mrs Kinsella laughed, and Juniper momentarily forgot her butterfly, looking over at her and joining in. 'I do declare, Maudie, that isn't the most romantic story I've ever heard.'

Maudie joined in with the laughter, seeing the humour in her story now, which for some reason made things even funnier – until Mrs Kinsella's laugh turned to a rasping cough, alarming Maudie.

She filled a jelly jar with iced tea. 'Here, sip this.'

Mrs Kinsella's hand was shaking as she took the cup, and after several slow sips interspersed with wheezing, she gradually regained her equilibrium.

Juniper had gone back to her exploring, her attention now

fixed on the azalea bushes, and it saddened Maudie that the little girl was so used to Mrs Kinsella's coughing that she no longer seemed to hear it.

The two women sat in silence, swatting at the odd cheeky mosquito flying too close, and Maudie longed to ask Mrs Kinsella how she'd met her husband but felt it would be too impertinent to ask her outright.

'Were your people happy with your match?'

'No. I can't say they were. Maybe if we'd been living in peaceful times, in a free Ireland, they might have viewed Ronan more kindly, but they were frightened he'd bring trouble upon the family.'

'In mine and Declan's case, it was fear of scandal. We didn't meet like most of my peers – there was no dance card marked at a cotillion. In fact, it was as unromantic as it gets. We've a lot in common, you and I.'

Caroline Kinsella's words were light, but they sent a flush creeping up Maudie's neck because never a truer word had been said.

Her eyes cut to Juniper. 'No, Juniper.' Maudie got up, the grass soft and spongy beneath her feet, and took the petals from the little girl's vice-like grip, then picked her up and plopped her down on the rug. She sat there looking about, as if perplexed as to how she'd come to be there, while Maudie returned to the bench, hopeful Mrs Kinsella would continue her story.

'The first time I saw Declan he'd called to the house with papers my daddy needed to sign. He was understudying my daddy's banker, who was older than the hills and due to retire. I thought Declan was the most handsome man I'd ever laid eyes on, but I think he was too intimidated by my daddy to notice me. Winnie was with me when I orchestrated "accidentally" bumping into him outside his place of work as he took his lunch break. Being a Southern gentleman, he was too polite not to invite me to join him for lunch. Winnie said she had errands to run and left us alone.'

Maudie was listening raptly.

'Do you think me terribly conniving?'

'I'd say resourceful.'

Mrs Kinsella smiled. 'That's exactly what I told Winnie, who thought I was being terribly forward. Still, she was my partner in crime – she helped me come up with all manner of excuses to meet up with Declan after that initial luncheon. I'd never have been allowed to court him, or him me, what with him being a Catholic and me a Baptist. But, Maudie, you and I both know the heart wants what the heart wants.'

'It does,' Maudie murmured, glad Winnie wasn't in earshot because she was certain she wouldn't approve of their conversation. Was she overstepping the line between employee and employer by even listening like this? She was the nanny, after all, not one of Mrs Kinsella's fine lady friends. Despite these thoughts, she couldn't resist adding, 'And you and Mr Kinsella lived happily ever after.'

'No, child, we didn't. There was heartbreak and plenty of it.'

'Oh, I'm sorry. I didn't know.' Maudie sat up a little straighter.

'How could you know? I lost babies, Maudie. Four of them, one after the other, before I was even three months gone. My body wouldn't hold on to them. The doctor told me I had a weak constitution and my heart wasn't strong enough to continue trying for a baby. It nearly broke me. I wanted so badly to be a mama and to give Declan a child to love because we had far too much of it for just the two of us. And then a miracle happened. Juniper. I knew the moment I held her in my arms I'd love that child as though she were my own for the rest of my days.'

Maudie reached up and touched her face. It was wet. She'd

had so many preconceptions of this woman – that she was a baby snatcher for one – but how could she feel anything but tenderness toward someone who loved her daughter as much as she did.

'Don't cry.' Mrs Kinsella patted her hand once more. 'I did get my happy ending.'

Maudie wiped her cheeks with the backs of her hands, and they both looked to where Juniper was entranced by the swaying Spanish moss overhead.

'I think you and I will be good friends, don't you?'

Maudie smiled. 'I'd like that, Mrs Kinsella.'

45

In the blink of an eye, Juniper's first birthday was looming, and in the months Maudie had been living at Millard House something wonderful had happened, tempered by something none of them wanted to accept. Maudie had discovered it was possible for a child to have more than one mother and had come to understand it was impossible for a child to have too much love. Families weren't all built the same, and they were her family now: the Kinsellas; Winnie, who'd finally begun to thaw where she was concerned; and Birdie, who no longer tripped over her feet since Mr Kinsella – every bit as kind and generous as Maudie's first impression of him had suggested – had insisted she get her eyes tested, which meant she now wore glasses.

Mrs Kinsella had been adamant Maudie address her as Caroline since their picnic in the square. Birdie too, though the younger girl had refused, saying it wouldn't be right. As with Cecelia at St Patrick's, Maudie and Mrs Kinsella were bonded by motherhood, despite their different backgrounds, even if Caroline Kinsella was unaware of it. Either way, Millard House had become home. Then there was Aunt Annie, who was like a mother to her and a grandmother to Juniper, whom the pair of them visited every week.

None of which meant there wasn't still hope in her heart that Ronan would soon be part of her new family. They'd find a way to make it work. When he finally came for her, she prayed he'd understand why she could never leave her position at Millard House because to do so would be to take Juniper away from a home filled with more love than she could ever have imagined for their child. Somehow it would all work out, she reassured herself as she lay in bed listening to the crickets.

Nora's letters arrived regularly, and Maudie would tear them open and scan the pages for Ronan's name, her shoulders slumping when it didn't leap out at her. Then she'd reread the letter properly, savouring the updates about Nora, Martin and their children, along with the rest of family. Her thoughts strayed to Cecelia and little Nessa every day too, along with all the other girls at St Patrick's. Guilt plagued her that Cecelia, despite Maudie's parting promise to her, was still trapped in that terrible place. Cecelia had nowhere else to go and she'd never leave without Nessa. She'd had no reply from Sister Louise as yet, so she'd written again regularly, begging for her help, and would keep doing so.

Sometimes, Maudie felt as though her whole life was a lie festering with secrets, and one day she hoped to bury the past because she was building a good life in Savannah. It was where her heart belonged and where she'd stay, waiting for Ronan.

None of these thoughts were on her mind this morning, however, as she jiggled Juniper – who had a strong independent streak – on her hip. She was bringing her into the parlour as Mrs Kinsella had requested and was surprised to see Mr Kinsella standing with his back to her, staring out the window, which overlooked the live oaks in Chatham Square. Strangely, he didn't acknowledge their presence, but his wife – seated beside him at the writing desk – spun round in her seat when she heard Juniper cry out, 'Mama, Dada.'

The little girl's limited vocabulary consisted of Mama, Dada, Nay-Nay for Maudie, Wah for Winnie, and for Birdie she'd make a sort of chirping sound, like the birds that fascinated her. It made them all smile to hear it. She brought joy on a daily basis.

Maudie set her down so she could crawl over to the busy chinoiserie bird-scene wallpaper that Caroline had confided had fascinated her when she was little too. *This room's filled with happy memories of my parents, Maudie, she'd said. And that there wallpaper was imported all the way from China at Mama's request. I used to find a new bird in it each time I looked at it and thought for sure it had to be a magic wallpaper.*

For Maudie's part, Millard House was a far cry from the spartan cottage by the coast where she'd been born. Aunt Annie had drummed into her how she should never forget where she came from, no matter how lofty the heights she might scale, because the higher the climb, the further the fall. The Southerners had a saying that summed it up nicely, she'd told her, and it had stuck in Maudie's mind. *You could be a rooster one day and a feather duster the next.*

Juniper, on all fours and midway to the wall, gave a piercing shriek of excitement when she saw the warm body brushing against Maudie's bare calf: Biscuit, a one-eared, scruffy ginger tomcat. She looked around for Gravy, his sandy-coloured sister, who was never usually far behind, but there was no sign of her.

Biscuit and Gravy were partners in crime. After being abandoned, they'd decided to make Millard House home a few months back, and their names, though at odds with their colouring, made sense given that the first time they'd inadvertently made their presence known was when Winnie had caught them helping themselves to the buttermilk biscuits and sausage gravy she served up each Sunday morning.

The little girl did an about-turn and gave chase, ever hopeful of pulling the scruffy cat's tail. Biscuit, having been burned once before, was faster, however, and shot up to the safety of Caroline Kinsella's lap, where he flopped down, front paws hanging over the side of her green cotton dress like a leopard resting in a tree as he waited to be petted.

'He's a naughty, plump lump, so he is, and he'll get cat hair all over your pretty dress, Caroline,' Maudie tutted.

Biscuit fixed a beady eye on Maudie while he revelled in Caroline scratching behind the ragged remains of his right ear. It was strange, Maudie thought fleetingly – Mr Kinsella had yet to turn from window.

The thought drifted away at the sight of Juniper now trying to grab the rainbow shards falling on the timber boards by her mother's feet. Caroline's engagement ring, which these days seemed too big for her finger, was catching the mellow morning light, creating a colourful floor show.

'It won't be long until she's up on her feet. There'll be no stopping her then.' Maudie smiled at the little girl indulgently. 'We'll all of us need eyes in the back of our head then, so we will, Caroline.'

Then she shifted uncomfortably, wondering if the reason Mr Kinsella was still standing at the window like a soldier saluting was because they'd had a marital row. It would be a first if that was the case.

She turned her questioning gaze on Caroline, alarmed by the sadness she saw flickering in her eyes. But then, with a blink, it was gone, and it was as if Maudie hadn't spoken. 'Where's Gravy got to then?' she asked.

'I've just finished making the beds, ma'am, and the last I saw of her, she was tracking straight for the sunny spot on the end of your bed.' Birdie had entered the room and came to stand alongside Maudie. 'It don't matter how many times I pick her up and carry her out of there, she trots straight back in like she owns the place.'

Caroline began to cough then, so Biscuit shot off her lap and charged from the room, causing Winnie, who had one foot in the door, to squeal as if a mouse had run past her.

'That ornery cat!' Winnie regained her composure and bustled into the room. 'Those party invitations piled high on your desk there won't write themselves, Caroline – not unless your fountain pen has magic powers.'

Her tone was short, but Maudie knew her well enough now to pick up on what lay beneath it – fear. The annoying cough Caroline had been unable to shake had worsened rapidly since Maudie had come to stay, and she'd realised something else: Mr Kinsella's shoulders were shuddering now. She glanced to Birdie and Winnie, who she could see had no clue as to why they'd been summoned here. From their expressions, they were as wary as she was.

Caroline, meanwhile, wiped her mouth with her handkerchief then swiftly balled it up out of sight. 'Winnie Jackson, I do declare you're about as patient as a gnat at a picnic, and don't you be fretting. I'll get them written. Junebug's first birthday party is going to be the talk of Savannah. Sure, Declan here will tell you the same thing.'

Mr Kinsella turned around then – slowly. His eyes were rimmed with red, and there was a slump to his shoulders as he moved to rest a hand on his wife's delicate shoulder.

'It will be – you can count on it,' he said, the enthusiasm he injected sounding forced.

His wife gave a small nod then, and Maudie wanted to turn and run from the room because the nausea in the pit of her stomach was telling her she didn't want to hear what he had to say next.

It was too late, however; he was already speaking, 'Winnie,

Maudie, Birdie, I'm afraid Caroline and I... well, we've some bad news to tell you.'

The only sound was the creeping ivy, embedded in the porous bricks of Millard House, rustling at the edges of the window, as if trying to get inside. Juniper, perhaps picking up on the sombre mood of the adults, abandoned her rainbows and sat quietly staring up at her father.

'Caroline has tuberculosis.'

As if she understood her mama was sick, Juniper crawled toward her, but Caroline shrank in her seat and raised a hand to ward her off. 'No. She mustn't come near me!' Her voice was shrill.

Juniper stopped and looked up at her mama, startled by her reaction, while Caroline burst into noisy tears. Maudie stepped forward then picked Juniper up and held her close.

'Take her away, Miz Maudie,' Mr Kinsella pleaded. 'Please.'

Caroline's broken-hearted sobs at no longer being able to hold her child echoed in Maudie's ears as she hurried from the room before her own tears fell.

46

True to her word, Caroline Kinsella sent the invitations for Juniper's party out the very next day, and the cards of acceptance piled up on her writing desk soon after. But it was as if Mr Kinsella, having said tuberculosis out loud, had conjured the disease like an evil djinn because Caroline had been confined to bed, having insisted on moving to a guest room, since her diagnosis. On the morning of Juniper's first birthday, however, she rallied.

The party was to be held in the parlour that afternoon, and Maudie and Maisie spent part of the morning draping the crepe-paper streamers they'd made in quieter moments, while Winnie beavered away in the kitchen. Maisie had been in charge of filling the vases with fresh flowers, while Maudie lay the two tables – one for the children and another for the adults – draping an Irish lace cloth over the latter. Then it had been all hands on deck in the kitchen.

At first, it had seemed to Maudie that all this fuss and expense to hold a party Juniper wouldn't even remember was a waste of the ailing Caroline's precious little energy. The way she'd taken it upon herself to ensure everything ran like clockwork on the big day was ridiculous, yet for someone wasting away before their eyes, she issued instructions like a sergeant major, and Maudie, Winnie and Birdie had been run off their feet, with barely a moment to themselves in the days leading up to it. But as they'd busied themselves in the kitchen, the night before the party, it had been Winnie who'd pointed out the method behind Caroline's madness.

'She wants to take all our minds off her being sick, and the only way she knows how to do that is by keeping us busy,' she'd said, slathering buttercream over the bottom layer of the birthday cake she'd baked earlier.

'It has been a tonic – not having to think, I mean,' Birdie had piped up from where she was churning the ice cream.

Maudie had been thoughtful for a moment as she'd continued peeling the hard-boiled eggs she'd been charged with mashing for the sandwiches. Then it had dawned on her. 'This party's not about Juniper at all.'

'Yes it is.' Birdie had bristled, resting her arm for a moment. 'How can you say it's not when it's her first birthday?'

'Hear her out, Birdie,' Winnie had chided.

'What I mean to say is Juniper's birthday is the excuse to hold the party, but it's not because Caroline wants a big fuss for her. Rather, she wants to give us all something to focus on and to remember her by.' Because she was a kind woman who put others' needs before her own.

'Maudie's right. And one day, when she's older and can understand, Juniper will be able to look at the photographs taken on her birthday and see for herself how much her mama loved her,' Winnie had added.

Her use of the past tense hadn't escaped Maudie's notice.

Mr Kinsella brought his wife through to the parlour shortly before the first guests were due to begin arriving. He helped settle Caroline on the sofa, telling her she looked pretty as a peach. Then Maudie passed Juniper to her father, the skirt of her dress caught up in her cardigan in the process. Maudie had dressed her that morning in the peter-pan-collared, pastel-pink cotton dress Caroline had chosen for her with a matching cardigan beneath which she had on a pair of wool stockings. The silver bracelet on her wrist was engraved with her name, a birthday gift from her parents.

'And as for you, well, you're sweet as sugar and twice as nice,' Declan declared, arranging Juniper in his arms.

'Her skirt, Declan,' Caroline pointed out.

He pulled it down while the photographer set his camera up on a tripod then instructed Maudie, Winnie and Birdie where to stand in relation to the Kinsellas. At last, they were posed to his satisfaction.

'Look lively!' he said, and the snap of the shutter was swallowed by the parp of a motor car pulling up, signalling the party was about to get underway.

Mrs Kinsella was helped to a chair by an open window and a blanket draped over her lap. She clasped a handkerchief watching from afar as guests trickled in, queenlike and aloof.

In no time at all, the parlour was abuzz with conversations and filled with overexcited children charging about in frilly dresses and sailor suits. Declan held court to the gentle swell of 'The Blue Danube' waltz on the gramophone. Meanwhile, the birthday girl, who'd quickly become overwhelmed by all the fawning attention, had decided to bury her face in her Nay-Nay's shoulder, refusing to acknowledge any other well-wishers, gift or no gift. Maudie caught Caroline's weary eye and fancied she'd happily do the same to her husband if she could.

The photographer was sure to freeze-frame the various guests as they milled about, and he took aim at the children, their excited eyes flitting to the buttercream-filled birthday cake in the centre of their table, eagerly anticipating a slice.

Laughter and a smattering of applause sounded as Juniper roused herself long enough to jam a wedge of cake in her mouth.

As the festivities began to wind down, Mr Kinsella surprised them all with a song, his melodic baritone bringing a tear to more than one pair of eyes as he serenaded his wife and child with 'Let Me Call You Sweetheart'. When the song reached its conclusion, everybody pretended not to notice the violent coughing fit that wracked Mrs Kinsella's frail body – or what it meant.

47

Maudie saw the ghostly figure of a man in uniform for the first time one month after Juniper's first birthday. She woke in the depths of the night feeling chilled, despite her bedcovers being tucked around her. Assuming she'd left the window open, she tossed them aside, intending to get up and close it. But as she sat up, her arms pimpled with goosebumps, and she became aware of a strong draught.

She took a moment to allow her eyes to adjust to the darkness. Maudie expected to see the curtains fluttering, but instead her lips parted and her jaw dropped in a silent scream – beside the window stood a soldier, his form flimsy, but yet frighteningly clear.

Juniper! She had to save Juniper!

She wanted to run next door to the nursery, but fear had immobilised her, and she couldn't tear her eyes away from the otherworldly apparition. She felt as if a blanket of sadness had been tossed over her. It was mixed with an equally unsettling sense of foreboding, and she knew instinctively that he'd come to warn her. But of what?

Before she could make sense of what she was experiencing,

however, he began to fade, and soon it was as though he'd never appeared to her in the first place. The room returned to its usual temperature, and Maudie wondered if she'd been dreaming. It was so real, yet how could it have been?

Wide awake now and no longer frightened, she checked on Juniper, relieved to see she was sleeping soundly. Trying to convince herself her subconscious had conjured the entity, she slipped back between the sheets and closed her eyes.

Morning rolled around far too soon; when she prised open her gritty eyes, Maudie felt like she'd only nodded off minutes ago. The milky light of dawn greeted her, and then she heard Juniper calling for her, which was no surprise given she always woke with the birds.

'You just missed Caleb with the bread delivery.' Birdie smirked over at Maudie from where she was dishing up breakfast for the three women.

Maudie pulled a face at her as she sat at the table. Birdie slid a bowl of creamy grits under her nose.

'Winnie, come and have your breakfast. He was asking after you, Maudie; Winnie will tell you the same.'

Winnie, doing three things at once at the counter, replied, 'He's sweet on you – ain't no mistaking that.' After finishing her tasks, she took the bowl Birdie had scraped out and sat at the table.

Birdie, spoon halfway to her mouth, even though she was still beside the stove, giggled.

'Well, I'm not sweet on him. I've no time for a man in my life.' That wasn't true, but Maudie couldn't imagine her heart ever belonging to anyone except Ronan.

It was only a matter of time now until Birdie married her beau, and as annoying as she could be, she'd be a loss they'd feel keenly in the Kinsella household. As for Winnie, well, like Maudie, she had her secrets too. Her good friend Esther for one, whose husband had run off, leaving her to raise their young daughter, Sarah. Winnie visited them on her day off, often staying over. Maudie suspected that Esther and Winnie's relationship was more than just a friendship – not that she'd ever mention this to Winnie, just as the housekeeper had never breathed a word about her inklings as to who Maudie really was to Juniper. It was an unspoken agreement between the two of them that some things were better left unsaid.

'Everybody needs a sweetheart, Maudie,' Birdie chided.

'Not me.'

'If you say so,' Winnie said.

'I do.' Maudie imagined Winnie was secretly pleased Maudie professed no interest in men because she wouldn't wish to lose her too.

She recalled her dream then and relayed it to them, partially to change the subject but also in the hope that Birdie and Winnie would pooh-pooh it as a nightmare of sorts.

Winnie dropped her spoon in the bowl with a clatter. 'That weren't no dream, Maudie.'

Birdie, meanwhile, had pressed herself back into the stove and crossed herself.

Maudie felt a cold trickle of fear drip down her spine.

'That was George who came to see you. I ain't never seen him myself, but Birdie's sister Lizzie did. She left not long after.'

Birdie nodded furiously, sending her glasses sliding down her nose. 'Lizzie was always teasing me growing up, and with me due to replace her when she married and left Millard House, I decided she'd made up the story of a ghost haunting Millard House to frighten me.'

'I don't understand.' Maudie swung pendulum-like between Winnie and Maudie. 'Who's George?'

Winnie was too busy praying so left it to Birdie to explain.

'Millard House was commandeered for Union soldiers' quarters some sixty years ago, after Sherman's army captured Savannah. Ain't no one knows for sure who that poor soldier is or who decided to call him George, but what is certain is he only appears when someone's about to die. The last time he showed himself was when Lizzie saw him, and Miz Caroline's parents passed soon after.'

The three women looked at one another. They all knew what George had come to tell Maudie.

The Kinsellas left quietly for the Banks County sanitorium the next day. The sky was filled with storm clouds, and the last words Caroline Kinsella managed to rasp to Maudie as she was carried from her home to the waiting Buick were, 'I can go in peace knowing our dear lil Junebug has you, Maudie.'

48

The funeral of Mrs Caroline Kinsella was held in Bonaventure Cemetery, the statue chosen to watch over her the tallest angel in the avenue of graves. It was a solemn affair under a solemn sky, arranged by her husband, who hunched over the hole in the ground where her casket had been lowered, consumed by his grief. A who's who of handkerchief-clutching Savannah women and their menfolk, the three remaining women of Millard House, and a bewildered and fractious Juniper, who couldn't possibly understand the significance of the occasion, were also in attendance.

Birdie said she felt like she was wading through molasses in the days following their final goodbye to the lady of the house. Maudie thought this summed up exactly how grieving felt, and she wished she could close her ears to Juniper's plaintive cries for her mama and Winnie's mutterings of, 'It ain't over. There's more coming. I can feel it.' Mr Kinsella chose to bury his grief in his work. leaving the house early and coming home late.

All the while, the black clouds continued to hover over Savannah, and while George might have given Maudie, Winnie and Birdie an inkling that Mrs Kinsella's time had come, they weren't prepared for the knock on the front door just shy of a month later.

It was Winnie who opened it to a policeman, clad in a navy wool uniform, cap in hand. His voice was grave as he explained there'd been a terrible accident earlier that morning as Mr Kinsella walked to his offices. It seemed he'd stepped off the pavement and straight into the path of an oncoming motor car. 'I'm sorry to tell you he died at the scene, and I have to say, ma'am, it's a mystery t'me how he never saw that car coming.'

The three women chose to believe it was an accident, that Mr Kinsella had simply been blinded by grief, and they found comfort in the thoughts of the couple being together again, at peace.

Maudie, despite her broken heart, did her best to keep wading through that sea of molasses, as did Winnie, aware it was what the Kinsellas would have wanted for poor little Juniper. Birdie, however, had gone to pieces upon hearing the news, and when she'd wrung her hands, declaring Juniper a poor little orphan child, Winnie had slapped her just hard enough to bring her to her senses.

'She's no orphan child while she has us. Ain't that right, Maudie?'

Maudie nodded. Juniper had lost her parents, but she still had her mother and the love of Winnie, Birdie and Aunt Annie. She wasn't alone.

Declan Kinsella's three sisters – with what Winnie sniffed were their 'highfalutin ideas' and 'husbands far too big for their britches' – descended on Millard House like locusts as soon as word of their brother's passing reached their ears. Ironic given none of them had visited since his scandalous mixed-religion engagement to Caroline Millard years earlier. The sisters had begun quibbling over who would take what before the first handful of earth was thrown on his coffin, which was buried next to his wife's, and not once was Juniper's welfare mentioned.

The thought of what would happen to her child and herself, along with Winnie, compounded Maudie's grief. With a wedding on the horizon, Birdie would be all right, although with all the sadness of the Kinsellas' passing, she was talking about postponing it. Maudie had already resolved that if guardianship of Juniper fell to one of the awful sisters, she would snatch her daughter and run. She'd take Winnie with her too, if she'd come. Aunt Annie would help them, although where they'd run to she had no clue, but she wouldn't be separated from Juniper again, no matter what.

Then, three days after Declan Kinsella's burial, Maudie was unexpectedly summoned to the offices of Fry & Farrell, Attorneys at Law for the reading of Declan Kinsella's will that coming Friday.

When Winnie heard this, she steepled her hands to her mouth, eyes glistening as she said she'd known the Kinsellas wouldn't abandon them. Then she launched into a diatribe about God being good and merciful that Maudie tuned out as she pondered why she was to be present. The only conclusion she could draw was that she was Juniper's nanny and therefore to serve as her representative. This unusual turn of events meant she could feel the calculating eyes of the sisters upon her whenever she emerged from the nursery. As for Juniper, she'd begun waking in the night once more, and the smallest things could set her off into wailing fits as she expressed her upset at the disappearance of her parents in the only way she knew how.

So when Friday morning came, Maudie – after a squeeze from Winnie and a hug from Birdie, along with a promise that they'd keep an eye on Juniper, who'd had to be prised from Maudie's arms – dressed in her best blouse and skirt she walked to the lawyer's offices. There'd been no offer of a ride in any of the three motor cars that glided away from the kerb outside

Millard House, despite them all heading to the same destination, though Maudie wouldn't have accepted anyway.

As she hurried along the streets, cloaked in her grief, she was barely aware of the moody sky or the closeness in the air making the tendrils of hair around her face curl.

At 10 a.m. on the dot, she presented herself, flushed and sticky, at the offices of Fry & Farrell, where the secretary led her to a boardroom. She took in the expanse of polished wood, spiralling cigar smoke and the presence of the loathsome sisters and their spouses, who were already seated around the table. Another man – Mr Conrad Fry, presumably – sat at the head of the table and rose to greet Maudie as his secretary shepherded her to the last vacant seat. Maudie thanked her then clasped her hands beneath the table to hide her anxiousness, ignoring the pointed glance at a fob watch from one of Mr Kinsella's brothers-in-law.

Mr Fry was a florid-faced man with a thick white moustache, tinged nicotine yellow at the ends, otherwise it would have matched his sideboards perfectly, and Maudie could see from his generous girth – glimpsed before he sat down once more – that he had a love of home cooking. He proceeded to make a show of opening the folder in front of him, rustling the papers it contained and clearing his throat. All the while, Maudie kept her eyes trained on him, refusing to look at the others gathered, and listened intently as he ran through the formalities.

'Get to the meat and potatoes of it man,' an impatient voice grumbled.

'Hush now, Henry-John. Mr Fry's just doing his job,' a woman – the man's wife, she assumed – replied. Maudie didn't know the sisters or their other halves by name, nor did she wish to.

Mr Fry, however, would not be rushed, and he peered solemnly overtop of his bifocals at every one of the seven parties present. 'I can assure you this won't take long. Mr Kinsella was clear in his instructions.' Then he began to read in a deliberate and precise manner from the legal document he held in front of him.

'"It is mine and my late wife's express wish that Millard House and our entire estate be bequeathed to Miz Maude O'Connor to run as she sees fit until our daughter, Miz Juniper Kinsella, comes of age. This bequest is made upon the condition that Miz Maude O'Connor shall draw a generous allowance while continuing to oversee the upbringing, care and well-being of Miz Juniper Kinsella in all respects until she reaches the age of twenty-one. Winnie Jackson is also to be given a position for life at Millard House."'

Maudie felt faint as someone slammed a fist down on the table.

'The nanny! They've left it all to the nanny and the orphan child.'

A fat finger jabbed in her direction. 'You planned this, strutting in here all gussied up!'

'Why that's – that's cattywampus is what it is!'

'I declare we'll contest the will!'

'If you think you're gonna be livin' in high cotton, girl, you've got another thing coming!'

Mr Fry interrupted the furore by slapping his big hands down on the table. 'I can assure you all as Mr Kinsella's attorney, he might have been grieving when I last saw him, but he was very much of sound mind, and he explained to me that while his wife Mrs Caroline Kinsella's body was ailing' – he tapped his head – 'her mind was not, and that he was making the changes to this, his last will and testament, in accordance with her wishes. As I have already said, his instructions were clear. All that's left for me to do now is congratulate you, Miz O'Connor. The Kinsellas held you in high regard, as is evident in the trust they are placing in you. Mr Kinsella also asked that I should give you this in the event of his passing.'

He produced an envelope, and he heaved himself up from the table in order to pass it to Maudie personally. She took it from him, too stunned by what she'd just heard to thank him.

'It's to be read in private.'

There was nothing further to be gained by sitting at the table, so Maudie left Mr Kinsella's awful siblings and spouses bickering around the table, taking satisfaction from turning on her heel, just before Mr Fry opened the door for her, and imparting her final words to them.

'I'd thank you all to vacate Millard House by midday today.'

She caught the twitching of Mr Fry's mouth beneath his moustache as she nodded good day to him then swept from the building.

Somehow she made her way to the nearby Johnson Square – it was a mystery to Maudie how she'd come to be there, sitting on a bench, her mind whirring with the news she, Juniper and Winnie would remain a family, and Millard House would continue to be their home.

The letter couldn't wait any longer, though she knew Winnie and Birdie were desperately awaiting her return in order to hear their fates. Besides, Mr Fry had said it was to be read alone.

She tore the envelope open and tried to hold the letter it contained steady, her eyes skimming then rereading the words that were Caroline Kinsella's but written in the strong hand of her husband.

Dear Maudie,

I shall get straight to the point. I've always known who you are, from the very first moment you approached me in Chatham Square. I could see it in your face when you caught sight of

Juniper. I knew because the way you looked when you held her was how I felt when Juniper was first placed in my arms. That little girl might not have been born of my body, but she was born of my heart, and I believed she was a precious gift meant to be mine and Declan's – until I saw you. We could never give Juniper up, nor could we deprive a mother of her child, so I decided there and then to invite you back to Millard House in the hope we could find a way to share her, and we did.

You, Winnie and even dear Birdie have been like sisters to me, and I can slip from this world to the next knowing Juniper will be well loved. Declan has assured me that whatever happens, you will remain in Millard House with her, as will dear Winnie.

Please, Maudie, speak of me to her from time to time, and tell her how very much she was loved.

All my love,

Caroline Kinsella

The letter, signed with a spidery flourish, fluttered to Maudie's lap. The couple had known who she was – they'd always known. Of course they had.

49

Six months had passed since the reading of the will. In the immediate aftermath of the funeral, Juniper had constantly asked for her mama and dada, breaking everyone's hearts all over again each time she cried for her parents. At her young age, she couldn't grasp not seeing them again. Time was a great healer, however, and with the passing of the months, the little tot had stopped asking for the Kinsellas. So while the shadows of grief still lurked in the corners of Millard House, Juniper helped keep them at bay with her infectious giggles.

The routines of caring for a child rapidly approaching the age of a busy-bee toddler helped Maudie, Winnie and Birdie – who was married now but still dropped by Millard House most days – forge forward as they clung together. They were a different sort of family but a family all the same.

On this particular blue-skied morning, Maudie was chasing Juniper about the nursery on her hands and knees. She was attempting to get her dressed, and it was slow going. Thus far, all she'd managed was the nappy – or diaper as she'd begun to think of the cloth that kept her child dry – and a pair of socks. All in all, it was a chaotic scene, especially as Biscuit and Gravy had decided to join in. The cats thought it a great game, digging their claws in and shooting up things they'd no business climbing while Maudie shrieked at them to get down and Juniper clapped her hands, laughing. The little girl was surprisingly nimble given how chubby her legs were, and Maudie scrambled for her again.

'Come on now, Junebug. It's a beautiful day for a walk. The sooner you get dressed, the sooner we can enjoy it.' Then she played her ace. 'We could call by Grandma Annie's.' Her daughter loved to visit the woman she called Gamy, who was always sure to give her a treat.

At the mention of her grandma, Juniper plopped obediently down on her backside, and Maudie wasted no time, scooping up the dress she'd picked out and tossing it over her shoulder while Biscuit swung from the curtains and Gravy stared down at them from her bookshelf perch.

As she slipped the dress over Juniper's head and threaded her arms through the sleeves, Maudie smiled. 'Your mama always thought pink was your best colour. She was right too. You're pretty as a picture.'

'Mama gone.'

'She's not gone, Junebug. She's with you here, in your heart.' Maudie put her hand on her heart and then placed it on Juniper's. It beat rapidly beneath her touch from all that running about.

'Jun-pah's heart.'

'That's right.' Maudie knew what was coming.

'And Dada there.'

Maudie smiled. 'Yes.'

'Day-Day too.'

Tears prickled in Maudie's eyes, and she nodded. She'd made a promise to the Kinsellas as she'd said her final goodbye at the cemetery that Juniper would grow up knowing the kind and generous couple who'd loved her so fiercely. She would keep their memory alive, and she spoke of them often to Juniper, just as she did Ronan. She'd decided Day-Day was a good name for him, as Day-Day and Nay-Nay just fitted together. She'd explained he was someone special to them both, but that was where it ended. She would never tell Juniper the truth of her parentage. It would remain buried with the Kinsellas.

Maudie wasn't married, and to announce to Juniper and all and sundry who she really was would be to tar her child with the stigma of illegitimacy. Society wasn't ready to accept the truth, and the need for the truth to be told and acknowledged publicly no longer mattered to Maudie. For all intents and purposes, she was Maudie's mother and Nay-Nay suited her just fine.

She still pined for Ronan. He was her soul mate, and while gentlemen callers sniffed around, eager to court her, she gave each of them short shrift. She'd told Winnie in one of their late-night conversations across the kitchen table that the way she saw it, you only had one soul mate in the world, and hers was out there somewhere, lost in it and unable to get word to her. It was then Winnie had confided the truth about Esther, her own soul mate, confirming Maudie's suspicions. Maudie had just squeezed her hand and smiled – she'd find no judgment from her on the matter.

Winnie had opened up to her, and so Maudie had decided to trust in the woman who had initially eyed her with suspicion but now treated her like a sister. Besides, she was going to need Winnie on board, because Sister Louise had at long last written to her, explaining that she hadn't received the earlier letters – otherwise, she would have responded sooner. The Mother Superior had succumbed to a period of illness, and in her absence, Maudie's last letter had finally reached her. She said she had prayed for God's guidance and would do what she could to help Cecelia and Nessa. There were plans that needed to be put in place to ensure a fresh start in America for them, and Maudie couldn't do it alone, but there was hope now she had Sister Louise on side. Still, she'd need Winnie and Aunt Annie too.

Winnie was no fool, however, and as Maudie had once feared, she'd also known who Maudie was to Juniper all along. She hadn't known the cruelty behind the story of how the Kinsellas had come to adopt the baby girl, though, and she'd wiped her eyes more than once as she'd listened to Maudie's tale. When Maudie had finished unburdening herself, Winnie had wrapped her in a warm embrace that had told Maudie she was exactly where she was supposed to be. Home.

Now, Winnie's voice was shrill. 'Get down from there this minute. Heavens to Betsy, I do declare these cats will be the death of me!' she exclaimed, having appeared in the doorway. She whipped off her shoe and threw it at Biscuit, who scrambled down the curtain and out the door, Gravy hot on his heels. Then she retrieved her shoe, slid it back on and fetched an envelope from her apron pocket. 'A letter came for you, Maudie.'

Juniper broke free from Maudie and stampeded toward Winnie with her arms outstretched. 'Wah!'

Winnie's face lit up as she bent to scoop the little girl up and cuddled her close. 'Good morning to you, lil Junebug.' She covered her head in kisses while Juniper giggled. 'I'll take her downstairs and give her breakfast while you read your letter in peace, Maudie.'

Maudie was grateful, and when she took the envelope from Winnie, she recognised the handwriting on it immediately and smiled. 'It's from Nora. I'll be down shortly. It's looking like it will be such a beautiful day, and I'm eager to sniff the air.' She waved the envelope. 'Thank you for bringing this up to me. Will you be off to see Esther later?'

'It's Wednesday, ain't it? I'll swing by River Street Sweets and pick you up some of that taffy you love so much. I'll be home around four. Esther says next time you and Junebug are to come for lunch. She and Sarah are itching to see you both. No argument.'

'I'd like that. Juniper too – she adores Esther and Sarah.'

Maudie's mouth watered at the thought of the sweet, chewy treat, and with a nod and a smile, she left her dear friend to cart Juniper – now shouting that she was 'hungwy' – downstairs. She settled herself in the chair in the corner of the nursery, eager for a family update.

But the single-page letter wasn't full of her elder sister's usual light and breezy anecdotes of life in Rush. Instead, Nora's words saw Maudie's hand begin to tremble and a cold flush slowly creep through her body.

She'd a strange sense of hovering outside her body, looking down on herself, as she forced herself to read the letter again. When she'd finished, Maudie let the piece of paper flutter to the floor and put her head in her hands. The letter was the death of hope.

50

Maudie's beloved Ronan was dead. Nora had relayed this in a short and straight-to-the-point manner because dressing it up wouldn't change the fact the man she'd loved with her entire being was dead and buried. Her sister had written that Daniel, Ronan's youngest brother, had got word to her, and she'd written to Maudie immediately to relay what he'd conveyed. The Quinn brothers had decided it was safer for them to split up and hide rather than stay together after that dreadful day they'd escaped the burning farm, but it seemed Daniel hadn't stopped looking for Ronan. He was the only brother who'd failed to reunite with him.

His search had led him to a priest's notes and a gravedigger's records, where he'd discovered Ronan's body was buried in an unmarked grave in a small church yard cemetery south of Dublin near Kilternan. He'd been shot and killed only days after he'd fled Rush. Gone, all this time.

Maudie had thought she'd know in her soul if Ronan was gone, but she hadn't, and each sob came in a gasp as she murmured, 'No, no, no.' A rallying cry against the loss of the future they'd planned together.

The lump in her throat threatened to choke her and never allow her to swallow again as she cried too for the father Juniper would never meet. Her body ached with her loss, and in the fog of immediate grief, she thought of who was to blame for what had come to pass and remembered the letter her little sister, Caitie, had written her. The letter she hadn't opened and read as per her promise to Nora until the ship had set sail. She could remember it almost word for word.

Dear Maudie,

I'm writing this letter to you because I think it's only right I own up to you first before I sit in the confessional box and ask Father Doyle for absolution. The truth of the matter is your forgiveness matters more to me than what God thinks, but don't ever tell Mammy I told you so or she'd eat the face off me.

I wish I'd been brave enough to say sorry to your face. I felt so bad in those days before you left home, hearing you crying yourself to sleep. My stomach was in knots with everything I wanted to tell you, but mostly what I wanted to say was I wished I'd been kinder. It's not in my nature, though, not like it is yours and Nora's. I was born with this terrible affliction where things, sometimes mean things, jump out of my mouth before I even know I've said them.

That's another thing I might as well own up to, and I'm not proud of it, but I was always mad with jealousy over how you and Nora were together. I felt left out and even more so when you began stepping out with Ronan Quinn. I'd see you talking to Nora, heads together giggling, and wish I was older so you might include me in your conversations. Maybe that's why I did it. Then again, I don't really know why I did now when I look back on it. I only wish I could go back and change things, but I can't.

I'd been out late playing with my friend Mary-Kate, and I

was on my way home one night when I saw you, Maudie. You were headed for the beach road, and I could tell you were up to something by the way you kept looking back over your shoulder, so I followed you, but then you disappeared into the dunes. That's when I saw Ronan a little way ahead, and when he vanished in the dunes as well, I knew you were still seeing him even after Mammy and Da forbade you from doing so.

I ran home and told Mammy what I'd seen, and I thought you'd be in terrible bother when you got home, and it's awful to admit it, Maudie, but I hoped you would be. When nothing happened, I got so mad that I took to following you all the time, waiting to catch you out. I should have been in school, but I'd convinced the sisters I was poorly, and they sent me home early, the day I saw you rushing out of the grocer's. I trailed after you, and when you reached the bóthar I knew where you were headed. Quinn's Farm. I hid near the path's entrance out of the rain, and then the Tan appeared. I saw him follow you up the bóthar, and I didn't know how to warn you without getting myself in trouble. So I did nothing. I stayed where I was, even though the rain was lashing by then. The shot when it rang out terrified me into movement, and I ran home. I was so frightened, Maudie, when Mammy asked me what had me in such a flap, it was out my mouth what I'd seen and heard before I could stop it.

You arrived home soon after, and it was clear you were sickening, and I tried to forget about it all, but when the Tan's body washed up on the beach, I knew Ronan had killed him. Mammy did too thanks to me. I saw her go to the barracks. It was Mammy who betrayed the Quinns, and if I hadn't told her what I'd seen that afternoon, none of it would have happened.

I hope you can forgive me, Maudie. I hope you can forgive Mammy one day too.

Your loving sister,

Caitie

Maudie knew you couldn't change what had come to pass – trying to would only mean holding on to bitterness and never being happy in the present moment. She forced down a swallow and sniffed. She'd forgiven Caitie for the naivety of her actions the moment she'd screwed her letter up and tossed it out to sea, but her heart was dead to her mother. There were some things you couldn't forgive but could learn to live alongside. To live was what Maudie had to keep doing. She owed it to Ronan to be here in the present, raising their daughter.

Accordingly, she raised her head and whispered, 'I'll never stop loving you, Ronan Quinn, and I promise you I'll raise our daughter to know what a strong, brave and kind man her day-day was.'

Maudie's tear-stained gaze was pulled toward the window, and her lips flickered with a smile when she saw a brown-and-white Carolina wren fluttering there for a moment before it alighted on a branch of the magnolia tree. As it began its strange, whistling tea-kettle song, Maudie knew Ronan was there with them after all. He always had been.

She wiped her cheeks with the backs of her hands before going to blow her nose and splash her face with cold water. Then she ventured downstairs to where Juniper, their daughter, was waiting for her.

51

IRELAND, 1985

Maudie stood outside the gates of St Patrick's Mother and Baby Home, seeing the wild-eyed girl who'd climbed out of the Mother Superior's office window in the deep of night and run away. By coming back here today, she'd come full circle.

St Patrick's was their last stop for today. Tomorrow there would be cups of tea and slices of buttered brack or apple cake as they called in on Caitie and her family, along with those of her younger brothers, all of whom had spread far and wide from Rush. They'd visit Ronan's final resting place in Kilternan too. His grave was no longer unmarked, his brother Daniel having organised a proper headstone to mark where he lay. Maudie, too, had written to the parish priest not long after she'd learned of Ronan's death and, with the help of a generous donation, had secured the church-yard plot next to his. Thus ensuring they'd lie together for eternity. Death didn't frighten her. It simply meant she'd be with Ronan again – finally.

She wasn't dead yet though. The news St Patrick's had been sold for development had reached her ears in Savannah, galvanising her into coming back to Ireland because this was her last chance to speak her truth where it had begun.

Maudie was no longer that beaten and cowed girl, berated into believing she was a fallen woman, and as they made their way arm in arm to the front entrance, there was no fear or apprehension. It was just a building. A building that contained painful memories and sadness, so much sadness, for all the other girls, women and babies it had once housed. She'd tried to help, but... She closed her eyes momentarily, thinking she heard a baby's cry, but it was just the past calling her, telling her it was time.

She turned to the woman by her side, her reason for being, and took in the features so dear to her. As she'd grown, they'd taken on a curious mix of hers and Ronan's. She reminded Maudie of Ronan in lots of ways too, especially when she got the bit between her teeth for a cause she believed in. Her heart was fluttering and her mouth dry as she cleared her throat.

'Juniper, I've brought you here because it's where you were born. I gave birth to you in that building there, and you were stolen from me by the Mother Superior who ran it.'

Juniper was a woman of sixty-five now, who'd married and raised a family of her own, who'd given her great-grandchildren. Her daughter's hair was streaked silver, and her blue eyes crinkled behind her glasses in understanding as she took her mother's hands in both of hers. She stroked the nobbled knuckles with her thumbs. 'I know, Nay-Nay. I've known since I was ten years old.'

EPILOGUE

The wooden box in Juniper's line of sight had a mother-of-pearl inlay and was the size of her late mama's jewellery box. This box, just like the one containing Mama's sparkling necklaces, rings and brooches, was out of bounds; it was also locked, which, to a curious child such as herself, was the equivalent of catnip to Biscuit and Gravy.

The box's contents had intrigued her from the moment, she'd seen it on Nay-Nay's dressing table. She'd asked her what treasure lay inside only to be told it was Nay-Nay's Pandora's box and that some things weren't for sharing. This was by no means a satisfying answer because Juniper didn't know who Pandora was. It was also unfair because she didn't have any secrets from Nay-Nay. Not one and never had in all her ten years.

Today, however, Juniper was queen of the castle. The sun, moon and stars had aligned to leave her alone in her home, Millard House. A never-before occurrence and one that had only come about because Nay-Nay had business in town and Winnie was visiting her friend Esther, while she was supposed to be playing at her friend Ruthann's house for the afternoon –

only Ruthann had got sick. Too much cake eaten too fast would do that to a girl.

Juniper had had the sense to stop at one big wedge, but there was no telling her friend, who'd convinced her to sneak downstairs to the kitchen, where she'd helped herself to the rest of the strawberry shortcake cooling on the countertop until there were only crumbs left. So Juniper had assured Ruthann's exasperated mama – busy trying to calm an irate cook and sick child with a stinging red handprint on her leg – that she would be perfectly fine to go home and there was no need to arrange a chaperone.

How she'd enjoyed the freedom of skipping the entire two blocks back to Chatham Square, stopping wherever the fancy took her, until she'd arrived at the house where she'd always lived. Once, she'd had a mama and papa – Dada she'd called him – who lived there with her. Now it was just her, Nay-Nay and Winnie. Although Birdie and her little ones along with Gramma Annie called by most days, so the house never felt too big for just three of them.

Oh, the thrill of letting herself into a deserted house, hers to roam and explore. Which was how she'd come to be standing there, with one toe in and one toe out of Nay-Nay's bedroom.

'Best mind your own biscuits, and life will be gravy,' was a phrase that had been thrown at Juniper more times than she could count by Winnie, and she hesitated as it ran through her mind now. But as the grandfather clock in the front hall below began to chime, Juniper forgot all about biscuits and gravy and minding her own business. She hurried across to the dressing table and snatched up the box, giving it a shake to see if it would give up its secrets easily. There were no clues like a rattle or clink to be gleaned, though, and, frustrated, she cast her eyes about the bedroom, wondering where she would hide a key if she were in Nay-Nay's shoes.

It didn't take her long to find it tucked away under the

mattress of the neatly made bed, which was exactly where she'd have hidden it herself.

Juniper's hand trembled as she inserted the key into the lock. She held her breath, but it turned smoothly, suggesting that whatever was inside the box was something Nay-Nay often looked at. What was it? Her heart was beginning to pound, and she was careful to keep an ear open as she slowly opened the lid, knowing she'd be deeply ashamed if she were caught in the act of not minding her biscuits.

For a moment, she stared blankly at the scant contents, then her fingers rifled through them. She didn't understand the two plain baby booties and the folded, torn newsprint sheet. The newspaper clipping snagged her interest, so she unfolded it and gazed at a photograph of a cluster of women and small children flanked either side by women wearing the silliest hats Juniper had ever seen. They made her think of the seagulls that scavenged around River Street waterfront because it looked like they had white wings sticking out the sides of their heads. The group was overshadowed by a big brick building that looked nothing like the row houses of Savannah. This house looked cold and unloved, and Juniper imagined the windows were eyes spying on those posed below.

Annoyingly, there was no headline or text to tell her anything about the scene, so her mind took a leap and decided it was an orphanage. Inquisitive she might be, but Juniper also felt things deeply, and she'd read a sad story about children at an orphanage. And sadness was what she sensed as she stared at the picture.

Nay-Nay often talked about Day-Day and her brothers and sisters, but she never talked about her mama and dada or the house they'd all shared back in Ireland before she'd sailed on a big ship to America. Was this why? Had she grown up with no parents to love her, somewhere cold and scary, ruled by women in seagull hats? She inspected the clipping more closely and decided they had mean faces too. Tears threatened as sadness for Nay-Nay swelled.

Juniper blinked them away and scanned the young women and girls, who were all dressed the same in shabby sacks. Some of them didn't look much older than she was. A magnetic pull dragged her focus to the young woman with an enormous belly in the middle of the group. It was a strange sort of orphanage, Juniper thought, unable to make sense of what she was seeing. She stared at the newsprint image so hard, her eyes burned, and her breathing became ragged as she scrambled to understand what she was seeing.

It was Nay-Nay looking back at her, but that didn't make sense. Juniper shut her eyes and counted to five slowly before reopening them. It was still Nay-Nay, but what had happened to the baby in her belly?

Juniper realised she knew exactly where that baby was, and a slow smile of understanding spread across her face. She was Nay-Nay's baby! She didn't know how she knew this to be true – she just did. Nor did she care what had happened to make her Mama and Dada's baby too. It didn't matter because Juniper figured she must have been an extra special baby to have not one but two mamas.

She carefully put the things back in the box, locking it and placing it back on the dressing table before hiding the key away where she'd found it. Then she closed Nay-Nay's bedroom door and skipped off down the hall to the nursery, where she planned on amusing herself until either Nay-Nay or Winnie got home.

She wouldn't say anything to anyone about what she'd discovered, Juniper decided. Not because she didn't want to have to explain how she knew but because nothing had changed. Millard House was still her home, and Nay-Nay still loved her, as did Winnie, Birdie and Gramma Annie. They were her family, and she was surrounded by love. It was enough.

Lost in these thoughts as she tipped a jigsaw puzzle out onto the floor, Juniper never saw the Carolina wren hovering in the window, watching over her, as it always did.

A LETTER FROM MICHELLE

Dear reader,

I want to say a huge thank you for choosing to read *The Irish Adoption House*. If you did enjoy it and want to keep up to date with all my latest releases, just sign up at the following link. Your email address will never be shared, and you can unsubscribe at any time.

www.bookouture.com/michelle-vernal

This story is deeply personal to me. As someone who is adopted, I understand how layered the journey can be. While Maudie's story is fictional, it's written from the heart and with deep compassion and respect for those who suffered at the hands of Ireland's mother and baby homes.

To birth parents, adoptees, adoptive families and anyone else for whom this book resonated – this book is for you.

I hope you loved *The Irish Adoption House*, and if you did, I would be very grateful if you could write a review. I'd love to hear what you think, and it makes such a difference helping new readers to discover one of my books for the first time.

I love hearing from my readers – you can get in touch through social media or my website.

Thanks,
Michelle Vernal

KEEP IN TOUCH WITH MICHELLE

www.michellevernalbooks.com

 facebook.com/michellevernalnovelist

ACKNOWLEDGEMENTS

I'd like to say a huge thank you to the fantastic team at Bookouture who work tirelessly to bring the best version of each book into the world across all formats. You make the publication journey seamless, and I feel so fortunate to have you all behind my stories. Thank you for bringing *The Irish Adoption House* into the hands of readers.

A special thanks to my amazingly talented editor, Natalie, whose careful eye, patience and suggestions have coaxed this book into a story I'm proud of. I love working with you and appreciate your hard work.

A thank you to my mum and dad, whom I love and miss every day, and who helped shape me into who I am. To Julie and Ian, Lisa, Jon and the boys, life is all the better for having you in it. I love you all. And to my wonderful mother- and father-in-law, Pam and Bob Vernal.

I couldn't do what I do without Paul. So thank you to my lovely husband. I never stop pinching myself over how lucky I am to have met you, and of course to our boys, who are doing us proud.

PUBLISHING TEAM

Turning a manuscript into a book requires the efforts of many people. The publishing team at Bookouture would like to acknowledge everyone who contributed to this publication.

Audio
Alba Proko
Melissa Tran
Sinead O'Connor

Commercial
Lauren Morrissette
Hannah Richmond
Imogen Allport

Cover design
Eileen Carey

Data and analysis
Mark Alder
Mohamed Bussuri

Editorial
Natalie Edwards
Charlotte Hegley

Copyeditor
Laura Kincaid

Proofreader
Liz Hurst

Marketing
Alex Crow
Melanie Price
Occy Carr
Cíara Rosney
Martyna Młynarska

Operations and distribution
Marina Valles
Stephanie Straub
Joe Morris

Production
Hannah Snetsinger
Mandy Kullar
Ria Clare
Nadia Michael

Publicity
Kim Nash
Noelle Holten
Jess Readett
Sarah Hardy

Rights and contracts
Peta Nightingale
Richard King
Saidah Graham

Dear Reader,

We'd love your attention for one more page to tell you about the crisis in children's reading, and what we can all do.

Studies have shown that reading for fun is the **single biggest predictor of a child's future life chances** – more than family circumstance, parents' educational background or income. It improves academic results, mental health, wealth, communication skills, ambition and happiness.

The number of children reading for fun is in rapid decline. Young people have a lot of competition for their time, and a worryingly high number do not have a single book at home.

Hachette works extensively with schools, libraries and literacy charities, but here are some ways we can all raise more readers:

- Reading to children for just 10 minutes a day makes a difference
- Don't give up if children aren't regular readers – there will be books for them!

- Visit bookshops and libraries to get recommendations
- Encourage them to listen to audiobooks
- Support school libraries
- Give books as gifts

There's a lot more information about how to encourage children to read on our websites: **www.RaisingReaders.co.uk** and **www.JoinRaisingReaders.com**.

Thank you for reading.

www.ingramcontent.com/pod-product-compliance
Lightning Source LLC
LaVergne TN
LVHW041623060526
838200LV00040B/1403